FAR FROM HOME—
AND SAFETY

Charis Winslade had successfully resisted Major Daniel Hammond's brilliant campaign of conquest when she had first attracted that incorrigible rake in England.

But now, accompanying her brother to the dazzling social whirl of Brussels as the cream of society gathered to view the approaching showdown with Napoleon, Charis once again found herself face-to-face with the handsome officer who was too charming to be true.

Caught in a maze of intrigue, and pursued by the flagrantly insistent and insidiously attractive Comte de Mallon, Charis needed the help that only Hammond could give her . . . even though it might mean that she, like Napoleon, was heading for her Waterloo. . . .

THE
INCORRIGIBLE
RAKE

⊘

Other Regency Romances from SIGNET

The Incorrigible Rake

Sheila Walsh

A SIGNET BOOK

NEW AMERICAN LIBRARY

NAL BOOKS ARE AVAILABLE AT QUANTITY DISCOUNTS
WHEN USED TO PROMOTE PRODUCTS OR SERVICES.
FOR INFORMATION PLEASE WRITE TO PREMIUM MARKETING DIVISION,
NEW AMERICAN LIBRARY, 1633 BROADWAY,
NEW YORK, NEW YORK 10019.

SIGNET, SIGNET CLASSIC, MENTOR, PLUME, MERIDIAN AND
NAL BOOKS are published by New American Library,
1633 Broadway, New York, New York 10019

First Printing, October, 1984

1 2 3 4 5 6 7 8 9

PRINTED IN THE UNITED STATES OF AMERICA

1

The thunderstorm erupted with sudden and quite astonishing ferocity, as summer storms so often do. It caught Charis Winslade still some way short of home, her arms laden with books from the circulating library.

Even as she paused to look about her in hope of finding a roving hack, the fast-darkening sky was rent with jagged light, and a long menacing growl of thunder echoed in response. Then the rain came, lashing slantwise in solid rods of water that soaked her muslin dress in seconds.

The little maidservant staggering in her wake with the remaining parcels uttered a frightened moan.

"Oh, God help us, we'll be struck down for sure!"

"Humbug!" Charis exclaimed in bracing tones. "And if we are, we won't know a thing about it! Come on—keep close to me—if we run we can be home in no time!"

She rounded a corner and met the full implacable force of the wind and rain which flung itself against her, driving the breath from her body. Head down, she clutched despairingly at her bonnet with her one free hand just as a particularly violent gust plucked it from her ineffectual fingers, dragging it backward to flap crazily around her neck in a tangle of rain-soaked ribbons that threatened at any moment to choke her.

In her preoccupation, she quite failed to notice the figure advancing in her path and so ran full tilt into an unyielding, unmistakably masculine chest. The books slithered irretrievably from her grasp and splashed one by one into the fast-forming river at her feet.

"Oh, devil take them!" she gasped in disgust.

"Unladylike," returned a deep voice. "But pardonable in the circumstances."

The voice, resonant with amusement, came from somewhere above her head. Firm, steadying hands encompassed her waist as Charis lifted a face already awash with the little rivulets that came trickling down from a once fashionable fringe of Titian hair now plastered in dark, sodden tendrils across a wide, intelligent brow.

She looked up and blinked away the prismatic brilliance of the raindrops that beaded her lashes, to discover the bluest of blue eyes darkly ringed, regarding her with the liveliest interest from under lazy lids. The gentleman's smile deepened, his mobile mouth quirking upward at one corner.

Irresistibly, Charis found her own mouth curving in response and for the space of one crazy, heart-stopping moment it was as though the sheeting rain had locked the two of them together in a silent, timeless bubble; her body became pliant—she swayed a little toward him.

Then the lightning forked again, the sulphuric sky reverberated with an angry, crackling roar that made her flinch quite involuntarily, and Meg screamed.

"Easy, child," said the gentleman reassuringly.

It was to Meg that he spoke, but Charis was acutely aware of being drawn closer by the insistent pressure of his hands, of the way their warmth penetrated in the most intimate way the rain-drenched muslin that now clung to her like a second skin. She blinked furiously and found those extraordinary eyes very close above her, a disturbing gleam in their impertinent depths.

"You are not afraid, I think? Not of the storm at any rate."

Hot, embarrassed color suffused her face. In all her two and twenty years she had not been so discomposed by a man.

"Certainly not!" she retorted, mortified to find that her voice was stifled and that she was gabbling like an idiot. "One must expect storms now and then, so it's only sensible to get used to them."

"Enchanting!" he murmured appreciatively.

She tried to break free and could not; found his breath soft against her cheek and experienced a moment of sheer panic mingled with some other emotion that she could not or would not define.

"Sir!" she protested, only too aware that her heart was hammering against her ribs in a most *betraying* way. "You really . . . that is, please let me go."

There was a laughing devil in his eyes, pitiless—questing. "And if I choose not to? After all, you did fling yourself at me quite shamelessly."

"I didn't! You must *know* that it was an accident!"

"Perhaps. But it would be a pity to waste such a perfect opportunity, don't you think?"

As the full import of his words registered, she strove to collect her disorded wits—to assert herself, to muster the tattered shreds of her dignity, to demand that he release her. But already it was too late.

His mouth on hers was a gentle, lingering caress, and tasted of rain. It was over before she could struggle, and to her shame she didn't try.

"There," he said softly. "That wasn't so bad, was it? I would even hazard that you quite enjoyed the experience."

Even as she worked herself up into a fine fury, a small, traitorous voice at the back of her mind clamored to agree with him and had to be firmly quashed. Green eyes kindling, her cheeks flying flags of color, she fought strenuously once more to free herself, and was disconcerted when he suddenly released her, setting her away from him quite deliberately though his eyes continued to enjoy the exceedingly revealing spectacle she presented.

"Sir, you are not a gentleman!" she cried, the curious sensation of loss she felt serving only to fan her fury.

"So I have often been told," he admitted without shame.

"Were my brother here, he would call you out for your insolence!"

"I should think him a poor sort of brother an' he did not." He nodded gravely, though his eyes were still laughing at her. "But—not insolence, surely? I feel I must protest the word *insolence!*"

"Insolence," she reiterated, drawing herself up with dignity. "You used me like a . . ." she faltered over the word *whore,* and concluded lamely, "like a back-street trollop!"

His mouth quirked. "And what would a carefully nurtured young lady know of the way back-street trollops are used?"

It was a ridiculous conversation, born of an even more ridiculous situation, she concluded, stifling a sudden and quite improper desire to giggle; to be standing arguing in a state of near saturation—she with her feet squelching in a puddle of water, he with the rain dripping steadily from the curling brim of his hat—must rank as little short of high farce. It was well that the street was deserted.

But Charis had forgotten Meg. She remembered her now with a surge of embarrassment, and could only hope that the terrors of the storm had rendered her maid insensible to all else.

It was a vain hope, for the storm's violence had been short-lived. The rain was easing, the thunder gradually fading to an apologetic rumble, and already the sky was beginning to roll back the thick, dark banks of cumulous. With it, Meg's fear also began to subside, and she turned her attention to her mistress and the handsome stranger. Insensible of her own bedraggled state, she watched entranced what to her romance-starved soul appeared to be the most romantic of encounters, so that it came as a sad letdown to find herself on the end of a particularly quelling look as Miss Charis said in her most positive voice: "This is quite absurd! I must go."

"Must you?" said the gentleman with every appearance of regret. "Just when we were getting to know one another so well, too. Still, if you have quite made up your mind . . ."

"I have," she said firmly.

"Then, perhaps we should see if we can salvage your books?"

Charis had forgotten the books. Staring down now in dismay, she saw that their covers were beginning to curl and already some of the pages had been saturated beyond redemption.

Her tormentor, moving with remarkable agility, swooped to rescue one of the least damaged ones, and held it gingerly aloft between finger and thumb.

"Oh no! Now see what you have done!" Charis exclaimed, unjustly apportioning blame.

He accepted her censure with meek resignation, merely venturing the opinion that she might justifiably count them all lost, and abandon them to their fate. Charis had more or less reached the same conclusion, but now his complacence made her perverse.

"Certainly not," she declared, stooping and beginning to chivvy them into some kind of order. "They are not mine to abandon. I shall return them to the library— when they have dried out, of course."

"But, Miss Charis, they're ruined for sure!" wailed Meg, uncertain whether or not to put down her own parcels in order to help.

"Perhaps so, but that is no excuse for . . . for being too poor-spirited to own to one's carelessness."

She knew this for an unbearably smug pronouncement, an opinion confirmed by the gentleman's quizzical look as he applauded her intention; congratulated Meg upon her good fortune in having a mistress possessed of such high ethical principles, and took the books from her, cradling them with the air of one performing the supreme sacrifice.

"Pray allow me to find you a hack," he said solicitously.

The rain had now all but stopped. "Thank you," said Charis, "but that won't be necessary. I live only a step from here." She held out her hands imperiously for the books, but he clasped them to his chest with equal determination.

"Then I will carry them for you. No," he insisted magnanimously, "it is the very least I can do."

If her appearance was indecent, his was incongruous to say the least—his elegant clothes quite ruined by the deluge, his shoulders hunched a little against the knowledge. For a second time it was all she could do not to giggle.

"Very well." Charis turned and began to walk with as much indifference to her state as could be managed in squelching slippers. He fell easily into step beside her and Meg's hurrying feet brought up the rear. She made no attempt to converse further and he seemed preoccupied. They came presently to a quiet, genteel street—one of the many that clung with impecunious tenacity to the fringes of fashionable London—and after a few steps Charis halted before a pleasant house with a gleaming brass doorknob, and faced about.

She was not accustomed to being dwarfed by a man. Her brother and his friends were mostly of a size, being perhaps one or two inches taller than herself, no more. With a conscious determination not to be overwhelmed by his sheer physical presence, she drew herself up to her full five feet eight inches, prepared as a final gesture to be gracious.

"It is good of you to have taken so much trouble," she said politely. "This is where I live, so I will take the books now."

"You don't think it would be better if I carried them right up to the door?"

His blue eyes were creased against a blinding shaft of

sunlight as it pierced the gloom, so that she could not tell whether or not he was quizzing her. The faint movement of a curtain in the house opposite recalled her to her sorry state and how very singular it must appear, and quite suddenly she could not wait to run indoors.

"Thank you, but no," she said hastily. "I can manage perfectly well."

"I feared you might be of that mind." As he surrendered the books, he contrived an exaggerated sigh. "Am I to go without even knowing who you are?"

"I can't see that it would be of any use for you to know," she retorted firmly, evading the issue and turning a little pink.

"You don't wish to pursue the acquaintance?" he said regretfully. "Well, it is no more than I deserve. I daresay I was much too coming, though at the time the temptation was irresistible, believe me." His sleepy eyelids lifted hopefully. "You don't suppose I might yet redeem myself?"

His idiocy was infectious and she was in grave danger of behaving in a quite improper manner. Her dimple quivered and was sternly suppressed.

"I think not," she said firmly. "Good-bye."

"Such a very final word," he murmured, still showing a maddening disinclination to leave. "I confess I had hoped . . . after so intriguing a beginning."

Oh dear, this really would not do. She had made the mistake of looking at him, and an unwilling spurt of laughter escaped her.

"My dear sir, life is full of little disappointments. You must strive to give your thoughts a higher direction!"

She thought there was an answering echo of a chuckle, low and deep.

"You leave me little choice, fair divinity. I shall return to my lonely garret room to meditate upon my shortcomings."

On this note of mock humility he bowed, tipped his

hat, and went on his way with easy, loping strides.
Charis watched him for a moment and then hurried up
the path. Behind her, Meg sighed. "Oh, ma'am!"

Charis whirled around, with crimson flags flying in
her cheeks. "Not a word!" she charged urgently.
"Especially to Emily!"

But if Charis had hoped to gain the sanctuary of her
room undiscovered and uncensured, her hopes were
dashed upon finding her way to the stairs barred by a
small, elderly woman who waited like a plump, inquisitive blackbird, hands folded ominously across her rustling bombazine skirts.

"Well, it's a fine pair you make, to be sure!" she said.

Charis met Emily MacGrath's bright, roving eyes
with a defiance betokening guilt.

"We were caught in the storm, Em."

"I can see that, right enough," came the pithy reply.
"Meg, there is hot water on the stove. When you have
carried it up to your mistress's room, you had best
attend to yourself. Hurry now, child. We want no chills
or inflammations of the lungs."

The maid set the parcels down on the hall table, and
with a swift, speaking glance at Charis, scurried to
obey. The door to the kitchen slammed behind her and
the sound died away into silence.

Charis waited for the inevitable reprimand. Mrs. Emily MacGrath's somewhat singular position in the
Winslade household had from time to time vexed the
minds of unsuspecting newcomers to the little house in
Newsholme Terrace; too familiar by far to be dismissed
as a mere servant, she yet lacked that veneer of gentil-
ity which would comfortably consign her to the role of
ex-governess or companion, thus giving rise to the dreadful uncertainty as to how one ought to address her or
indeed respond to her forthright manners. If the new-
comer happened to be one of her brother Tristram's
more pompous acquaintances, Charis was not above

deriving a degree of innocent amusement from prolonging their uncertainty for as long as possible.

The simple truth was that Emily MacGrath had brought the twins—for twins she and Tristram were—into the world, more than twenty years ago, and when their mother's frail hold on life had proved inadequate, their distraught father had begged Mrs. MacGrath to remain and care for them. Widowed some years previously and with her own children grown and off her hands, she had been pleased to agree. Long before her charges had outgrown their need of a nurse, she had become an indispensable member of the family. In due time she advanced to fulfill with equal ease the duties of housekeeper and unofficial guardian of their behavior and morals. And with the untimely death of Mr. Winslade just over two years since ("taken before his time, God rest him!" as she confided to her bosom-bow, Mrs. Arbuthnot—"and leaving behind him a parcel of debts fit to make a rich man quail!"), it was in this last capacity that she saw her true vocation.

"As for yourself, Miss Charis," she said now, making her mouth prim, "if you've come through the streets looking like that, it's to be hoped that the good Lord took it upon himself to shield you from the lewd stares of the hoi-polloi—to say nothing of your giving that Mrs. Huyton-Forbes opposite a nasty turn!"

The recollection of recent events caused Charis to flush bright crimson, but Emily's interest had already taken a different direction so that she scarcely heeded the indistinguishable reply.

"And what in the name of all that's holy is it that you have there?" she demanded.

Charis realized that she was still clutching the sodden bundle protectively to her breast.

"They are . . . or rather, were library books, Em. I'm afraid I dropped them."

"Tch! Could you not have left them outside? Dripping all over my clean floor—and that dress ruined, I shouldn't wonder, with the colors all running down! Here, give them to me."

Charis thrust the books at her and fled, thankful to have escaped a more grueling inquisition. In the safety of her room, she closed the door softly and leaned back against it, striving to assemble her disordered thoughts.

To be sure, the gentleman had behaved with shocking impropriety, but—she caught her breath on the thought—how must she have appeared in his eyes? She bit her lip, remembering that one crazy instant when she had known herself to be irresistibly drawn to him. Had he perhaps sensed that momentary lapse? If so, it might account for his having used her so . . . outrageously!

A sudden shiver recalled Charis to the present. With a discomforture that was not wholly physical, she moved away from the door, suddenly eager to be rid of all reminders of her foolishness, and in passing the dressing table mirror, caught a glimpse of herself.

Oh, good God! She looked like some dreadful demirep with her muslins deliberately damped down in order to make them cling! If that was how *he* had seen her, small wonder that he thought . . . Here she pulled up short, her imagination boggling at the probable trend of his thoughts. She stripped off the offending garment with fingers that trembled, crumpled it into a ball, and flung it into the farthest corner of the room.

How could she have allowed herself to become embroiled in such a compromising situation? It was useless to plead innocence. She was far from being a green girl, for in her two and twenty years she had been about a great deal (though sadly not of late), and with her brother's friends forever in and out of the house she was well used to dealing with young men— except, she amended with scrupulous honesty, that none of Tristram's friends would dream of treating her with such a ruthless disregard for her sensibilities. But then, the traitorous little voice at the back of her mind came again to taunt her, would she have felt that peculiar surge of exhilaration if they had? The unhappy truth had to be owned—she would not.

Charis was deeply shocked by this revelation of her own shortcomings. A gently nurtured young lady—his description, she ruefully recalled—must surely have swooned away, or at the very least have suffered an intense agitation of the spirit upon being forcibly kissed by a strange man.

Not quite knowing what this made of *her,* she fudged the issue and proceeded to rub herself down with a briskness that left her pink and glowing. By the time Meg panted upstairs with the hot water, she had donned a fresh gown and coaxed her hair into some kind of order, her normally ebullient disposition was in a fair way to being restored and she had managed to convince herself that it would be foolish indeed to refine too much upon a trivial incident that would be much better forgotten.

The decision was easily made, but less easily accomplished with the experience echoing over and over in her head. And then Tristram arrived home with a piece of news that drove all else from her mind.

ᔆᔆᓬ 2 ᓬᔆᔆ

She was on her knees in the linen closet when Tristram arrived, shattering the peace of the house with his exuberant shout which vied with the reverberation caused by the slamming of the front door.

"Charis? Are you there?"

She looked up eagerly from the reproachful contemplation of a hitherto undiscovered thin patch in the best pair of sheets.

"Up here, Tris."

"Such a turn up! Just wait until I tell you!"

Her brother could be heard taking the stairs two at a time.

"That boy has no moderation in him at all," declared Emily in the reproving tones of one who, having raised the said boy from a muling infant, reserved the right to treat him as though he were still in short coats. "Skimblebrained!" she added for good measure, as though by thus berating him she could in some measure disguise the fact that she adored him. "The good Lord alone knows how he ever got to be taken on as secretary to such a great government swell!"

Charis sat back on her heels, hugging the offending sheet to her with a blithe disregard for the way she was crushing it.

"Oh, Tristram isn't anything so grand as a secretary, Em. In fact, I should be surprised if he has so much as laid eyes on Lord Rowby since he went to work for him. I'm sure that his lordship only made a place for Tristram out of a sense of obligation. Both he and Lord Castlereagh thought very highly of Papa, you know."

"And why wouldn't they? He was a grand man, your father—took his diplomatic duties seriously whatever his other failings." Emily's attention was momentarily diverted as she held up a towel. "Will you look at that, now? There's no saving this one, I'm thinking."

"Tear it up for dishmops," said Charis absently, her mind dwelling with uncomfortable persistence upon Emily's reference to Papa's failings. She hoped devoutly that Tristram had not inherited the unsteadiness of character that, in Papa, had shown itself in a passion for gambling that had left them near penniless at his death. To be sure, Tristram had not so far as she was aware succumbed to any specific vice—but dear as he was to her, she could not but wish for a little more ambition, some evidence in him of a determination to seek advancement.

"Oh well." She shrugged philosophically. "I suppose even diplomats must sometimes begin as lowly clerks, and Tris is still young enough to prove himself."

"Young, is it?" Emily's tone was so dry that it crackled. "When I was his age I'd been married to Mr. MacGrath for all of five years and had borne him four lusty children, including a brace of twins the same as yourselves."

Emily's irrefutable brand of logic always confounded Charis, and she blessed Tristram's whirlwind arrival, which relieved her of the necessity of making some reply. He filled the narrow doorway—a slim young sprig of fashion—his infectious smile a mirror of hers, the words spilling out of him in his eagerness to impart his news.

"You'll never guess—it's the most tremendous piece of luck—Lord Rowby has been posted to Brussels, and I'm to go with him!"

The sheet billowed to the floor forgotten as Charis was lifted to her feet and crushed in a triumphant, suffocating embrace. Her kiss landed somewhere just below his left ear, her words of congratulations being muffled by the stuff of his stylish blue coat as she turned her face swiftly into his shoulder.

"Isn't it perfectly splendid, Em?" he said above her head. "Aside from Vienna, there isn't anywhere likely to be half so gay, for everyone who isn't going to the Congress is following the Army of occupation to Brussels. I daresay the place will be simply crawling with nabobs, and there's no knowing what a fellow might not achieve!"

Emily MacGrath swooped wrathfully on the crumpled sheet and began busily to smooth its creases. "If you achieve one half of what's expected of you, it'll be a miracle, I'm thinking! Now, out of me way, the both of you—and let somebody in this house do a day's work."

Tristram realized that Charis had said very little. He held her away from him, his merry eyes quizzing her as she forced a bright smile to hide a fast-engulfing dismay.

"What's wrong, little sister? I thought you'd be pleased."

"I am," she insisted.

"Liar," he said softly.

There was a wryness in her grin. "You're right, of course. Indeed, I am very happy for you, my dear. But I'm also pea-green with jealousy . . ." She threw her arms wide in a curiously helpless gesture. "And, oh lordy, I am going to miss you quite dreadfully!"

"So that's what ails you. I thought as much." Tristram reached out for her hands, bringing them together in a warm, possessive clasp against his chest. "Well then, we'd better see what can be done about it, hadn't we?"

Charis could hardly bear to speak lest she should be reading more into his words than he intended.

"*Stoopid!*" he murmured in mock reproof as eye to eye he met her now brilliant, questioning gaze. "You didn't really think that I would leave you behind?" His fingers squeezed hers reassuringly tight. "How could I possibly survive without my good right hand?"

At this they collapsed against one another in a spontaneous explosion of merriment which on her side was part relief, part sheer exhilaration.

"Without a doubt it was my superior command of languages that clinched things for me," Tristram concluded with an absence of modesty that in anyone else would have been odious. "That, and the fact that his lordship's private secretary made particular mention that, though my work was erratic, I could upon occasion pen a remarkably neat hand."

For some reason that Emily couldn't fathom, this sent them into fresh paroxisms of mirth. She watched them with a baleful eye and went on folding her linen as Charis, catching her breath, gasped, "Oh, you can indeed!"

Overgrown children, that's all they were—just a pair of silly, irresponsible children! Not but what Miss Charis hadn't sense enough and to spare for the two of them when all came to all, only that she let her brother have his head far too often. Emily sighed. Well, for that she must take her own share of the blame, since she was no more proof against his charm than the rest.

They were off down stairs now, the two of them, all else forgotten as they fell to arguing amiably over the how and the when of the remove to Brussels.

"Skimble-brained," muttered Emily again, listening to their animated chatter. She leaned stiffly over the bannister rail. "Listen now—when you've the time to spare from arguing over how many new clothes you'll be needing, perhaps you'll give some thought to me, and this house, and what's to be done with the both of us while you go galavanting off to foreign parts, for I give you fair warning that I've reached the time of life when I'd be loath to uproot meself in order to come traipsing after you on any kind of hair-brained scheme!"

From the landing below, the two heads lifted as one; two pairs of eyes the color of jade, thickly fringed, regarded her, wickedly aslant, from under winged brows—Miss Charis's faintly troubled and his teasing as he said: "Oh, come on, Em—you're not that old!"

"Did I say anything about being old?" she came back at him, quick as light, acutely aware that she would not see sixty again. "A body doesn't have to be old to want her feet under her own table of a night and her own friends about her instead of a lot of pesky strangers who don't even have the sense to converse in a decent tongue!"

Charis threw her brother a warning look and said soothingly: "You know you don't really mean that, dear Emily. And anyway, we wouldn't dream of making any definite plans without consulting you!"

"I'm glad to hear it," she grunted, somewhat mollified. "But fine words butter no parsnips, and I'll thank you to remember it."

This being one of her most favored pronouncements, they received it with equanimity, gave her a reassuring smile, and went blithely on their way.

There was no denying that they were a handsome couple, Emily acknowledged with grudging pride—she a little on the tall side for a girl and he as slim and elegant a young man as you could wish for—and the likeness between them quite marked since the day Miss Charis had gone out and had her lovely auburn hair cropped so that it would better resemble that new-fangled swirly style with the fancy foreign name her brother had taken to wearing. All the crack, he'd said it was! For him, maybe, Emily had retorted, but what was allowable in a man might well be deemed fast in a young lady. They had simply laughed at her.

They were laughing now as they vanished from Emily's view, Master Tristram with his arm draped casually about his sister's shoulders and she chiding him indulgently. They were too close, of course, always had been, and their father's habit of taking them abroad with him whenever possible, employing the services of a tutor instead of sending his son off to school like a sensible man, had forged an even closer bond between them.

Perhaps, if their mother had lived? Emily sighed. She had done *her* best, as the good Lord would bear witness, but it wasn't the same. And their mother's sister, who had married Viscount Weston and might have been looked to for help, was a silly butterfly of a woman without a thought in her head beyond balls and the like, though to be fair, she had taken Miss Charis about as much as could be thought reasonable in a woman with a daughter of her own to bestow.

And if Miss Charis didn't choose to make the most of such opportunities as were offered, she had no one to blame but herself. Emily knew for a fact that she had discouraged at least two most promising suitors—and for why?

"Because she was content as she was, if you please," the old lady had confided to the ubiquitous Mrs. Arbuthnot, "and wouldn't, in any case, dream of abandoning her brother to fend for himself! I could have slapped her! Well, fond as I am of him, it's small hope there'd be of him showing her the same consideration . . . and I didn't scruple to tell her so!"

Mrs. Arbuthnot had nodded sagely and wondered how such frankness had been received.

Emily grunted. "Much as you'd expect. 'Emily, dear Emily,' the child told me, blithe as you please. 'Of course, I wouldn't expect Tris to make any such sacrifice—nor would *he* expect it of me, I promise you! The plain fact is, I have no wish to exchange my present, very agreeable mode of life for any other, and until someone comes along who can make me change my mind, I am quite resolved to eschew marriage.'" Emily's eyes kindled anew at the telling. "Did you ever hear the like?"

Mrs. Arbuthnot was clearly moved by such transports of idealism, and was rash enough to say so.

"Romantic twaddle, more like!" her exasperated friend

had snapped. As if marriage had anything to do with such silliness! Miss Charis needed a man—a real man—and small chance she had of finding one among her brother's friends, who were all as light-minded as himself. A scapegrace he had been as a boy and a scapegrace he would always be.

This Brussels business now might have been the very thing to separate them, but it would be a waste of good breath suggesting it. Miss Charis was set on going, and go she would, though Emily might wish it otherwise. Which meant that, notwithstanding all her protestations, she too must bestir herself, for let them out of her sight she would not, come what may.

Down below in the hall, brother and sister were still wrangling amiably, oblivious of her concern.

"Honestly, Tris—you have no tact at all! It will probably take me the best part of the afternoon now to smooth Emily's ruffled feathers."

"She'll come around," he said with a careless grin. "Em's bark was ever worse than her bite."

"Yes, but you have touched upon her age, my dear—and that is a very sensitive area these days. Even you must have noticed that poor Emily isn't as robust as she was used to be . . ."

"Stuff! She's as tough as an old warhorse! Anyway, she don't have to come with us."

"Oh, but she'd be so hurt if we so much as hinted that she might stay behind!"

Tristram lifted a laconic eyebrow. "My dear, soft-hearted sister, it is not many minutes since she was avowing that such was her intention."

"Only because she is confident that we can't survive without her," Charis explained patiently.

"Heaven defend me from feminine logic!" he exclaimed.

"And *us* from the ruthlessness of men!" she retorted with spirit.

He grinned. "I can't stay to argue. Neill, that dragon of a private secretary, don't know I've slipped my leash."

"Oh, Tris!"

"It's all right," he said airily. "Ned's covering for me, and anyway, they'll never miss me. Lord Rowby's nephew and heir is due home from the war—the *conquering hero* is to have a hero's welcome—and the entire household is in a ferment of anticipation." He turned away to pick up his valise and when he turned back his voice had grown softly coaxing. "Dear little sister, I know you will have a million things to do, but—" he produced a folder of papers—"could you find a minute or two to copy these?"

When Tristram looked at her like that, she was incapable of refusing him anything. Not that she wished to do so. It wasn't the first time he had brought work home for her to complete. Her ability to produce a reasonable facsimile of his hand was a skill tried and perfected in the schoolroom where Tristram had frequently shown an engaging indisposition toward work. And when, in his early days at Lord Rowby's, he had found so much of his work deadly dull and had thus fallen behind with it, it had seemed no more than a harmless prank to slip some of the papers into his valise and bring them home for her to finish.

But sometimes of late the ethics of what she was doing troubled Charis.

"I suppose it *is* all right?" she said now, taking the folder from him with sudden reluctance. "I mean, there might be things I shouldn't see . . . documents that outsiders should not be privy to."

Tristram lifted a quizzical eyebrow. "Lord, Charis— you don't imagine old Neill gives us lowly minions so much as a sniff at anything of significance, do you? We are but specks of dust in the corridors of power, fit only to copy out mundane agendas and other such tedious stuff!"

"Oh, but I don't find it in the least tedious."

He pressed a finger to her mouth in mock horror.

"Never say so, my dear! I don't want it noised abroad that my sister is a blue stocking!"

"Idiot!"

He laughed and gave her cheek an affectionate peck. "What a pity society don't hold with young women of good character being employed as clerks. His lordship might then engage you in my place. With your aptitude you might in due time rise to the giddy heights enjoyed by private secretaries like Neill and would then be able to keep me in prime style!" He snapped his bag shut, made her an exaggerated leg, and sauntered to the door. "I give you good day, Madam Secretary. Mind now, don't pen *too* neat a hand or I am sunk!"

His unrepentant laugh floated back, tugging the corners of her mouth into an answering smile. It was impossible to be angry with him. Emily vowed he was spoiled and maybe he was, but his ready charm easily outweighed the more irresponsible tendencies in his character and made one eager to smooth his way.

Charis stood hugging the folder until the door had closed behind him. Then she wandered into the parlor and laid it down on her father's handsome rosewood desk near the window and began to mend her pen.

In White's Club in St. James's that same evening, three gentlemen sat in friendly fashion over a bottle of port exchanging the latest *on-dits*. The atmosphere was pleasantly relaxed, disturbed only occasionally by a sudden burst of laughter from the far side of the room which caused irate frowns from the older members.

"Makes one feel deucedly staid, don't it?" observed one of the three, a bored exquisite, quizzing glass raised to view the enthusiastic horseplay. "Were we ever that young, Dan?"

From the depths of a capacious armchair his sleepy-eyed companion sank his chin a little deeper into the folds of his cravat as he too watched the youthful revelers over the rim of his glass.

Unhurriedly he stretched his exceedingly long legs, encased in black knee-smalls, and crossed them neatly at the ankles.

"I seem to recall," he reflected, deep-voiced, "that a certain marquess of tender years once introduced within these hallowed portals a pair of violently disruptive monkeys."

"Dammit, so I did! Vile-smelling creatures they were, too!" A faint gleam lit the Marquess of Verney's eyes. "Perhaps you will also recall that it was a long-legged young devil of a rifleman, still wet behind the ears, who procured 'em for me!"

A chuckle reverberated through Major Dan Hammond's ample frame. "I was ever a resourceful fellow."

"Egod, what a time ago it all seems," sighed the marquess. "Must be all of eight or nine years."

"The thing *I* remember," said Sir Edwin Booth, the third and most senior member of the group, "is that his grace, your father, was not best pleased when it fell to him to foot the bill for the damage caused—and generally smooth ruffled feathers."

"Very proper of him," drawled the marquess. "What else, after all, are parents for?"

A further outburst of laughter drew their attention back to the group of young bucks. One voice rose above the rest. "Three hours, forty-two minutes! Dammit, that's crawling! I'd wager that Ceddie's new team could do it in less!"

This brought shouts of derision mingled with excitedly issued challenges.

"Plus ça change—plus c'est la même chose!" murmured the marquess. "Young men were ever thus."

"The older ones ain't much different," said Sir Edwin.

"Do you know any of these particular hotheads?" Dan Hammond's voice was casual. He was seemingly intent upon the rich ruby liquid swirling gently around in his glass, but his veiled glance observed covertly the young man who had spoken, his vivid face framed by a head of swirling auburn hair.

Verney lifted an eyebrow. "Depends what you mean by *know*, dear boy. They ain't exactly among our set, though I am, of course, acquainted with Ned Kent—and the Bartholomew Babe in the wasp-waisted coat with the absurd shoulders is Weston's youngest, the honorable Cedric, I believe."

"What of the lively sprig with the red hair—his face has a familiar look to it. Should I know him?"

"That's young Winslade—Cedric Weston's cousin," Sir Edwin put in. "His father put him up for membership here not long before he died." He shook his head. "A tragic business, Charles Winslade going like that—in his prime. Left his family in queer street, too, so I heard. With a sister to support, the boy must needs knuckle down to the harsher realities of life, though to look at him, there don't seem much evidence of it. Come to think on't, that's most probably why he seems familiar to you—your uncle has taken him on his staff, I believe."

"Really?" said the major easily. "Yes. That will be it, then."

❦ 3 ❧

It was long past midnight when Tristram arrived home. Charis heard him singing bawdily as he mounted the stairs and prayed that he would not disturb Emily, who had retired early to bed with the morose pronouncement that the rain had brought on her twinges "something chronic."

This was patently an untruth, but after a day given over to long silences accompanied by much heavy sighing, Charis was not disposed to argue her out of her fit of the sullens.

Left to her own devices, however, she had felt unable to settle, and passed the time as she waited for Tristram to return by laying out on her bed the most presentable of her dresses, the better to assess their potential. Anyone of a less sanguine disposition must have been instantly cast down, for it had to be acknowledged that three morning dresses, and a further three better suited to evening parties and balls—most of which dated from happier, more affluent days, and all of which had been refurbished more times than she cared to think—constituted a pitifully inadequate wardrobe to carry one through a stay of indefinite duration in a city that was fast becoming one of the social hubs of Europe.

But Charis was seldom able to resist a challenge, and the strong vein of creativity in her nature which had served her well over the past two difficult years now found ample scope for expression. With a modest outlay, it should be possible to contrive something for herself. She had already decided that this could well be Tristram's opportunity for advancement, and if he was to make the desired impression, it was clear that the bulk of their available funds must be given over to turning him out in prime style, for then, surely, her brother's natural ease of manner, together with an ability to converse fluently in both French and German, must bring him to the attention of his superiors in a way that being able to pen a neat hand would never do.

She quickly fetched her drawing block and, curling up at the end of the bed, began a series of swift sketches culled from her recollection of the exceedingly modish creations illustrated in her aunt's most recent copy of *The Lady's Magazine* which she and her cousin Lavinia had been sighing over but a few days since. There had been a half-robe, in cream silk she remembered, that had been quite ravishing in its simplicity, and she was sure that with a little judicious alteration, her own ivory crepe could be made over to resemble it tolerably well.

She worked on, thoroughly engrossed, and it was not until the downstairs clock chimed one o'clock that she realized how numb her feet had grown with sitting. She swung them to the floor and wiggled her toes. As they came painfully back to life, she distracted herself by leafing idly through the drawings. They were good— very good, some of them, she decided with a small thrill of satisfaction. And then she was pulled up short, a slow, hot tide of color flooding over her.

A man's face stared back at her—a long sensitive face with strong bones, a sensual mouth quirking up at one corner, and pitiless laughing devils in his lazy lidded eyes. She had sketched it on the evening of their meeting, and had then pushed it away out of sight, consumed with guilt over her continuing obsessive thoughts of him and anger with herself at what she considered a shocking weakness of character.

Now, Charis forced herself to look at it objectively. It was an excellent likeness, rousing in her momentarily that curious melting awareness of him that she had felt that day in the rain. Was that why she had not destroyed it? Why, even now, she could not bring herself to do so? It was foolishness of a kind she had not until this moment been prey to, but though she might castigate herself for what she termed weakness, the sketch was nevertheless almost furtively returned to its hiding place.

It was perhaps fortunate that at this point she heard the door close none too quietly below, to be followed by the sound of Tristram's lusty rendition of a somewhat lewd ballad. She ran to hang over the bannister rail and saw him negotiating the stairs in a decidedly haphazard fashion.

"Tris—do be quiet!" she urged. "You'll wake the house!"

He came level with her, put an affectionate arm around her shoulders, and planted a kiss on her cheek amid wreaths of brandy fumes. "My pardon, sweet sister, I shall be as silent as the grave," he promised in a solemn, carrying whisper.

Charis smothered a giggle. "You are foxed, my lad!" she accused him.

His eyes, so like her own, crinkled into a beatific smile. "Devil a bit, my dear," Tristram stumbled and held on to her. "Well—a trifle bosky, perhaps."

He pushed himself erect and walked carefully into his own room. Charis followed in time to see him take out of his closet a pair of buff breeches and an olive green coat.

"Tris—what are you doing? Have you the least idea what time it is?"

"Late, I guess—or early—late for yesterday, but early for tomorrow . . . if you take my meaning." He began to struggle out of his coat, pausing only to grin at her. "D'you mind, love? I mean, deuced fond of you and all that—but a fellow don't in the general way care to drop his inexpressibles in front of a beautiful young lady . . ." His grin grew irrepressibly lewd. "Not, at any rate, if she happens to be his loving sister!"

His sportiveness brought a little color to her cheeks, but Charis stood her ground. "Tris, I am not moving from here until you explain to me why you are changing your clothes in the middle of the night."

"Simple, m'dear. Can't drive Ceddie's curricle and four in this rig, can I? Stands to reason."

"Drive Ceddie's curricle?" Charis decided that he must be more badly disguised than she had thought. "In the middle of the night?"

He looked at her pityingly. "Of course not, stoopid! Who ever heard of anyone trying to race at night with no moon to show the way? Thing is, we set off at first light. Someone—I don't just recall who, but it don't signify—said it couldn't be done in less than three and a half hours, and I said that with that new bang-up rig of Ceddie's I'd engage to do it in less, and before we knew it, the race was on . . . last team to reach Newmarket buys a slap-up breakfast for everyone at the White Hart."

She found the whole idea nonsensical, and did not scruple to tell him so. "You cannot possibly drive to Newmarket and be back in time for work."

"Fear not—all is arranged," Tristram said airily. "Ned ain't coming with us, so he will engage to tell old Neill that I am sadly indisposed."

"Oh, Tris! You can't ask Ned to lie for you! If the truth does come out—and you know how these silly races get gossiped about—you could jeopardize his future as well as your own!"

Tristram took her by the shoulders and propelled her backward through the door, gently, but with irresistible force, while his eyes laughed down at her.

"Out, woman! You are very much *de trop*. Besides, if I don't hurry, Ceddie will grow tired of waiting and come rattling the knocker, and we don't want that, do we?"

Charis gave in, knowing that in his present state further argument with Tristram would be useless.

"Don't forget Aunt Lizzie's ball tomorrow night," she besought him urgently from the landing as the door closed.

"I promise—hand on heart," the reply floated back.

The following morning she was up early, heavy-eyed with lack of sleep, but unable to rest. Emily's persistent probing about Tristram's whereabouts had to be fended off with vague half-truths, and the old lady's reminder that she was away to visit her daughter in Islington for the day came as profound relief.

With the house to herself, Charis made a conscious effort to keep busy and cheerful by tipping out her box of trimmings so that she might decide what must be bought. The discovery of a forgotten length of the ivory crepe lifted her spirits considerably and sent her hurrying to fetch the ball gown she wished to alter. She passed the next hour happily stripping away all the old trimmings until only a simple sheath remained. Then, with the aid of her sketch pad, she cut out the overdress and pinned it into place before trying it on.

Even in its unfinished state the effect was all and more than she had hoped for. The simple line complimented her tall, slender figure and with the addition of some particular pearl fastenings that she had seen in the Pantheon Bazaar only yesterday, it would do very well, she decided, for Aunt Lizzie's ball.

Without further ado she dispatched Meg to buy the trimmings that were needed and by the time she remembered that there was no one to help her out of the dress, the girl was beyond recall. Oh well, it was no great matter. She made some minor adjustments to the set of the brief sleeves and was just deciding how best to extricate herself from all the pins when the knocker sounded below.

Drat! Charis ran to the window, craning forward in an effort to see who could be so vexatious as to call at this precise moment. There was a sporting phaeton with a pair of prime-looking horses being walked by a groom farther down the street, but apart from that she could see nothing but a carriage, vaguely familiar, disappearing from view.

Of course! Lavinia. She had said she might call. The knocker sounded again, more imperatively this time. Charis abandoned a halfhearted attempt to wriggle out of the dress and, lifting her hands in a helpless, amused gesture, gathered up her skirts and the book of sketches and ran down the stairs. She arrived, breathless, at the front door and flung it open with a flourish.

"Oh!" It was more a squeak than an exclamation.

A figure filled the doorway, almost blotting out the light. A most elegant gentleman. It seemed to Charis, suspended in a state of shock, that she had all the time in the world to note how advantageously his shoulders were set off by a coat of superfine whose tailor Tristram would instantly have recognized; to observe that not a wrinkle marred the buff pantaloons encasing slim tapering hips and fine long legs, distinguished by a pleasing muscularity of thigh. She caught her errant thoughts and schooled them severely; lifted her eyes and found that, from beneath the curling brim of a beaver hat amused blue eyes were subjecting her to a similar scrutiny, marking particularly the incongruity of the pinned dress, and watching every nuance of the many conflicting emotions that chased across her all-too expressive face, the wild color that came and went.

"We meet again, fair divinity," he said in that well-remembered voice. And as she still stood, transfixed, he smiled. "Well, am I forgiven, or do you still mean to deny me admittance?"

And if I did, you would be well served, she decided as a healthy indignation began to stir. Only a man so totally devoid of sensibility as to flout the more conventional codes of social behavior would presume to turn up on one's doorstep without benefit of an acceptable introduction. And why, oh why, if he must do so, had a perverse fate chosen to place her yet again at a disadvantage?

"In point of fact, sir . . ." she began primly, only to be halted as he interposed with deceptive meekness:

"I had meant to send up my card."

Charis took the proffered card, curiosity overriding prudence. Major Daniel Hammond. The name meant nothing to her, yet she felt a sudden inexplicable unease.

"I had hoped for a brief word with your brother," he added helpfully.

"With . . . with Tristram?"

"With Tristram," he agreed.

This threw her into fresh confusion. She had assumed, not unnaturally in the circumstances, that he had come in pursuit of her, so why should he want Tristram . . . unless he wished to apply to him for permission to pay his addresses to her . . . At any other time such an idea would have sent her into whoops, but if she really allowed her imagination full rein, there was no telling what it might not devise. After all, with this mad major, if major he indeed was, anything must be a possibility!

"A trivial, but tiresome little matter of some papers that are needed by my uncle, Lord Rowby—or, to be more accurate, by my uncle's secretary, Neill—a fussy man . . . likes everything to be just so. I happened to be coming this way, and in view of your brother's indisposition . . ."

He watched with interest as consternation replaced bewilderment in her expressive face, until full realization dawned at last.

"Heavens!" she exclaimed, the words spilling out before she could stop them. "*You* must be the Conquering Hero!"

"Must I?" he mused, one eyebrow quirking irrepressibly upward. "How very gratifying for me!"

"Oh! I didn't mean . . . that is . . ." Her cheeks were aglow with embarrassment. "Well, you don't wear a uniform . . ." This was very much in the nature of a reproach, and as such invited explanation.

"Worn to rags, I fear," he offered apologetically. "You would not have me appear shoddily clad?"

Charis tried hard to control the feeling of helpless exasperation that his quixotic flights seemed to rouse in her. "It is of little interest to me how you choose to appear," she declared with what she hoped would pass for a distant coolness. "Except," she added with sudden spirit, "that nothing in our brief acquaintance would lead me to connect you in any way with Lord Rowby!"

The major's eyes gleamed with appreciation. "A regular coxcomb, in fact. I freely admit that my behavior has been despicably misleading from the first. We Peninsular fellows, you know, aren't at all fitted for polite society. Incorrigible, my aunt calls me. I can only beg your pardon and promise to do better in the future."

Before she knew what he was about, he had taken her hand and carried it gallantly to his lips. The thought of Mrs. Huyton-Forbes opposite being privy to this absurd charade from behind her muslin curtains made Charis snatch her hand away at once.

He was doing it again! Dispelling her indignation with that insidious charm, so that the blow to her vanity upon first discovering that he had not come solely in search of her was almost dispelled, and her mouth began to curve in answer.

And then the sudden recollection of why he *had* come brought her sharply down to earth. He had come to see Tristram, who was *indisposed*, and somehow she must convince him that such a visit was out of the question. All else faded into insignificance before the pressing need to prevent him from learning of Tristram's escapade.

A gentle cough reproached Charis, reminding her that the major still waited patiently on the doorstep. She stifled a moment of panic which urged her to slam the door in his face. There was a kind of implacable

force about Major Hammond which belied his nonsensical ways and suggested that he would not submit to
being summarily dismissed. And to confess that she was
alone in the house would be to admit that Tristram was
not there. Only one course remained. She had fortunately completed work on the papers, and must out of
courtesy and to allay any suspicion admit him for as
long as it would take to return them to him. She smiled
brightly and bade him enter, conversing with admirable
composure over her shoulder as she led the way to the
sunny back parlor.

"You must forgive me if I seem a trifle distraught,"
she said, comfortable in the knowledge that she did not
have to actually look him in the eye as she spoke. "I am
all on end this morning—not able to settle to anything,
which is why you find me in some disarray."

It was at this point, having ushered him into the
room, that she turned rather suddenly and found him
very close, towering over her in a disconcerting fashion
that quite took her breath away.

"Please, do sit down," she implored, driven by something akin to desperation. "I believe you will find the
chair near the window very comfortable."

He made no immediate attempt to move, but stood
looking down at her consideringly. "The likeness is
certainly marked," he mused in that deep, pleasant
voice. "The moment I saw Winslade I knew him for
your brother, for all that you resembled nothing so
much as a startled water sprite at our previous meeting!"

Charis bit back the retort that sprang to her lips and
instead said sweetly, "Such acute powers of description
you have, major—but you were much more complimen-
tary at the time. You thought me enchanting then, as I
remember. . . ."

She stopped abruptly, appalled to discover where her
desire to score a point off him had led her. His slow,
delighted grin confirmed how well he appreciated the
excellence of her recall.

"So you were—still are, my dear Miss Winslade.

Utterly enchanting, pins and all, only I was so sure that you would bridle if I ventured to say so yet again!"

"Well, of course I would if I were not so sure that you were quizzing me!" she exclaimed. "It would be most improper, and besides . . ."

"Yes?"

The query was so deceptively meek that Charis bit her lip, half-laughed, and said, "Nothing." And then, resolved to try treating him in much the way she did Tristram's friends, "Oh, do please stop being so nonsensical, sir. I refuse to come to points with you! Will you take a glass of Madeira?"

"That would be very pleasant."

There was a smile in his voice, but this time she did not make the mistake of looking into his eyes. Instead, she put her drawings down on the table and walked across to the dresser.

"Concerning your brother," he said conversationally, "is his indisposition of a serious nature?"

Her hand froze on the decanter while she chose her words with care. It suddenly seemed very important to avoid an outright lie.

"Oh, well," she prevaricated. "It has all been rather worrying. I am not sure what to think. Poor Tristram!"

"Poor Tristram, indeed," he murmured. "And poor Miss Winslade, too. Perhaps I might be of some help when I see him. I have had considerable experience in dealing with the kind of afflictions that young men so often fall prey to."

For a moment her composure almost deserted her. The decanter in her hand trembled over the glass and there was a distinct ringing sound as the two touched; a few drops of wine spilled onto the dresser's polished surface and she made a small, incoherent grunt of annoyance.

In a moment he was at her side, removing the decanter from her tense fingers and replacing the stopper.

"Forget the drink. It doesn't matter. . . ."

His voice was clipped, strangely unlike him, and his expression when she could bring herself to look up at him was enigmatic, questioning, even a little forbidding. It was as though those hooded blue eyes had seen right inside her to the growing morass of deception in which she floundered. Perhaps he had already guessed the truth, or, worse still, had known it from the very first.

Her faith in Ned's ability to tell convincing bouncers had never been great, but now her own aptitude was shown to be equally shaky. A part of her wanted desperately to confess the whole, to make light of it and see the laughter come back into his eyes. But it was already too late for that, and for Tristram's sake she was committed to continue.

"You are very kind, but . . . I think it might be better if you did not see my brother just now. You see, he is probably sleeping and . . . and I expect that sleep is the very best thing in such cases, don't you?" she continued, quite unaware of the note of supplication in her voice. "It would be foolish to risk disturbing him?"

There was a moment of silence, and then, unexpectedly, his expression, his whole aspect softened.

"Quite so," he said almost gently. "No doubt Neill can wait for his papers."

"The papers! Oh, but I know where they are!"

Relief flooded through Charis, and as though released from a spell she practically ran to the bureau, took out the folder, and returned to find the major leafing through her sketches.

"Did you do these?" he said without looking up. "You have a decided talent, Miss Winslade."

With one hand still clutching the folder, she quickly put out the other to stop him, but she was too late. He caught her hand in mid-flight and held on to it, his thumb smoothing it gently as he studied the drawing she had done of him for what seemed like an age without speaking. Then:

"A decided talent," he said again softly, "though I fear you have flattered me."

Charis did not know where to look. His clasp became more insistent and in the end, she could avoid his eyes no longer. What she saw in their expression confused her further, almost robbing her of breath as she said valiantly, "As to that, sir, I am no judge. I . . . simply find faces interesting. . . ."

She tugged her hand free and thrust the folder at him. "Please . . . take it," she implored, striving for normality.

For Daniel Hammond, too, it was a moment quite unlike any other he had ever experienced.

He was thrown, temporarily, out of his stride, and needed time to think. What had begun as a light flirtation—or had it been more than that, even at the first—had suddenly assumed a quite different aspect.

"Miss Winslade . . ." he began, but she would not let him continue.

"No, please, I beg of you . . . take the folder and go! If you remain any longer, you will say things you might regret and so might I, and it would all be quite improper." She urged him once more to accept the folder and when he presently did so, said with finality, "The work is completed."

"Is it?" He looked down at it, sounding surprised. In truth, he was not accustomed to being so summarily dismissed. It piqued him faintly.

"Naturally," Charis said, hoping that her blush would pass for indignation rather than guilt. "Tristram is most conscientious in such matters."

"I am delighted to hear it," he said, dryly formal all of a sudden. "Though you might give him the hint that Neill don't care to have papers removed from the premises. Give him also my good wishes for a speedy recovery." He took up his hat and turned to leave, but the tenseness of her face moved him to brush it lightly with one strong, slim finger. "Easy, fair divinity—my teasing is done."

He bowed and was gone.

Charis wandered back into the parlor and stared down at the picture which still lay on the table, the half-smile in the eyes seeming to reproach her. Her gaze lifted to the small looking glass on the wall beyond. She felt so strange that surely it must show! But there was nothing different to be seen, except perhaps a certain haziness—a suspicious brightness about the eyes.

"Fool!" she told her reflection sternly. "You are behaving exactly like Lavinia and her silly friends, and you ought to be ashamed of yourself!"

And before she could weaken, she took up the drawing of Major Hammond and tore it into little pieces.

4

Charis had never been able to enter her uncle's house in Berkley Square on the occasion of a grand ball without being filled with a sense of awe. This stemmed not from any feeling of inadequacy, but rather an amused disbelief that Aunt Lizzie should consider it necessary to embellish such a beautifully proportioned mansion almost to the point of vulgarity in order to achieve an effect. She sometimes found it difficult to believe that her father and dear feather-brained Aunt Lizzie had been brother and sister, for he had been such a high stickler in matters of taste—a truly elegant man.

Although darkness had not yet fallen, every window was ablaze with light as Charis arrived. Red carpet covered the steps and flowed out across the pavement beneath an elaborate awning, while the open door afforded any curious passer-by a tantalizing glimpse of what lay beyond.

Banks of flowers and potted palms filled the hall, drenching the air with their mingled perfumes; greenery swathed its six Corinthian columns, twining upward, around and around, and spilling over to envelope the bannister rails.

Charis knew from experience that the theme would be repeated in all the main reception rooms and was momentarily glad that Tristram was not with her, for his comments would surely have reduced her to giggles. Not that she had wholly forgiven him for letting her down.

"You promised!" she had accused him roundly as he tumbled into the house, bespattered in mud and grinning sheepishly when she was already dressed and ready to leave.

"So I did," he returned with feeling. "And it's no fault of mine that I wasn't here sooner! If you mean to hurl reproaches, pray direct them at Ceddie's door. That boy has the worst pair of hands I've ever come across—overturned us in a ditch on the way back, if you please—miles from anywhere! You may think yourself lucky to see me at all!"

Charis cut short this tale of woe to issue an ultimatum. Either he must be changed and ready within fifteen minutes, or she would not stay for him.

"Don't be cork-brained, love!" Tristram's expression was one of comical dismay. "I cannot vouch to be ready one minute under a half hour, and then only if all goes swimmingly, which it won't, you know, if I'm obliged to snatch at things and tie my neckcloth in a hurry! You had much better go on without me."

"Dandy!" she taunted him. "Aunt Lizzie will be furious if you ruin her table arrangements, and you really can't expect her to put dinner back on your account."

Tristram's grin was back, tinged now with audacity. "You leave Aunt Lizzie to me. With any luck, Ceddie will already have drawn the worst of her fire—and in any case, you know that I have never yet failed to turn her up sweet!"

"Oh, you are quite shameless!" she had exclaimed, trying not to laugh. "And will be well served if you find the door barred to you!" On the point of leaving the room she paused, looking back. "By the by, did you win your wretched race?"

"Of course," he said with maddening complacence. "Knocked a clear four minutes off the time."

In her aunt's double drawing room the guests invited to dinner before the ball were already foregathering with, here and there, a red uniform making a bright splash of color. Many of those present were known to

Charis and her progress across the room in search of her cousin was frequently halted by kindly greetings. In the end it was Lavinia, a floating vision in white spider gauze liberally sprinkled with tiny silver stars, who found her.

"Charis—at last!" she exclaimed. "I declare I had almost given you up for lost!"

As they embraced, Charis could not suppress a twinge of envy; everything about her cousin was perfection, from the delicately rounded figure so artlessly exposed by the brief bodice of her gown to the exquisite oval of her face where each feature vied for beauteous symmetry. Even her curls, shimmering now under the light of the dozens of candles which picked out the silver ribbon threaded through them, were guinea bright. Had she been less amiable, Charis sighed, one might comfortably have disliked her, but the worst that could be said of Lavinia was that she was light-minded and a trifle spoiled—and on the credit side, however volatile her nature, she was quite devoid of malice.

She tugged now at Charis's arm, pulling her to one side. "I cannot wait to tell you!" Her cerulean blue eyes were wide and brilliant with some inner excitement, the words tumbling over themselves. "I have just made the acquaintance of the most devastating man!" she announced breathlessly, and seeing the twinkle of amusement in her cousin's eyes, protested, "No, truly—he is an officer, a rifleman, just home from the war where he distinguished himself most nobly! And oh, Charis . . . everything about him is handsome, and he has *such* engaging manners. Of course, he is being feted by simply everyone, but . . . well, I hardly dare to think it, but I am almost certain that there was something quite particular in his eyes . . . in his manner, when he addressed himself to me!"

Charis had heard a similar catalog of superlatives so often before, and applied to so many different gentlemen that, with her own somewhat painful experience still fresh in her mind, she was inclined to treat it with less indulgence than usual.

"Naturally. I should think him both blind and stupid if he did not find you wholly irresistible," she said lightly. "But you will be a greater widgeon than I take you for if you pay too much heed to his attentions. Military gentlemen are notorious flirts. Remember Captain Manners?" (Not to mention Major Hammond. She had almost said it aloud.)

"Oh, but . . ."

Before Lavinia could rush to the defense of her latest would-be inamorato, however, her mama arrived upon the scene, resplendent in a most becoming feathered turban secured with ribbons tied strategically so as to disguise the least suspicion of a sagging jawline. She was a plumply pretty lady of middle years, whose likeness to her daughter was so marked that one could see exactly how Lavinia would look in twenty years time.

"Charis, dear child!"

As she clasped her niece dutifully to her bosom, Lady Weston could not but give thanks to the divine Providence which had decreed that her own dear Lavinia should be built on softer, more womanly lines! There were many, she knew, who admired, nay envied, Charis her careless boyish elegance, together with that openness of manner which her ladyship privately considered at times to be a trifle too lively—and seemed quite undiminished by the downward trend of her fortunes. Still, she would be the last to deny that her niece was possessed of many excellent qualities.

"You are looking very fine this evening," she said, a shade grudgingly, eyeing the newly-renovated gown which was attracting more than the occasional glance. "I am sure I don't know how you contrive to dress so well. . . ."

She did not add "purse-pinched as you are," but as the unfinished sentence hung in the air, Charis was very conscious of her meaning, and was at once put on her mettle.

"It is only my old ivory silk, dear aunt, made over dagger-cheap," she said sweetly.

"I would never have recognized it," Lavinia put in, seeing the light of battle in her cousin's eye. "It looks perfectly splendid!"

"Did I say otherwise?" demanded her mama a little querulously. "Charis knows very well that I have the greatest admiration for her many accomplishments. . . ."

"Oh, you would be surprised what may be achieved when one has a talent for design and some small skill with a needle. Tris calls it my knack of creating something out of nothing." A little devil within prompted her to add, "He has suggested more than once that I should set up as a seamstress . . . I might do rather well, don't you think?"

"Hush, child!" Lady Weston glanced about her in some agitation. "I pray you will not say such things, even in jest! By the by, I do not see Tristram. Was he not with you?"

Charis explained that he would be along very soon.

"Well, I am sure I hope he may be! And I shall have something very pertinent to say to him when he does come, I can tell you! Leading my poor Ceddie astray! His father was most displeased!"

Charis exchanged a speaking glance with her cousin, knowing full well that her uncle was quite indifferent to the minor peccadillos of his youngest born.

"Aunt Lizzie—Tristram is to go to Brussels. . . ."

"Brussels!" cried Lavinia. "Oh, how splendid!"

"Really?" Lady Weston's thoughts were clearly still elsewhere. "Tiresome boy! Now, I wonder—is everyone arrived? I had better just—"

"So you see, I won't be able to come to the country with you," Charis persisted.

"Not come?" Lady Weston's blue eyes opened very wide as though debating where else she might go, and yet again Charis was made aware of being regarded, however unintentionally, as a poor relation. There was, in consequence, an added lift to her chin as she explained the sudden turn events had taken.

"And so, you see, I mean to go to Brussels with him. It will be like the old days."

"Oh, how I envy you!" Lavinia sighed. "It will be such fun! The guards are stationed there now, you know, and oh, so many people are taking houses there. Mama—" she was at her most coaxing—"is not Charis fortunate, indeed?"

"Fortunate? I would call it foolishness!" exclaimed her flustered mama, who was not a little put out at being told rather than consulted. She rescued her silk shawl as it slipped from her shoulders and carefully rearranged it. "To be going among strangers—foreigners, at that, in such a harum-scarum way—you and Tristram setting up house together, just the two of you—"

"And Emily," Charis put in swiftly.

"Oh, Mrs. McGrath don't signify where appearances are concerned. She can hardly go about with you in the guise of a chaperone!"

"Nor does she here. Oh really, Aunt Lizzie!" Charis wasn't sure whether to laugh or be annoyed. "We are more than two and twenty, and shall be living very much as we do at present."

"Just so. But abroad. A vastly different situation! Apart from any other consideration, it will give them such odd notions of how the English go on!" At this point a splutter of laughter from the two girls made her toss her head. "Oh, you will no doubt think me sadly old-fashioned . . ." They protested that they did not. "Well, it is ever the way of the young that they care nothing for the opinions of their elders, but *you will see!*" she concluded darkly. "And now I must go . . . I am neglecting my guests!" And she bustled away, bristling with injured pride, leaving Charis feeling the pangs of guilt.

"Don't let Mama put you in a pucker," said Lavinia with the indifference of one used to such megrims. "She will come about presently." Her eyes sparkled. "I can't wait to see Nugent's face when he hears . . . he won't like it above half!"

Charis said that she couldn't see what business it was of Lord Weston's firstborn.

"None at all, but you know how my dear brother loves to pontificate!" Lavinia linked fingers with Charis, and pouted prettily. "Oh, how I wish I was coming with you! London is going to be so dull this winter with everyone of note either in Brussels or Vienna. I shall just have to be very clever and drop hints in Mama's ear and then perhaps the thought of what she might be missing will outweigh her fear of crossing the water!"

As they laughed together, Lavinia looked up and saw a pleasant-faced older lady in an unfashionable puce silk gown approaching. She drew her hand away from her cousin's and whispered mischievously, "Here comes Lady Rowby. Forgive me, dearest . . . I shall leave you to entertain her. I have already paid my respects, and though she is charming in her rather odd fashion, I can think of better ways to pass my time!"

She drifted away with a dreamy smile for the lady in question, leaving Charis to stand waiting with mixed feelings, not because she did not like Lady Rowby—in fact, she liked her very well. But should her husband be here also, and Tristram came swaggering in, full of pride in his success with the ribbons, there could be little hope of his deception remaining undiscovered. Also, there was the vexed question of her relationship to Major Hammond.

"Miss Winslade," Lady Rowby was nodding kindly at her and Charis did her utmost to respond with ease. "I was hoping to see you this evening."

"Indeed, ma'am?" Charis said.

"I understand that your brother is to accompany my

husband to Brussels next month. That will please him, no doubt?"

"Yes," Charis replied, with perfect truth. "He is looking forward to it with great enthusiasm."

"And you mean to go with him?"

Charis betrayed her surprise. "However did you know that?"

Lady Rowby smiled her dry little smile. "Oh, you would be surprised what one may learn if only one keeps one's eyes and ears open!"

Charis wondered if there was not rather more behind her ladyship's words than was immediately apparent, but for once her normal forthright approach deserted her and she veered off at a tangent.

"Do you disapprove of my wishing to go?"

"My dear child, it is not for me to approve or disapprove what you do," said Lady Rowby briskly. "You have always seemed to me to be an eminently sensible young woman, not given to foolish starts."

"Why, thank you," said Charis, surprised to learn that her ladyship had interested herself to such an extent. "Aunt Lizzie thinks it quite improper that I should wish to set up house for Tris and myself abroad, though I really don't see why. I am hardly a green girl, and we have always been together, you see," she explained. "Of course, I do realize that we can't continue indefinitely, living in one another's pockets, but . . ."

"But you do not feel that Mr. Winslade is quite ready yet to be loosed upon the world alone," Lady Rowby said shrewdly. "Yes, I see I was not mistaken in you." She smiled. "What you say simply serves to convince me that your presence in Brussels can only have a beneficial outcome."

Charis was now certain that Lady Rowby had heard about Tristram's escapade. It made her say with some urgency: "There is no real unsteadiness in Tris, you know. But when Papa died . . . well, it has taken him longer than me to come to terms with our changed circumstances, and just occasionally, when he sees the greater freedom enjoyed by his friends, he kicks against his lot. That is why—"

"Miss Winslade, do not go on, I beg of you." The older lady held up a hand, her eyes twinkling. "Anything that needs to be said must be between your brother and Lord Rowby . . . though if I might venture a small piece of advice . . ."

Charis assented eagerly.

"Then I suggest you urge Mr. Winslade to confess the whole to my husband. I am not saying he won't give him a rare dressing down, but he appreciates the straightforward approach and is not yet so old that he can't remember the follies of his own youth!"

"Oh, thank you, ma'am! I'm sure you are right," Charis exclaimed. "I think Tristram got a little carried away with his celebrations upon hearing the news about Brussels."

"Very likely, my dear," said Lady Rowby dryly. "So let us say no more about it. You must come to visit me in a day or two, and I will see what can be done about finding you suitable lodgings in Brussels." She glanced over Charis's shoulder and the tone of her voice changed suddenly to encompass a wealth of pride and affection. "Miss Winslade, here is someone I should very much like you to meet . . ."

Charis knew instinctively who the someone would be and so was afforded a valuable moment in which to school her features if not her racing pulse into a suitable degree of expectancy. Her composure almost suffered a reverse upon turning to behold Major Hammond approaching with Lavinia on his arm, looking quite odiously like the cat that had stolen the cream, and her cousin with the possessive glint in her eye that said clearly "This one is mine!"

It was pointless to try to convince herself that she was not mortified to reflect upon the ease with which

Lavinia had captivated Major Hammond, though a further moment's thought obliged her to recognize the inevitability of their mutual attraction; she was beauty itself, while he—in the distinctive dark green elegance of his dress uniform, much braided with black and embellished with silver lace, all set off by a dashing scarlet sash, and with his wickedly expressive eyes and his light brown hair arranged *à la Brutus*—was enough to turn any girl's head. Seeing them together, Charis acknowledged the absurdity of supposing that he had ever regarded her as anything but a brief, amusing diversion.

The spurt of anger triggered by this acknowledgment enabled her to respond with equanimity to the drawled formality of his "Your servant, Miss Winslade . . . delighted to make your acquaintance." She was able to curtsy and murmur his name, and even—just for an instant—to meet those sleepy eyes with just the hint of amusement in their depths as he complimented her on her gown, with more more than a faint flutter of her traitorous pulse.

The suspicion that he was making game of her turned the anger to indignation, which carried her very adequately through the brief conversation that followed before Lavinia imperiously led him away to be introduced to others of her friends.

"Make a handsome couple, don't they?" observed Lady Rowby, blithely unaware of the tumult raging in her young companion's breast. "Though I do hope Miss Weston will not lose her heart to him too drastically! Dan is the dearest boy. He is like a son to us. Indeed, I am sometimes hard put to it to remember that he's *not* our son, for he was still in short coats when his parents died, leaving him in our care. I was never able to have children, you know." She sighed, and then became brisk once more. "However, that is neither here nor there. The thing is, soldiering is his life—we are so proud that both Lord Hill and the duke have praised him so highly—and since his commitment is quite unwavering, I suppose he is destined to remain forever a bachelor!" Lady Rowby said this with a certain degree of regret, adding with a sudden twinkle, "Besides which, he is an incorrigible flirt—and would, I fear, make the very devil of a husband!"

It was quite clear to Charis that the major could do no wrong in her ladyship's eyes. There was much that she could have confirmed about his character, but confined herself instead to something suitably noncommittal. After only a short time more, several newcomers approached and the conversation became general and she was presently able to slip away.

Tristram's arrival just when she had convinced herself that he would not come caused a pre-dinner diversion not without its hilarious, if somewhat embarrassing, moments. He carried off his meeting with Lady Rowby with great aplomb, recovering almost instantly from the shock of coming face to face with her, to inquire with a disarming audacious charm whether he was to have the pleasure of meeting Lord Rowby also, and showing every appearance of regreat upon learning that he was not present.

"I should have very much liked to have had a word with him about Brussels," he told her with an engaging smile.

Since the news of his curricle race with Ceddie had by then percolated through the assembled company, Charis hardly knew where to look. But Lady Rowby seemed to find Tristram's audacity amusing and prophesied that his capacity for instant and utterly convincing extemporization would stand him in excellent stead so long as it was kept in check.

"I take it the old girl knew," he said unrepentantly as Charis managed to drag him away.

"Well, of course she knows, Tris. Practically everyone knows!"

He grinned. "Bound to, I suppose. Still, I like Lady

R—for all that. She's a bit of a prosy old thing! She won't carry tattle!"

Charis despaired of him. She told him what her ladyship had said about telling Lord Rowby the truth, and he was much struck.

"Damn me if I don't march straight into his office in the morning and bare my soul," he said. "After all, he's bound to find out sooner or later, and it will spike old Neill's guns if I confess. That alone's worth humbling oneself for!"

There was a small shriek and Lavinia was upon them. "Tris! You've come at last!" She greeted him with cousinly fervor and advised him to avoid her mama at all costs. "She is all set to give you the most tremendous scold for leading my baby brother into perilous paths!"

Tristram grinned. "If she knew her son as well as she ought, she'd know that I was the one in need of protection!" Lavinia giggled and introduced him to Major Hammond, whom he eyed with a certain degree of envy. "I've heard a great deal about your exploits," he said with an enthusiasm that surprised Charis.

"My family been boring on about them, have they?" drawled the major. "I advise you to discount at least half of what you hear, and you'll be somewhere near to the truth." He raised a laconic eyebrow. "By the way, permit me to return the compliment and commend *you* on the speed of your recovery."

"My . . .?" Tristram shot a glance at Charis, and closed one eye in a solemn wink. "Oh, aye, my recovery. Thanks, but I'm never out of sorts for long, am I, love?"

Charis could cheerfully have wrung his neck, and dared not meet Major Hammond's eyes. Lavinia, however, was puzzled and was all set to ask questions when, thankfully, Lady Weston's butler announced dinner.

It was not a comfortable meal. Charis was placed almost opposite the major and several times glanced up to find his gaze resting on her somewhat enigmatically.

Each time she made a point of returning her attention to the rather dull government official on her right, who needed little encouragement to continue his exceedingly tedious dissertation upon how he considered that the Allied Powers should deal with the disposition of Napoleon's vast European acquisitions. In consequence of all this, her appetite was quite ruined, and so was her temper.

As the Honorable Nugent Weston found to his cost when he made it his business to seek her out as the people began to assemble for the ball.

Mr. Weston was a stolid gentleman of some thirty-five summers who contrived to seem considerably older by dressing with sobriety and cultivating a prosy disposition which lacked even the slightest leavening of humor. From his present frowning air of constraint, Charis deduced that news had reached him of her intended remove abroad.

"I assumed at the first that Mama had mistaken the matter," he informed her gravely. "But Tristram informs me that it is no less than the truth."

"Tristram?" She sounded surprised, for he did not usually deign to exchange more than half a dozen words with her brother.

"I was venturing to point out to him how damaging his want of conscientiousness might be to his future prospects, when he grew quite short with me, and accused me of meddling in what don't concern me," Nugent explained with a distinct air of injured dignity. "I will not distress you with chapter and verse of his impertinence, but it concluded with the intelligence that since you were—both of you—on the point of embarking for foreign parts, I need no longer feel constrained to act as his conscience!"

Charis, though annoyed, was obliged to smother a laugh.

"Well, I'm sorry if Tristram was rude," she said, "but really, Nugent, it was no more than you deserved. It *is* no business of yours what we do with our lives, and if you mean to take me to task also, I shall very likely be even more uncivil than Tris, so do, I beg of you, let well alone!"

Astonished disbelief rendered him ludicrously deflated, robbing him momentarily of speech, but Charis, knowing from experience how quickly he would come about, felt that she must render the *coup de grace* to his pretensions once and for all.

She said, not unkindly, "We shall not change to suit your notions of propriety, my dear cousin, so you had much better wash your hands of us now and be thankful that we shall not be around to annoy or embarrass you for some little time at least!"

The glittering ballroom was filling rapidly and the musicians were beginning to tune their instruments. As he still lingered, she added with a smile, "I am sure Aunt Lizzie must have finished receiving her guests by now, so do go and put her out of her misery, Nugent. You know how she will be cast into high fidgets if you are not there to lead Lavinia out in the first dance."

While he still hesitated, tense with conflicting emotions, she happened to glance over his shoulder. "There now," she exclaimed, seeing her chance of escape at last. "I have just seen Ned Kent! Forgive me, cousin, but I must have a word with him." And she left him before he could protest.

The Honorable Edward Kent was a stocky young man with sandy hair and pleasing gray eyes that frequently held a vaguely harassed expression. He was as different from Tristram as was possible, but they were good friends for all that.

"Charis!" he exclaimed as she hurried toward him. "Is T-Tristram back safely, do you know?" he said in a low voice, glancing furtively about him as though afraid of being overheard.

She was quick to reassure him, aware from his slight stammer just how ill-at-ease he was.

"Yes, of course. He is here, if you please, wretched creature, positively basking in his success, for news of the race has become public property just as I expected it would, so you need trouble your head no more about it!"

"As long as he d-doesn't get into t-trouble on my account," Ned said apologetically. "Only I wasn't sure what I was supposed to say, d'you see? T-Tris being a trifle bosky and . . . and not very clear about it. . . ."

"My dear Ned, don't! It was monstrous of him to expect you to tell lies for him. . . ."

"Oh well, as to that," a rueful smile gleamed in his eyes. "I didn't actually lie, you know. It was more an evasion of the t-truth . . . about his being not t-too clever, last night . . . that sort of thing . . . very likely indisposed, and all that. . . . I'd never have carried through an outright b-bouncer with old Neill staring at me, gimlet-eyed!"

"Very likely not." She laughed, linking arms with him. "You are a better friend than Tris deserves and have nothing to reproach yourself with! Now, for reward, you may have my hand for the first dance, if you are not already bespoken."

His stammered assent was so fervent with relief that Charis resolved to take Tristram to task about it later.

After this, the evening improved considerably. Charis did not want for partners, and her obvious enjoyment did not go unnoticed. The Marquess of Verney and Sir Edwin Booth, on their way to the saloon set aside for gaming, paused in the ballroom doorway to survey the scene. A lively country dance was just ending and the marquess put up his glass, training it on one particular set. Sir Edwin followed the direction of his gaze.

"That's young Winslade's sister, ain't it?"

"H'm," mused Verney with an air of preoccupation.

"Fine gal. Pity about her circumstances . . . bound to limit her chances."

"Now here's a pensive-looking pair," murmured an

amused voice. "Whose character are you dissecting, I wonder?"

They turned to find Dan Hammond beside them.

"Winslade's sister, if you must know," drawled the marquess. "Sir Edwin was just lamenting her want of fortune."

Dan watched Charis Winslade laughing at some comment made by her partner as they left the floor. "It seems not to have dimmed her popularity," he observed.

"I should say not, by jove! Nor, if all come to all, has she been entirely without offers, fortune or no fortune. I know for a fact she turned down Tubby Castleton. . . ."

"Sensible girl," said Verney. "Wouldn't wish Castleton on m'sister, for all his shekels!" He turned his glass on his friend. "You're very much *en grande tenue* this evening, Dan. Trying to outshine us all, are you?"

A lazy grin greeted this taunt. "I wouldn't presume, dear boy," Dan flicked the much-frogged coatee with a careless finger. "This lot was delivered this morning—everything else worn to shreds—and Aunt Sybil was insistent that I should wear it to escort her. However, I fear I am about to be eclipsed."

Dan indicated a familiar figure, severely resplendent in black and white, who paused briefly, eyeglass raised, to absorb the full impact of Cedric Weston's waistcoat before strolling across to join them.

"You look pale, George," observed the marquess, making room for him.

Mr. Brummell seemed much shaken. "So would you, m'dear Verney, if your sensibilities had just been exposed to such violent abuse. Purple and green stripes—with a blue coat!" He shuddered faintly. "And a neckcloth that defies description!"

"Best not to dwell on it, man," advised Sir Edwin with exaggerated gravity. "Youth and its vagaries, y'know. In both dress and manners, the young ever lacked discretion."

"I won't presume to answer for my manners," Mr.

Brummell's voice took on a plaintive note, "but I believe that even in my rawest salad days no one ever saw me in purple and green stripes!"

"I rejoice to hear it. Such an idea would be unthinkable!" drawled the marquess, the sardonic curl of his lip very much in evidence. "You are an enduring example to us all, my dear!"

As a cut it was scarcely more than a prick, but delivered with all the delicacy of an accomplished fencer, which Verney indisputably was. Dan thought his friend had been unnecessarily cruel as he watched Beau covertly from beneath half-closed eyelids. Rumor was rife that his affairs were in a sad way, and had grown infinitely worse since his estrangement from Prinny.

To the casual observer it might have seemed that Verney's thrust had missed its mark, but Dan, well used to assessing men for early signs of stress, noted an almost indiscernible tautness about Brummell's mouth; and the faint color that ran up under his skin following upon the barbed comment was curiously at odds with the careful blandness in his eyes. His voice, however, betrayed nothing beyond polite interest.

"I expect you are finding life a trifle slow here after all your exploits, Major Hammond?"

"It's certainly a great deal more restful. If you had ever been accorded the doubtful privilege of being detailed to keep pace with *old Nosey*'s demands once he'd taken the bit, you'd know what I mean! One could end up in some deucedly uncomfortable holes, I can tell you!"

"Manchester," murmured Mr. Brummell reflectively.

"Manchester?" The major lifted an eyebrow.

Sir Edwin chuckled. "Did you never hear tell of George's brief but exemplary military career? Quite the dashing Hussar in his youth, was Beau—one of Prinny's very own regiment of pretty toy soldiers! Nothing but the best for George, even in those days!"

"It was an agreeable life," reflected Beau, "but in the

end, you know, I was obliged to resign . . ." He looked
from one to the other, his eyes opening a little wider as
he concluded in his drollest way, "But, what else could
I do? The regiment was posted to Manchester!"

Amid laughter the marquess drawled, "Ah, but Dan is
made of sterner stuff. He may prate about restfulness,
but he don't know the meaning of it. Beneath that
languid pose churns a fount of tireless energy which can
become exceedingly tedious, I may tell you! When he
ain't laying seige to Froggy bastions, it's pretty women's
hearts! Dammit, he's actually spent most of this evening dancing!"

A gleam lit the major's eyes. "Thank you for reminding me, Gideon. Valuable time is passing and I have to
see a young lady about a waltz."

He found Charis at last surrounded by a group of her
friends. For a few moments he was content just to
watch her. She stood, slim and straight, the deceptive
simplicity of her dress now free of its pins and quite
uncluttered by jewelery, while the rest of them fluttered
around her like gaudy butterflies, and the brilliant crystal
chandelier above her head turned the swirling cap of
copper curls to flame and lent an added radiance to her
vividly expressive face.

Only when the people around about began seeking
out their partners did he step forward with an indefin-
able air of authority which his height and the splendor
of his uniform seemed to accentuate, so that it seemed
the most natural thing in the world when a place was
instantly made for him.

"Miss Winslade, will you do me the honor of waltzing
with me?"

Charis had been so sure that he wouldn't ask her;
that her capacity for deceit, by now so abundantly clear
to him, must inevitably have given him profound disgust of her, so that even if he had not been slain by
Lavinia's beauty he would surely not wish to pursue her
acquaintance. The fact that he had made no attempt to

do so until now, though he had danced with almost every attractive woman in the room, served only to confirm her opinion. And now that he had sought her out, she could find no trace in his eyes of that irresistible smile; instead, they held a compelling, implacable glint that seemed to convey that he would brook no denial. It was a situation spiced with danger—a challenge which she ought to resist.

Most of her friends had melted away. Only Ned remained. She turned to him impulsively. "Ned?"

He looked from one to the other of them and grinned, good-naturedly. "Don't m-mind me, m'dear. Not much of a dancer, as you know. Two left feet—always had! You'll do much better with Major Hammond!"

"My thanks," said the major with the hint of a smile, and without waiting for Charis's consent, he grasped her arm with a tingling sureness and led her toward the assembling dancers. Finally, when they were almost there, she found the wit to resist.

He looked down at her. "What is it?"

She sought desperately for the right words, but they refused to come.

"I know that you *do* waltz, for I saw you doing so in the most accomplished way earlier, so it isn't that you are afraid of being thought fast—"

"No, of course not!"

"Well then?"

She lifted her chin. "If you must know, I am not at all certain that I care to be so summarily . . . appropriated!"

"Oh, if that is all!" He laughed softly. "Sound military tactics, dear girl—I didn't mean to give you the chance to repulse me!"

The music began, and his hand found the curve of her waist with unerring ease. A tiny shiver ran through her.

"Easy," he murmured as he drew her close and whirled her into the dance. "After all, it isn't the first time I have held you like this."

She had meant to be so sensible—to cling to her best instincts, which told her that it was all a game to him! But common sense was already spinning away dizzily, splintering into bright fragments as the light from crystal chandeliers above her was splintering, cascading around her, taking with it all coherent thought and leaving her prey to a myriad of sensations. The sensual lilt of the music seemed to be inside her, making her doubly aware of him, the increased pressure of his hand through the silk of her dress, the taut line of his thigh against hers as he swirled her around, and through it all, a reckless giddy impression that she was drowning in her own delight.

"If you keep on looking like that," he said softly, "I shall have to kiss you—in front of all these people."

"Like what?" she answered breathlessly, still half-seduced, entranced by the way he was looking at her.

"You have hundreds of little jade green stars shimmering in your eyes and your mouth is almost irresistibly, invitingly, vulnerable. . . ."

"Oh, no!" Charis came back to reality with a stifled skirl of dismay. Her step faltered, but he took her through it with expert precision until they were once more moving in unison.

"How can you say such things to me?" It was a low, anguished sob.

He smiled indulgently. "Very easily—when they are true."

The knowledge that she had been so lost to all sense of decorum as to give him cause . . . that she had so betrayed her feelings . . .

"You are right," she admitted in a stifled voice. "No blame attaches to you. I knew very well how it might be! The fault is mine! My damnable weakness for getting my fingers burned! But oh, I never meant . . . never wanted . . . Oh, please, take me off the floor. I cannot continue!"

Her distress had the oddest effect upon Daniel

Hammond. It was compounded all at once of tenderness, impatience, and anger born of injured pride. And in that moment, the last emotion was by far the strongest.

"To do that would be to really draw attention to yourself," he said harshly. "Surely a folly far greater than suffering a few more moments of my company?"

The whiplash impact of his contempt acted like a douche of cold water which, after the brief numbness of shock, summoned up the blood so that she was able to say with adequate composure, "Yes, of course."

Never had a few moments seemed so long. Never had she been more in need of the resolution necessary to carry her through his scrupulously polite leave-taking and the subsequent good-natured teasing of Tristram and her friends upon her conquest. Several times she found Lavinia looking at her in a puzzled, almost resentful fashion—and prayed that her cousin would not try to quiz her about Major Hammond.

For her own part, the sooner the evening was over and forgotten, the better she would be pleased.

Lady Rowby leaned back against the comfortable squab of her town carriage watching the shadowy outline of her nephew's face, chin sunk in the folds of his cravat, illuminated every now and then by the swaying torches of the link boys who lit their way. For someone who had danced the night away with any number of pretty women, he looked remarkably pensive.

"An enjoyable evening, Dan," she remarked conversationally.

"Hm."

His preoccupied grunt being the only answer vouchsafed, she tried again.

"Eliza Weston is not to everyone's taste, of course. Too twittery by half. But there is no real harm in her, and one can always be sure of being royally entertained!" The dryness of this last remark brought the faintest of reaction, which encouraged her to pursue her thoughts aloud. "That youngest gel of hers has developed into quite a beauty." The encomium brought no response, so she continued, "Though for my part, I much prefer her cousin, Miss Winslade. A very pleasing, remarkably *sound* young woman, Miss Winslade, and devoted to her brother. I mean to take her under my wing a little. She will do very well in Brussels, I think . . . steady that young man down. He has great charm," she mused, remembering, "but I suspect he is as feckless as they come!"

"So Miss Winslade goes to Brussels, does she?"

Daniel Hammond's position did not alter, nor was there any particular interest discernible in his voice, yet Lady Rowby knew him well enough to wonder just a little. She was not, however, so foolish as to press the matter further, saying merely, "Yes. Which reminds me, I must have a word with your uncle so that suitable lodgings can be found for them."

❦ 5 ❧

The days passed in a whirl. There was so much to be done, so many arrangements to be made, and the house to be cleaned from top to bottom before being put under holland covers. Charis's energy seemed unremitting.

"Will you for pity's sake slow down, child!" Emily grumbled. "You're making me giddy with all this *rush, rush, rush!*"

"I'm sorry, Em. But the more I can do now, the less there'll be at the last minute. I don't want you worn to shreds before we even set out."

"Worn to shreds, is it? I could get that way just watching you! Anyone would think you had the devil on your tail!"

Perhaps she had. But such an insidious, beguiling devil! And the only way to keep the thought of him at bay was to keep so busy that there was no time in which to indulge her misery.

She had not seen him since the night of Aunt Lizzie's ball, but Lavinia had called on her more than once, expressly, or so it seemed to Charis, for the purpose of talking about Major Hammond. She had met him, quite by chance it appeared, in the park on the day following the ball, and again at Lady Melchett's Venetian breakfast. "Such a pity that you weren't able to go, after all, my love. It was prodigiously romantic!"

Charis, with her head inside the closet searching for a missing spencer, muttered something unintelligible, but Lavinia wasn't really listening. She picked up her cousin's second best muslin, laid upon the bed waiting to be packed, and waltzed around the room with it held against her.

"And, of course he is to be at the Carlton House fete which the Prince Regent is giving in the Duke of Wellington's honor . . ." She sighed dreamily. "He really is quite the handsomest, most charming gentleman ever! Wouldn't you say so, Charis?"

Charis emerged from the closet, flushed and clutching the missing spencer. "Who, Wellington?"

"No, idiot!" she giggled. "Major Hammond! And he has such a divine way with a compliment, too." Lavinia crushed the muslin to her in an excess of fervor and whispered confidentially, "If you'll promise not to tell Mama, I'll let you into a secret. At Lady Melchett's I was alone with him in the conservatory. Oh, only for a few moments, and of course his behavior never went beyond what was proper—" a note of regret quickly turned to ebullience once more— "But he did manage to convey the extent of his admiration, and he vowed that I had quite the loveliest blue eyes he had ever seen, like twin sapphires! There," she declared triumphantly, "what do you say to that? I declare, I almost swooned away at his feet!"

At any other time Charis might have laughed at Lavinia's flights of fancy, but now she averted her gaze and stared blindly out of the window. *You have hundreds of little jade green stars shimmering in your eyes* . . . She could hear his voice as clearly as if he were in the room, and a sudden desire to hurt—someone—anyone—made her say sharply, "Tris said he told Ned's sister that waltzing with her was like waltzing with an angel! So I shouldn't set too much store by Major Hammond's pretty speeches. Clearly he has one for every occasion!"

Lavinia threw the dress in a heap on the bed and flounced to the door. "That's a perfectly horrid thing to say!" she cried, close to tears, "and I can't imagine why you should be so crabby, unless it is sheer jealousy!"

She spun around. "Yes, I believe that's it! *You* danced with him at Mama's ball, too, didn't you? I remember thinking at the time that you were a great deal too coming with him! I daresay you are miffed because he didn't offer you any pretty speeches!"

The slam of the door made Charis wince. She sank onto the edge of the bed, knowing that she ought to go after Lavinia but too angry and ashamed to move.

When Tristram came home that evening, he brought with him an invitation from Lady Rowby for Charis to take tea with her. The thought that she might encounter Major Hammond made her demur.

Tris shot her a surprised look and then, coming closer, took her by the shoulders. "I say, love, are you feeling quite the thing? Only you look a bit hag-ridden!"

A laugh that verged on a sob broke from her. "Charming, brother dear. You know just how to set a girl to rights!"

"Sorry!" His grin was rueful, but the pressure of his fingers tightened a little. "I'm right, though, aren't I?"

"Oh, Tris!" Just for an instant she rested her head against his coat.

"Want to tell?" he asked quietly.

If it were only that simple! She pulled herself upright, blinked away the mist, and said with determined cheerfulness, "Not much *to* tell. I have quarrelled with Lavinia . . . my fault entirely . . . and so must eat humble pie. In consequence, I am feeling confoundedly blue-deviled!"

"Not like you at all! You've been overdoing things, my girl," Tristram chided with mock severity. "Don't think I haven't noticed. Em may dismiss me as a frippery care-for-nothing, but I ain't entirely blind to what goes on." He gave her a quick, affectionate hug and let her go. "What you need is a treat—like taking tea with a charming lady who is feeling a trifle down-pin herself, having for the present lost her much-prized nephew."

"Is Major Hammond no longer with Lady Rowby, then?"

Charis hoped her voice sounded suitably casual—and was relieved to find that her interest was received without comment. The major had gone into Gloucestershire, said Tristram, to see a friend who had been sent home with injuries sustained at Toulouse in April.

And so Charis was able to accept Lady Rowby's invitation without fear of a confrontation. It was an agreeable visit, her first to the house in Cadogan Square where Tristram and Ned carried out their, it seemed to her, something less than exacting duties.

There was no sign of them, however, or of the despised Mr. Neill, as she was shown up to Lady Rowby's saloon—a curious room full of mingled styles; a richly-worked Chinese carpet covered the floor, and was in turn covered by little round tables, some standing on central columns fashioned like palm trees and flanked by winged cats, others held up by three lion-like back legs each topped by a lion's head; chairs of strange foreign design abounded, and everywhere were busts in stone and bronze.

"Extraordinary, isn't it?" said Lady Rowby dryly, crossing the room to meet her.

Charis caught her lip ruefully between her teeth. "I'm sorry. It is quite ill-bred of me to stare so. . . ."

"Nonsense! It is a perfectly normal reaction. I should stare myself were I not so accustomed to it. Such a heterogenous muddle of styles must always invite disbelief!" Lady Rowby drew her forward. "Do come and sit down. Most of these chairs are exceedingly uncomfortable, more ornamental than useful, but I do keep a small oasis of sanity in front of the fireplace!"

When Charis was settled on a shabby but reposeful sofa, the tea was brought in, and while Lady Rowby busied herself infusing it and pouring it into shallow Japanese dishes of exquisite paper-thin fragility, she watched with absorbed interest, surprised to find herself feeling instantly at home.

"We traveled a great deal in our younger days, Miss Winslade, and everywhere we went in the world we made friends. And when the time came for us to move on, we were inevitably presented with mementoes of our visits." Lady Rowby indicated the room with a wave of her hand. "So you see all of this is, if you like, a kind of potted history of our lives. Each item recalls a special person or some incident which might well be forgotten were there not something positive to shape the memory. Many people, I have no doubt, see me as an agreeable eccentric to be humored, but it gives me much pleasure to know that when I am old, I will need only to pick up . . . say, that exquisite little gilded elephant to be immediately transported back to the sights and sounds and smells, and the unbelievable beauty of the tiny Indian state whose maharajah presented it to my husband as a mark of his esteem."

Charis, watching the pleasant, unremarkable face framed by wispy, graying hair come alive with enthusiasm, found her fingers itching for pencil and paper—and fell to wondering what Lady Rowby had been like as a young woman.

"It's a splendid idea! I don't think you in the least eccentric," she exclaimed. "So many people's drawing rooms say absolutely nothing about their characters, except that they have commissioned the most fashionable architect of the day to surpass what he has designed for their bosom-bow friend the week previously!" She looked about her yet again. "*No one* could reproduce a copy of this!"

Lady Rowby laughed aloud. "Oh, Miss Winslade, I can see we shall deal excellently together. You clearly have as healthy a disregard of pretension as I do."

"I fear it is a sad fault in me that the conceits of others frequently make me laugh," Charis confided wryly.

"Tris and I share the same appreciation of the absurd, you see, and so we tend to feed off one another."

"Better that than becoming pompous," came the unequivocal reply.

The rapport established between the two women on that first visit, notwithstanding the difference in their respective ages, flourished in the days that followed, and with each succeeding visit Charis found her stomach less inclined to knot disagreeably at the prospect of meeting Major Hammond. She found herself listening with equanimity, even (if she were honest) with a concealed eagerness, to Lady Rowby's affectionate reminiscences of his youth.

"Such a mad, merry little boy. Always in scrapes and always endearingly repentant afterward. One never could be angry with him for long. I can see him now, head a little to one side, his hair flopping in his eyes—it was very much fairer in those days, of course—patiently enduring one's strictures, and then acknowledging the justice of them with that wry sleepy smile of his, quite melting one's heart and one's opposition on the instant!"

Oh yes, thought Charis with her own irresistible tug of memory, I know exactly what you mean!

Fortunately, Lady Rowby was too immersed in recollection to heed the affect her words were having upon her young friend. "Lord Rowby was always very sensible of his obligations, you know, not only toward Dan, who was now his heir, but also to his late brother's memory. He was very keen that Dan should go to Oxford, like his father before him, but there was never any question where the boy's mind and heart lay. . . ." She sighed. "I think he was born with a soldier's blood already in his veins and his resolve never wavered. Indeed, I have always found his single-mindedness once he was determined upon a course of action to be quite awesome! And all carried through with the greatest goodwill so that it is impossible to resist! And in the matter of his future his objective was quite clear—he had heard about the new *corps d'elite* of light infantry then in training at Shorncliffe under Sir John Moore, which incorporated the 95th Rifles, so as soon as he was old enough, my husband arranged matters for him."

"Major Hammond is fortunate in his family," Charis said. "You are very fond of him, I can tell."

"Oh indeed, yes! We both are. If he were in truth our own son, we could not love him more! *My* only regret is that we see so little of him, though he writes when he can." She sighed again. "Goodness knows where he will be sent to now that the war is over. One lives in constant dread of something terrible happening to him, but he seems to bear a charmed life, and in any case, it is the life he wants."

Lady Rowby's recollections, like an artist's brush, gave form and shape to Charis's sketchy awareness of the major's character, and in so doing fostered a deep need in her to know more, so that she eagerly took up her ladyship's invitation to her to come again. In spite of all that had still to be done, she found time to spend an hour now and then sitting in her comfortable sofa corner in that delightfully cluttered room with pencil and paper in hand, busily drawing while quite shamelessly encouraging her ladyship to talk about Dan's Peninsular exploits in which he had frequently distinguished himself.

It wasn't at all sensible, and she didn't entirely understand the need that impelled her to behave as she did, but she lacked the necessary strength of mind to resist the compulsion. But as the day of their departure loomed near and practical matters became more urgent, only one last visit remained, and that was partly business, concerning as it did final details of where and how they were to be housed in Brussels.

Lord Rowby had arranged for the Winslades to occupy an apartment on the first floor of a house belonging to a family sympathetic to the Allied cause—sentiments not shared by all the Bruxellois.

"It seems that some of them have made no secret of their Bonapartist leanings—and have little liking for the prospect of being ruled by the King of the Netherlands," Lady Rowby explained, with a philosophical shrug. "However, my husband has been assured that you will be recieved with every kindness. The Latours are a very old and well-respected family with aristocratic connections who have, by reason of the war, fallen a little on hard times. And as you will be no more than a step away from our own house in the Rue Ducale, you will not I trust feel at all strange."

"I'm sure we shall not," Charis exclaimed, her eyes sparkling with excitement. "You cannot imagine how I am looking forward to it. It will be just like old times!" She began to gather up her things. "Forgive me, dear ma'am, but I have already stayed too long. Emily is getting to the fidgety stage and will be fussing if I am not back within the hour—"

It was at this moment, quite without warning, that the door opened to admit a familiar tall, lithe figure, who stood for a moment on the threshold, taking in the scene.

"Dan!" cried Lady Rowby, throwing out her hands in welcome. "How splendid! We did not know when to expect you."

He crossed the room with that easy, loping stride and dropped a kiss on her cheek.

"And wishing, no doubt, that I were not back to pester you again, dear ma'am," he said teasingly. "Can you bear with me a little longer, do you think, up to your eyes as you are? Or shall I seek sanctuary elsewhere?"

"The very thought!" she exclaimed, patting his coat in a proprietorial way. "As if I would ever turn you from the door no matter how busy I was!"

He straightened up. "But I intrude now, I think?"

"Certainly not. You are just in time to see Miss

Winslade before she leaves. You do know one another, I think?"

He turned his glance on Charis, and found her sitting rigidly erect, hands tight clasped on a small folder, her gloves, a reticule—the face lifted to him as open and all-revealing as a full-blown rose with a deep blush spreading from its center, eyes still sparkling from something she had been saying as he entered.

It was the shock, she told herself, that had caused her heart to betray her so utterly, leaping into her throat and driving all the breath out of her. If only it might not wholly betray her!

"Miss Winslade." He was bowing with infernal ease. "This is an unexpected pleasure."

Determined not to be outdone in sanguinity, she swallowed firmly and made some reply in kind, hoping that it made sense.

Lady Rowby could hardly fail to observe the effect her nephew's arrival had had on Charis—and her heart misgave her. Oh, why had she not guessed? Rattling on the way she had about Dan, and all the time . . . She turned her attention to Dan, looking for some evidence that he might return the child's regard in similar fashion; to be sure, he was interested, but with Dan that meant very little. Oh, why could he not restrict his flirtations to the kind of women who knew how to play the game! Perhaps, a word in his ear . . .

"Miss Winslade has been doing some sketches of me," she said briskly into the silence. "I cannot think why, but she wishes to paint my portrait when we get to Brussels."

"Really? May I see?" Before Charis could prevent him, he had removed the folder from her clasp and was flipping through it. "Very impressive. Yes, you have a decided talent," he said blandly. "And you make an excellent subject, Aunt Sybil. I can see exactly why Miss Winslade finds you such a challenge. After all, much of a person's character is to be found in *his* or her face, wouldn't you say, Miss Winslade?"

"Sometimes." She pulled on her gloves with fingers that shook slightly and stood up, dropping her reticule as she did so. She bent swiftly to pick it up, but he was as quick. Their fingers closed on it together, touched, and held for a moment. Without conscious volition, she lifted her head and met his eyes, and behind their gentle smile, caught a glint of something more predatory that made her gasp.

Then he was helping her to her feet, handing her the folder, and slipping the reticule's handle expertly over her wrist.

"There," he said, and then, regretfully, "You are leaving?"

"Yes, I must." Her eyes went to Lady Rowby, unwittingly pleading. "There is so much still to be done. I doubt I shall be able to come again before we leave."

"Quite so, child. I understand perfectly. I'll ring for the carriage."

"Good-bye, then. Thank you . . . and Lord Rowby, for everything."

"Good heavens, as if we could have done less. Take care, now, until we meet again in Brussels."

"Yes." Charis hesitated, and then, "Good-bye, Major Hammond," she said, resolutely looking him in the eye.

"Not quite yet. I mean to see you home."

"Oh no!" The exclamation slipped out before she could prevent it. To soften its abruptness, she added with a light laugh, "There is no need. I have been coming and going for a long time now without benefit of an escort."

"Perhaps. But on this occasion you have one."

Charis looked appealingly to Lady Rowby, who said rather more sharply than was her wont, "You are not entirely irresistible, Dan. Perhaps Miss Winslade don't care to entrust herself to you."

He cocked a quizzical eyebrow at her and turned back to Charis once more, his voice softly persuasive.

"*Is* that your reason?"

She became flustered, which in turn made her annoyed. "I would not presume to question my safety, sir. But I cannot suppose that you really wish to turn out again so soon after your long journey, so—"

"Oh, if that is all, you may be easy. I don't account *that* as much of a journey. In fact, I am growing soft with so much spoiling!" He grinned at his aunt to remove any sting from the words. "The thing is, I have done little at Geoffrey's but lie in a hammock in the garden from morning until night, being waited on. The lucky dog has three young sisters, not to mention his old nurse, to pander to his every whim—and naturally I came in for similar treatment!"

Naturally, thought Charis.

"How is that poor boy?" asked his aunt, momentarily diverted.

A shadow crossed his face, and his voice took on the clipped quality that so dramatically changed his personality. "In a great deal of pain, and so damnably patient that it hurts one just to watch him," he said almost savagely. And then the hardness went from around his mouth and he was himself again, taking Charis's arm and walking her to the door with that blend of firmness and charm that brooked no argument.

And so, in a flurry of good-byes, she went.

❦ 6 ❧

Downstairs in the hall she made one last attempt to dissuade him and finally gave herself up to the inevitable. Once in the carriage, however, she sat a little stiffly, pressed into one corner until it finally dawned upon her that he was not bent upon pressing home his advantage, but rather appeared to be lost in thought. Gradually her body relaxed into the softness of the squabs, though her mind seethed with curiosity, not untinged with pique. He had been so very persistent, after all. The wheels bumped over a rut in the road, jolting her from her own reverie. She stole a glance at his face and found him regarding her with an absorbed, slightly puzzled frown.

In a funny kind of way it made him seem less disturbing; in fact, he looked for all the world like Tris when he had done something to displease her and wasn't sure how to get back into her good graces.

The comparison made her smile and say impulsively, "Cat got your tongue, major?"

A faint gleam came into his eyes. "I was wondering how best to say what I want to say without putting you into a fresh quake."

"You could try plain speaking instead of flummery."

A soft laugh greeted this forthright suggestion.

"Oh, I do *like* you, fair divinity! No, don't—please don't—shy away from me again. You want plain speaking—well, you shall have it, but I warn you, I shall expect equal frankness in return."

She experienced a momentary frisson of—what? Of danger . . . excitement . . . fear? For this was a different protagonist—this was the soldier who would give no quarter; still essentially charming as he sat half-facing her with his arm resting along the back cushions so that his fingers brushed her bonnet brim, still smiling—only now there was a pitiless quality in the smile, a disturbing *élan*, a relentlessness about him that suggested the invincibility of a tiger about to spring. She was being fanciful, of course—and yet?

"Very well," she agreed, chin lifting, and saw the surge of anticipation quicken in his eyes. It did nothing for her confidence.

"Good." He reached forward to rap on the coachman's box. "Take us around the park, Brooke."

"Right you are, Major Dan. The park it is," came the jaunty reply.

"I mustn't be late home," Charis said, too quickly.

"What I have to say won't take long." He considered a moment. "No wrapping in fancy ribbons. Quite simply—I love you."

The impact of his declaration was immediate and devastating. Whatever she had been expecting, it was not this unequivocal affirmation. Her breath almost snatched away, her cheeks flying flags of color, she gasped foolishly, "But you can't! There hasn't been time! You know nothing about me!"

He seemed unmoved by this somewhat incoherent reasoning. "Dearest girl, how long do you suppose it takes?" he said gently. "I loved you at our very first encounter—with the rain and the wind flattening your hair into shining coils about your face and lending it the freakish grace of a young Greek god! And when you smiled—oh, so reluctantly—the light began in your eyes and ran irresistibly down to meet your curving mouth! All I ever needed to know, I discovered in that moment . . . anything else is but an added delight!"

It was a beautiful speech—so beautiful that it moved her almost to tears. Yet even as Charis exulted that he should feel that way about her, a tiny worm of doubt was eating into her moment of glory. Was it too beautiful, perhaps, to be entirely spontaneous? Too glib? He had probably said it, or something very like it, a thousand times before—and at the time he had probably meant it.

She looked out over the park; it was too early in the afternoon for the majority of promenaders and with the exception of a few family parties all was green and still, the only sound above the faint crunch of the wheels being the distant echo of hammering as in the various parks preparations neared completion for what was to be a grand public celebration of the victory against Napoleon.

"Have I silenced you so completely?" he said, making her jump. "I had not thought it would come as such a surprise."

She shook her head slowly.

"Come—now it's your turn. Total honesty. You gave your word."

But how could she explain without sounding censorious . . . pious . . . ungrateful . . . all the things she hated. "I can't!" she whispered.

"Why not?"

Her head moved again, face averted from him, hidden by the poke of her bonnet.

He leaned forward a little, but made no attempt to touch her. "I think I must insist. You needn't have any fear of offending me, you know." And then, in a rallying way: "Don't shirk the chance of speaking your mind! Can't you at least tell me how you feel?"

"How I feel?" She flung up her head suddenly, gathering her courage to look him in the eye. "All right, I'll tell you—I *feel* confused! You will think me dreadfully commonplace, but I can't play this game the way you do—"

"Is that what you think it . . . a game?"

"I don't know! But you wanted complete honesty from me, and I am trying my best," she said doggedly.

"The fact is, I am two and twenty, and without wishing to appear complacent, I have never wanted for admirers, but none have ever moved me to—" she forced herself not to look away from him—"that is to say, I am not in any way an accomplished flirt."

At this his eyes narrowed into bright creases, but he only said tersely: "Go on."

"Perhaps it has something to do with Tris and me being so very close, but I have always found it difficult to take my suitors seriously. Our house is frequently filled with Tris's friends who have grown used to discussing quite openly in my presence the rival merits of their latest 'bits of muslin' and how to cast out lures to ensnare the more reluctant ones." She was unconsciously clasping and unclasping her hands.

"I found their strategems absurd, amusing, and at times amazingly instructive," she continued, striving for lightness, "and although I thought them amazingly fickle, I tended to judge my own sex more harshly, hazarding that those foolish enough to succumb to such blatant seduction must suffer the consequences. Until—" at this point she almost faltered under the unwavering intensity of his regard—"until that day in the rain. . . ."

She could not bear the light that leaped into his eyes, and looked down at her clasped hands.

"Until then, you see, I had no conception of how it feels to be subjected to that particular kind of persuasive charm."

"It mortifies me somewhat to be classed with those green young bucks, but . . . how *does* it feel, dear Miss Winslade?" he coaxed. "Tell me that I was not mistaken, that you are not indifferent to me."

She drew a deep breath and acknowledged the fact.

"I knew it!" he exclaimed.

"But I have no doubt I shall get over it," she concluded, firm-voiced.

"Get—?" He seized her hands. "My dear, exasperating creature, I don't want you to get over it! I'm in love with you! I want to marry you!"

The hands struggling under his went very still. "Look at me!" he commanded, terse once more.

She did so, and rather wished that she had not.

"Did you suppose I was about to offer you *carte blanche*?"

"No. At least. . . ." Against a weakening resolve came the echo of Lady Rowby's warning about her nephew's commitment to his career, her expectation that he would remain forever a bachelor, *"besides which, he is an incorrigible flirt and would make the very devil of a husband!"* Oh, but she would risk that, if only she could be sure! "I daresay," she stumbled miserably over the words, "that you have fancied yourself in love a hundred times before?"

She heard his breath sucked in. "Oh, at least!"

His biting sarcasm hurt her more than the painful tightening of his fingers on hers.

"Don't think I am reproaching you! I haven't the right! But I'm not experienced enough to distinguish between sincerity and mere dalliance."

"You could try trusting me," he said quietly.

"Oh, if only it were as simple as that! And besides, there's Tris to consider."

"Your brother is surely able to stand on his own feet? You can't hold his hand forever."

"Perhaps not, but our move to Brussels is all settled now, and then there is your career."

"None of which would matter if you were sure. Strange," he mused wryly. "I could have sworn that I had your measure—that you were the kind who would fling herself into love headfirst, and not care about getting hurt!"

"Then you were mistaken," she said angrily over the hurt in her throat, her eyes holding his defiantly.

He held her hands a moment longer without speaking, and then released them. As he did so, there was a shout and Lavinia broke from a group of people strolling under the trees and came running toward them. The time had passed unnoticed and there were now quite a few people taking the afternoon promenade.

"Charis!"

Lavinia's voice was reproachful. She looked from one to the other as Major Hammond ordered Brooke to halt the barouche, and was somewhat reassured. They didn't look as though they were enjoying one another's company, and Charis had insisted when they had made up their quarrel that she wasn't the least bit interested in Major Hammond.

"I thought you would be much too busy with last-minute packing to be taking the air," she added with a question in her eyes. "You said you would be when I suggested we might meet."

"I've just been to visit Lady Rowby and Major Hammond was so kind as to offer to see me home." Charis hoped that the tightness in her throat was not obvious in her voice, but Lavinia had already turned her attention to the major, her face artlessly lifted to him, framed by a bonnet, the underbrim of which was ruched in blue silk to exactly match her eyes.

"My cousin is indeed fortunate, sir," she sighed prettily. "I had supposed that you were still from home?"

"So I was until this very afternoon, Miss Weston. I confess I had forgotten just what I was missing by staying away so long!"

The lingering appreciation in his glance, the tone of his voice, left no doubt of the meaning in his words. Charis, wounded afresh by this example of his fickleness, was quick to put an end to it, reminding them of her pressing need to get home.

"Of course," he said soothingly. "Miss Weston." He touched his hat with a beguiling gallantry. "We shall meet, no doubt, at the Carlton House fete. Be sure to save me a dance."

Charis could not bring herself to speak for the remainder of the journey. Several times she felt his eyes on her, but she stared fixedly ahead and he spoke only once, to say with what seemed like odious cheerfulness: "I have been a great fool!"

Despite her protests, he insisted upon walking with her to the door where, determined not to be outdone in politeness, she offered him her hand and her thanks.

He held it for a moment in both of his and then raised it briefly to his lips, his eyes lifting to meet hers above it.

"Five minutes alone—really alone—with you, and the outcome might have been very different," he murmured enigmatically leaving her, not for the first time, with nothing to say.

Lady Rowby heard Dan come up the stairs. Her door stood half open and as he passed, she called out to him.

He pushed the door wide and stood, looking, she thought, rather like a leashed hunter in need of exercise. He inquired very civilly if there was something she wished of him.

"A word only, dear boy," she said with unusual diffidence. "About Miss Winslade."

One eyebrow quivered. "Miss Winslade? It seems to me that you and she are devilish close all of a sudden?"

"I have grown fond of the child, certainly," her ladyship acknowledged. "I find her decidedly refreshing when compared with most young women of today. Yet for all her composure and vivacity there is a curiously untouched quality about her. Wouldn't you say so, Dan?"

The question was innocently put, but he wasn't deceived for a moment.

"What you really mean, dear aunt, is would I refrain from attempting to seduce her! Am I not right?"

She gave a short bark of laughter. "That's frankness, indeed! But, yes, in effect, that is what I meant."

His mouth twisted into an ironic smile. "Then you

may rest easy, ma'am. The young lady's virtue is safe, for the present at least. My want of constancy would seem to present an insuperable barrier."

"Oh dear!" said Lady Rowby drolly. "How disconcerting for you, my dear boy. Do you mind dreadfully?"

"Yes. My strategy was damnable, and that touches upon my pride! But it is no bad thing occasionally to lose the opening skirmish." The smile became a grin. "It makes one all the more determined to win the war!"

✺❨ 7 ❩✺

Brussels was in high summer when the Winslades arrived to take up residence, the sky washed blue with occasional flashes of white, the gardens brilliant with color against the mingled styles of the baroque and neoclassical buildings, and everyone in festive mood.

Charis, who had thrown herself into the final arrangements with renewed fervor, felt her spirits lift the moment the journey began. Passage had been booked on the *Rebel Queen* sailing from Dover for herself and Tris, together with Emily and young Meg, whom Charis had decided could not be left behind. "It will cost very little more to take her," she had reasoned, "and we are the nearest thing to family she has in the world."

The ship was filled almost exclusively with pleasure-seekers, including ambitious mamas with daughters of marriageable age bent upon finding husbands among the Army of Occupation quartered in or close to Brussels. Many had brought with them carriages and horses, and so great a quantity of baggage that Emily spent the greater part of the crossing gloomily prophesying disaster.

"You mark my words! It only needs the weather to turn treacherous and there'll be pandemonium below and the whole lot of us drowned for sure!"

But in the event, a gentle breeze carried them across without incident. They rested overnight at a small, comfortable inn and on the following morning were able to hire a carriage to take them on to Brussels.

The house they were seeking lay in a quiet street just off the Place Royale, and upon first seeing it Charis wondered if some terrible mistake had been made. The gracious mansion with its high, elegant facade seemed an unlikely rooming house. But Madame Latour, who received them with a gentle courtesy, explained that the exigences and deprivations of war and occupation had reduced her husband's resources and position in society to the point where a painful choice had to be made between sharing their beautiful home with others, or selling up and moving to more modest premises.

"We have lived all our married life in this house," she sighed, glancing around her salon with a misty pride that took no heed of faded covers or the thin patches in a once handsome Aubusson carpet. "I think I could not bear to leave it now."

"I know exactly how you must feel," Charis said warmly. "And I think it is very courageous of you to contemplate allowing total strangers to occupy even a part of your lovely home. But you may be sure that we will treat everything with the greatest care."

Madame seemed reassured by this statement and, rousing from the reverie into which she had fallen, she put back a graying wisp of hair and collected that she had better show them to their apartment.

"We keep very little now in the way of staff," she explained apologetically, breathing a little laboriously as she led the way up the elegant curving staircase. "Our *chef de famille* is much troubled with pains in his joints and finds the stairs a trial, so I try to save him as much as possible . . . and in any case I would like to show to you the apartment for myself."

At the end of a corridor she opened a door on to a large room filled with sunshine which streamed in through three tall windows draped with faded rose velvet curtains.

"Oh, but this is charming!" Charis cried, turning to the others. "Tris—isn't it splendid?" She hurried across to the nearest window. "And the view! We are so high up that one can see right across the city!"

"When my children were young, I used this room as

a kind of family salon. In fact, this whole wing was given over to the children, and a separate stairs goes down from here to the *petit vestibule*, so you may come and go exactly as you please." Madame Latour's voice trembled with nostalgia. "Now, my family is scattered. I have only my baby, my Celestine, and we can manage very well with less. There are six rooms in all—some large, some not so large—mostly bedchambers except for a dining room and two other rooms up a short flight of stairs which used to be the schoolrooms, and a small kitchen, if you would care to see. . . ." Her voice trailed off.

"No, no! Please, madame, there is no need," Charis exclaimed. "For myself, I could not be more satisfied. Tris?"

She appealed to her brother, who was standing before a picture of an officer of Hussars seated astride a black hunter which hung above the fireplace. He turned and gave the older woman his most charming smile.

"My sister speaks for us both, madame. We shall make ourselves very snug here, never fear." He indicated the picture. "A member of your family?"

"The Comte de Mallon is my cousin, monsieur." There was a note of strain in her voice, but she did not elaborate, confining herself to saying simply: "If you do not care for it, I can have it removed."

They instantly reassured her and after a few further details concerning their well-being, she excused herself. "I would be grateful," she said, hovering uncertainly at the door, "if you would not mention the picture to my husband. Or to anyone," she added vaguely.

Emily's sniff summed up her opinion of Madame Latour, and feeling that no further comment was necessary, she took herself and Meg off to inspect the rest of the rooms, leaving brother and sister together.

Tris was the first to speak, observing with a studied nonchalance that he supposed they could have done a lot worse, but he could not maintain his gravity against the sheer rapture radiating from Charis; he grinned and opened his arms, and in a moment they were hugging one another and dancing round the room with inelegant, joyous enthusiasm.

"Oh Tris, we *are* going to be happy here, aren't we?"

He held her away a little, giving her an uncommonly penetrating look. "Well, I certainly intend to be, and if you aren't, I shall want to know the reason why." He read the evasion in her eyes. "No, I'm not asking questions, for the present, but that don't mean I've been blind to how miserable you've been these last days!"

She shook her head and drew away from him. "Well, not anymore. From now on, I mean to be heart-whole and fancy-free. You'll see!"

As Emily came back into the room at that point, she was spared any further need to dissemble, though she truly meant what she said. She had been incredibly foolish, surely unforgivable at her age, but it was all behind her now, and the lesson would stand her in good stead.

Emily was grudgingly approving of the apartment in general, though she doubted that it would be half so convenient to run as their own little house back in London. Charis tactfully refrained from comment and went instead to complete her own tour of inspection. The bedchambers were easily allocated; by virtue of their position, Tris was settled in the largest room at the front, and Charis the one adjoining it, while Emily, after a token resistance at the prospect of being ensconced in more luxury than she was used to, took possession of a very comfortable rear chamber.

The problem of Meg was solved when Charis ascended the next flight of stairs to view the remaining rooms. There was a small chamber beneath the eaves which had probably belonged to the Latours' nursemaid or governess and which proved to be ideal for Meg's use.

But it was the last room of all that enchanted Charis. It was reasonable in size, quite bare except for the floor-to-ceiling cupboards either side of the fireplace, and it had an enormous window facing north. Already in her mind's eye she was visualizing it stacked with canvasses—her easel in position where the light would best fall upon it; a studio, perfect in every particular, exactly as she had always imagined it!

"She's as happy as a flea on a dog's back!" Tris told Ned when they met several days later.

It had been Ned's intention to travel with them, but the sudden illness of his father had sent him hurrying off to the country. The earl had survived his visit by only a few hours, dying as he had lived, impoverished and leaving to the new Earl of Samwell, Ned's older brother, a pile of debts.

"There seemed little p-point in my remaining any longer," Ned said. "Getting under m'sister-in-law's feet. Nothing I could do to help Charles, d'you see, and I was b-beginning to feel distinctly *de trop*."

He had traveled with the Rowbys and was now settled into a pair of rooms at the top of a widow lady's home not too far away, and declared himself to be well content.

Charis allowed Lady Rowby a little time to settle in before calling on her, but when she finally did make her way to the Rue Ducale, she was received with a warmth that touched her deeply, while Lady Rowby was relieved to find her young friend relaxed and obviously none the worse for her brief involvement with Dan. In fact, the more they talked, the more it became clear that Charis had only one thing on her mind—the pursuit of art; to which end she entreated Lady Rowby to spare her an hour or two of her valuable time—"so that I may make a start on your portrait, dear ma'am."

Her ladyship's eyes twinkled. "You must not feel yourself under any obligation to go through with that, you know. I daresay you can find any number of pretty ladies here more worthy of your talents."

"Nonsense!" Charis declared. "Pretty ladies, as you

are pleased to call them, would be quite tedious to portray, whereas I have been greatly looking forward to attempting your likeness."

"Oh, if you mean to flatter me . . ."

"I shan't do that, never fear!" Charis said quickly, and then, fearing lest that should sound impolite, "You won't mind, will you? I mean, I would like my work to be an honest portrayal."

Lady Rowby laughed. "My dear child, if you attempted to prettify me, I should be really worried! I am past the age where my looks, or want of them, trouble me! I only hope you do not find it a shocking waste of time."

"I won't." Charis smiled back at her. "Besides," she added beguilingly, "only consider that if the picture turns out well, a great many people will see it and I may get other commissions."

Her ladyship was much struck by this line of reasoning and ceased her objections forthwith, expressing instead her pleasure that Charis had settled down so well and hoped that her brother was equally content.

"Everything is going to work out splendidly, I just feel it in my bones! And I cannot thank you enough, dear ma'am, for arranging matters so well for us."

"Oh goodness, child—I have done little enough. I did suggest the Latours to Mr. Neill as a possibility for I had heard that they were in a sad way . . . though to be honest, I was a little surprised when they agreed to take you. Monsieur is a proud, difficult man."

"You know them, then?"

Lady Rowby shrugged. "Only superficially. We met in a social way when Rowby and I were here some years ago. At that time they were still quite affluent, of course . . . he was a banker of considerable repute, but I fear that he was so outspokenly anti-Bonapartist that during the French Occupation he lost much of his business. Now, I believe, he is at the Hague trying to recoup his fortune."

"But Madame has aristocratic connections, does she

not?" Charis's curiosity about their hosts was stimulated anew by these fascinating disclosures.

"Ah, so you have heard about Mallon?" Lady Rowby's voice was dry.

Charis explained about the picture.

"How interesting! I'll wager that Monsieur doesn't know it hangs there. Their sympathies could not be less in tune, and I understand he will not have the count's name mentioned in his presence, which is unfortunate, since his poor wife has always cherished a particular *tendre* for her young cousin. And as two of her children died young, and two more are married, I daresay she clings to the youngest girl who was a late child."

"Ah!" Charis exclaimed. "That explains her."

"Mind you," her ladyship's tone grew even drier, "the count is an ambitious rascal for all his charm. I suspect that he was drawn to Napoleon's cause when it seemed certain that nothing could stop him. Now I am told he expresses complete disillusion and has embraced the Allied cause with equal fervor!"

"A rascal, indeed!" Charis agreed. "One would expect him to be shunned on all sides."

"Maybe, but I shall own myself very much surprised if he is not already being received almost everywhere. People develop surprisingly short memories when expediency rules, and the count *is* excessively rich—and unmarried!"

Charis knew she ought to be deeply shocked, but the fickle ways of fashionable society had long since ceased to surprise her, and anyway, if she were honest, she must own to a secret curiosity to meet Madame Latour's charming, unscrupulous cousin. One ought, of course, to hold him in aversion, but she knew, none better, how insidious a quality was charm! And knowing that must surely serve as a safety barrier.

Tristram meanwhile was finding life very much to his liking. He took his duties every bit as lightly as he had done in London, but as he and Charis found themselves drawn more and more into the social life of Brussels through the good offices of the Rowbys, his capacity for making himself agreeable on all sides tended to compensate for his *laissez-faire* attitude to other matters, and soon he was acting more and more as Lord Rowby's social aide.

Also, he had fallen in love. And since, unlike Charis, he was wont to wear his heart upon his sleeve, he could not wait to impart the wondrous news. To this end he sought Charis out in the garret room where she was busy at her easel.

She glanced up with a half-smile, her mind only partially absorbing the gist of his lyrical prose. She was well used to Tris's falling in love; he did so with unfailing regularity at least once in every two months, and was usually heart-whole again in half that time. So she murmured an absent, "H'm" and "lovely," and continued to direct her attention toward capturing that quality of wry humor about Lady Rowby's mouth which was so much a part of her character, and which was now proving elusive. Maddeningly so. She reached for the sketch in which she had caught it perfectly and studied it anew.

Tris, sensing that he did not have her whole attention, came to look over her shoulder. The light from the window fell on the canvas with unequivocal clarity, and he was momentarily surprised by what he saw—it was quite the best thing she had ever done.

"Not bad," he commented off-handedly, and advanced a critical finger. "I'd say it needs more shadow just there."

She tried it and sat back to view the result. "Yes," she said, glancing up with a grin. "For someone who can't tell a Tintoretto from a Rubens, you do sometimes have an uncanny knack of being able to see exactly what is needed!"

"That, sister dear, is the mark of true genius!" He

linked his arms casually around her neck. "Aren't you the least bit curious to know who the fortunate girl is?"

"Your latest inamorata?" Charis leaned her head back against him, eyes creased, looking up. "Do I know her?"

"You know of her," he said enigmatically.

It was hard to define his expression, seen upside down.

"She is Madame's *bebe*."

"The elusive Celestine?" They had gone two weeks without catching so much as a glimpse of her and had assumed her to be a child confined to a nursery existence. Charis sat up. "Then we were wrong about her?"

"Oh, indeed we were!" Tris said with feeling. "Honestly, love, she is a *vision*! Quite the most enchanting creature it has ever been my privilege to meet!"

Charis winced at his unwitting choice of description, but Tristram was too preoccupied to notice. Mademoiselle Celestine, it transpired, had been away with her *gouvernante*, which was why they hadn't seen her.

"Only fancy . . . I was taking the stairs in a great hurry and almost ran her down! She cannot be a day above seventeen, and so tiny, so fragile, that I might well have crushed her! She is incredibly fair . . . like blown thistledown, with a smile as sweet as any angel's!"

The very prodigality of his praise, that would ordinarily have made her smile, now drove Charis to bitter, irrational jealousy. "Well, don't attempt to seduce her, I beg of you," she said lightly. "We are very comfortable here, and I have no wish to be turned out of doors by her irate father!"

The moment the words were uttered she wished them unsaid, but the damage was done. Tris pokered up, accused her of demonstrating the insensitivity of a withered, embittered antidote, and flung out of the room, leaving Charis to bow her head in her hands while the tears ran unheeded through her fingers.

"I don't know what's got into the two of you," declared Emily McGrath the following day, surveying the silent breakfast table, the unwanted food fast congealing on the plates. "Such a fit of the sullens I haven't seen since you were both too young to know any better!" She snatched up their plates and marched out, the door closing behind her with a thud of disapproval.

Charis looked up and caught her brother's eye. She had slept badly and he, she knew, had stayed out most of the night—and now looked somewhat less than his usual urbane self.

Impulsively, she stretched a hand across the cloth. "Oh, Tris! I don't know what got into me! Forgive me?"

"Idiot!" Her fingers were crushed in his. "If you were insensitive, I was too touchy by half! Friends?"

"Friends," she agreed fervently. "And, incidentally, I have now seen your *vision*, and you did not exaggerate!"

But Tristram did not find it easy to pursue his suit with Mademoiselle Celestine. Her mama kept her very close and they went very little into company. Madame Latour did ask Miss Winslade down to meet her daughter, however, and though the visit was not an unqualified success—Madame falling into vague, uncomfortable silences and Mademoiselle being rather shy—Charis had every hope that a casual suggestion that the young girl might come and sit for her, might in time bear fruit.

Certainly the light of interest came momentarily into Madame's eyes at the prospect, but she was uncertain in spite of her daughter's soft entreaties.

"It must be for your father to decide, *cherie*. One would naturally enjoy very much to have a portrait of you." And to Charis: "My husband spends much time at the Hague at present. Business matters, you understand."

"Oh please, madame, do not misunderstand me," Charis said quickly. "I was not suggesting a formal portrait, though I should be happy to oblige if you wished it. I was hoping rather that Mademoiselle

Celestine would allow me to, as it were, practice on her! I am not yet greatly experienced in portrait painting and to be permitted to make some sketches of a young lady as beautiful as your daughter would prove invaluable, believe me."

Clearly the older woman was flattered and promised to give the matter some thought. And Charis, judging it to be prudent, left the matter there.

In the meantime, her portrait of Lady Rowby was finished and had already excited considerable interest, not least with her ladyship's husband. Lord Rowby was a bluff, genial man whose very direct gray eyes belied his apparent ease of manner. Charis had seen very little of him in London, but here in Brussels they had become much better acquainted, and she found that she liked him almost as much as his wife. It was not difficult to see why they were so attached to one another.

"I can't tell you how grateful I am to you, m'dear," he said. "You have caught Sybil's expression exactly—and I daresay that ain't an easy trick! But what's this she tells me about your refusing to take any payment for it, eh?" His grisled brows quivered. "Not going to be missish about it, are you, young lady?"

"No sir," she said lightly. "Not unless you mean to be tiresome." He gave a short bark of laughter and, emboldened by this, she added, "I've no doubt you think it quixotic of me, in view of our straightened circumstances, but I want the picture to be a gift—a kind of 'thank you,' if you like. And besides," her eyes twinkled, "as Lady Rowby has probably told you, I have great hopes of its being prominently displayed in her salon!"

Lord Rowby laughed again. "You may depend upon it. I have already been approached very discreetly by several matrons desirous of seeing their offspring captured forever in their prime!" He lowered his voice conspiratorially. "Wanted to know your charges. I told 'em!"

The figure he named made Charis go hot with

embarrassment. "My lord, I couldn't possibly ask so much!"

"Humgudgeon! They are well able to afford it. Anyhow, fashionable folk can be deucedly contrary—the more a thing costs, the more prestige they are like to attach to it! So be bold, my girl—grasp the nettle! We'll have you famous yet!"

As the days went by, it certainly seemed that his lordship had not been overoptimistic in his reading of the situation. The number of commissions, at first a trickle, soon came flooding in. The news that the Duke of Wellington would be visiting Brussels en route to Paris where he was to take up his post as British ambassador brought with it the expectation of a great number of balls and festivities of all kinds at which many officers and gentlemen of note would most surely be present. There would be morning calls and evening supper parties, and it became a point of fashion to have a painting by the talented Miss Winslade hanging in one's salon.

The duke's arrival could not have been more happily timed, coinciding as it did with preparations for a ball being held by the English residents to celebrate the birthday of their own Prince Regent. The official purpose of his visit was to inspect the frontier fortresses in the Low Countries, but with so many of his friends at present resident in Brussels, the duke was not averse to mixing a little pleasure with business. Nor, for that matter, was the Prince of Orange, who accompanied him. This dashing young heir to the Netherlands throne, known affectionately to his British army intimates as "Slender Billy," looked to be in excellent spirits despite the recent peremptory termination of his engagement to Princess Charlotte, the English Regent's willful young daughter.

"The gossips here will have a splendid time, no doubt," Lady Rowby said to Charis. "It really is, as Caroline Capel remarked to me the other day, the most gossiping place ever!"

"One cannot but feel for the prince in such a situation."

"I suppose so. And yet, at the risk of being thought unpatriotic, I strongly suspect that he will already be thinking himself well out of *that* connection!"

Charis smiled at her friend's forthright views. "I hear the Prince is to command the British troops in the Brabant. I expect that will please him, and at least he will be kept occupied."

"It won't please his father. The king is already complaining that his son is hardly ever at the Hague, and seems to prefer his British friends to his Dutch or Belgian subjects."

"Well, I suppose he is still very young," Charis said. "And speaking of the young, ma'am, I wonder if you would consider inviting Mademoiselle Latour to the reception you are giving for the Duke of Wellington? I feel so sorry for the poor child, immured as she is with her mama in that house and never going anywhere! She is not out yet, of course; indeed, I begin to wonder if she ever *will* make her bow to society, for her father spends all his time in Holland, pursuing his business interests at the Hague, and Madame Latour is . . ." Charis hesitated, not wishing to sound unkind.

"Becoming a trifle strange?" Lady Rowby finished her sentence for her. "Yes, I had begun to wonder, from certain things let fall by you and others, together with the fact that she doesn't seem to venture into society at all these days. Do you think she would permit the child to come with you?"

Charis said that she was sure that with a little diplomatic persuasion it might be possible. "The grand ball would be out of the question, of course, but an informal affair in your house is another matter entirely."

"Well then, I shall see to it that Madame receives an invitation for herself and her daughter, and leave the rest to you!" said her ladyship dryly. "Perhaps you might enlist the help of her cousin, the count!"

Charis had met the count only two nights previously at one of Lady Charlotte Greville's evening parties. He was older than the handsome young officer of the portrait, but in a curious way this merely emphasized his power to attract, and added a worldly-wise gleam to the bold dark eyes that bespoke danger even as they invited one's interest.

"So you are the young lady who is fast making a reputation for herself," he said as they circled the floor.

"Am I?" she prevaricated, striving to sound merely polite while being very conscious of the way he was holding her.

"Such modesty!" he mocked, laughing down at her. "A becoming virtue, if not carried to excess. But I would guess, from the way that Miss Winslade dances the waltz, that she does not despise the more liberal pleasures of life!"

His outrageousness was infectious, and it took every ounce of her resolve not to respond in kind; to remind herself that he was dissolute, intemperate—a self-confessed libertine.

"If that is the impression you have received, monsieur," she returned with spirit, "then I can only beg you to believe that you have been misled!"

"Oh, faint-heart!" he scoffed, laughing the more. "For your tongue denies what your body clearly reveals!" As she stiffened defensively in his arms, he added, "but if that is what you wish me to believe, then I am yours to command. Your frown is magnificent, but I would rather see you smile. So, tell me instead, how do you like lodging with my cousin, Marie? You have the nursery wing, I believe. Does my portrait still hang there?"

Charis admitted that it did.

"Dear Cousin Marie! Always my most ardent *admiratrice*! But I am much changed, I fear, since that was painted." His eyes challenged her. "You would perhaps like to attempt a more contemporary likeness? I vow I should account it an honor!"

She hastily declined the commission, and was more relieved than otherwise when the music ended. She did not know how to take his assurances that they would meet again, or his murmured reflection that he had neglected his cousin much of late, and she lived in a state of unease lest he should take it into his head to call.

But in the end she had cause to be grateful that he did. Her attempts to persuade Madame Latour to allow Celestine to accompany her to Lady Rowby's reception met with rather more resistance than she had foreseen. Madame did not feel well enough to attend, and kept murmuring that it would be most improper for her daughter to venture into company without her.

Charis was almost in despair. And then the half-expected happened and the Colonel Comte arrived to pay his respects, resplendent in his Dutch-Belgian uniform. The effect upon Madame was remarkable; she became almost animated, and when her *"cher Etienne"* was apprised of the difficulty in which she found herself, he at once came up with the solution.

How would it be if he were to go in her place?

Madame Latour, seemingly oblivious of the wrath such a course of action might arouse in her husband should he but come to hear of it, was relieved to have the matter settled and presently fell into a reverie.

When it became clear that she could not bestir herself, the Comte de Vallon looked at Charis in almost comical dismay.

"Does this happen often?"

"I'm not sure, but I think she has grown rather worse of late," Charis said unhappily.

"Pauvre Marie," he said as if to himself. And then, with sudden vehemence, *"He* should have known how it would be! What is he thinking about—to leave her so much alone?"

"If you mean Monsieur Latour—" she felt as though she was intruding into something that did not concern her— "I believe that there have been difficulties—and that Monsieur is now occupied in trying to re-establish his business connections."

"Which, if he had not been such a proud, single-minded bigot, he need never have forfeited in the first place!" said the count harshly. Then he seemed to recollect himself, shrugged, and smiled at her. "But this can be of no possible interest to you. Family squabbles are always tedious to outsiders. Now, about this affair of Lady Rowby's . . ."

Charis, faintly embarrassed by the knowledge that he had not been invited, scarcely knew what to say.

"It is just a small reception, monsieur, to enable the English people here at present to meet the Duke of Wellington informally."

"Yet Marie and my young cousin are not English, *hein*?" he mused softly.

"No." Charis bit her lip, aware that she was blushing. "Well, that was my idea—to try to introduce Celestine into society a little. You have seen how things are."

"Quite so. A most charitable thought, mademoiselle. But would she not feel strange, a foreigner among so many English people?" He seemed to be measuring his words with the skill of a fencer trying out his opponent; Charis knew it, but remembering the several Dutch-Belgian dignitaries who would also be present, she felt quite unable to dissemble. As if reading her thoughts, the count pressed home his point. "But then, perhaps she will not be alone? Perhaps it is only turncoats that my Lady Rowby would prefer not to be made known to the duke? He can be outspoken, I believe. How wise of her not to risk a scene. At such a small affair these things are not easily concealed."

He said it lightly, but she was almost certain that there was bitterness behind the words.

"I'm sure Lady Rowby would not allow that to be a consideration," Charis said in stout defense of her friend. "I will see her, explain matters. I'm sure there will be no difficulty."

To her relief, he seemed willing to leave the matter there, contenting himself with an ironic bow. And Lady Rowby, when approached, gave her a curious look, but made no objections.

Celestine, meanwhile, was overjoyed, her only fear being that sheer fright might cause her to swoon in full view of everyone.

"Nonsense!" Charis reassured her bracingly. "You will be enjoying yourself far too much to even think of swooning . . . besides, only consider what a sad waste of valuable time it would be!"

In order to give the girl's thoughts a more positive direction, they fell to discussing what Celestine might wear for the occasion, and in this Charis found an unexpected ally in the governess. Mrs. Grant, she discovered, was a briskly sensible Scottish lady who had lived most of her life in Europe; widowed in her early twenties, she had put her flair for languages to good use by becoming governess to successive families of good repute, first in France and then in Austria, before coming to the Latours.

Mrs. Grant proved to be an excellent needlewoman, and with a few suggestions from Charis and a lot of ingenuity, she devised the perfect gown for a *jeune fille* making her debut in society.

Charis determined that Tristram should know nothing of her scheming until the very last minute, but he wasn't easy to deceive and by the evening of the reception she had almost despaired of bringing it off. Her one fear was that he might be required to study the list of guests, but she ought to have known that he would not concern himself with such a trifling detail.

"You are looking uncommonly smug, my girl," he said, pausing on the way to his room to peer at her suspiciously. "Which means you're up to something. I can always tell." He seized her playfully by the shoulders. "Come now, confess."

"Oh pooh!" She shrugged him off. "Wait and see."

And then, unable wholly to hide her triumph, "I have been very clever, and shall expect to be suitably rewarded! But later. Go and get ready now, or we shall be late."

Charis had suggested that they should go downstairs to await the count's carriage and as they reached the *petit vestibule* Tristram was in the middle of saying teasingly that with all the money she was now earning from her painting they would soon be able to afford their own carriage, when his words faded away into silence at the sight of the slight figure waiting for them there.

She was dressed all in shimmering white, a wrap of some diaphanous material floating from her shoulders, and little clusters of silver fair curls framing a face that was almost transparently pale except for the wide violet blue eyes which shone with tremulous excitement; as her eyes met Tristram's, there was in them a kind of awed adoration that brought a lump to Charis's throat. She heard him murmur, "Oh glory!" as he stepped forward to lift Celestine from her curtsy.

When at last he managed to tear his glance away, it fastened in a dazed way upon Charis. "How *did* you do it?"

"Oh, it wasn't too difficult."

She lied with, she hoped, convincing gaiety in an effort to smother that freshly aroused pinprick of jealousy. It was unforgivably foolish, when none of his previous *amours* had caused her a moment's unease, to let the mere sight of the two of them together affect her so.

"Your sister 'as been so very kind to me, monsieur," Celestine was whispering shyly. "I do not know how I am ever to thank her."

Charis found that her brother was looking at her in a rather odd way, and was not at all sorry to hear the crunch of carriage wheels announcing the count's arrival.

Lady Rowby received the Comte de Mallon with equanimity, not by so much as a muscle betraying that his coming was anything but a pleasure. Not that she disliked him, precisely; rather she instinctively mistrusted anyone who so flagrantly set himself to please, to fascinate, and not for one moment did she believe his protestations of concern for his cousin's child. Such selflessness was out of character with all that she had heard of him, and besides, seeing them together, it was clear that Mademoiselle Latour was very much in awe of him. Her only hope was that he would not seek to use the child, and through her, Charis, in order to further his bid to ingratiate himself, for whatever reason, into their midst.

For the present, Celestine had eyes for no one but young Winslade; even her surroundings took second place. She really was quite lovely, with an appealing air of unworldliness about her that must present an irresistible lure to any young man. And he was not slow to succumb, by the look of him. Ah well! Time would tell.

"You will find Lord Rowby in the blue saloon, Mr. Winslade. I know he was wishing to have a word with you. Perhaps," she added with a droll glance at Charis, "you would like to take Mademoiselle Latour along with you."

Lady Rowby then hurried away to greet the Duke and Duchess of Richmond, who were at that very moment arriving, and Charis, left with the count, began to follow more slowly in Tristram's wake. After commenting with some amusement that his little cousin was undoubtedly head over ears in love with her brother—a sight quite affecting to behold—the count turned upon Charis a decidedly cynical smile.

"Your friend Lady Rowby is almost as accomplished a diplomat as her husband, Miss Winslade. One would never guess from the manner in which she recieved me, how deep is her disapproval of me!" He saw Charis searching desperately for some convincing words of mitigation and the smile in his bold eyes intensified. "You need not refine upon it, *chère mademoiselle*. My sensibilities do not bruise easily. Especially," he coaxed softly, "when there is a beautiful young lady on hand to console me!"

Charis blushed, not entirely displeased even as she disclaimed laughingly, "Oh, you must look elsewhere for succor, monsieur. I fear I shall be of little use in that respect."

"We shall see," he said with a touch of arrogance that half-annoyed, half-intrigued her, so that on the whole she was not sorry when the Duke of Wellington's arrival put an end to any further intimacy between them.

The duke was much slighter, much less impressive than she had expected; with no fancy uniform to set him apart—the Prince of Orange who accompanied him far outshone him in terms of gilded splendor—one might almost have been tempted to dismiss him, to conclude that the reputation had outstripped the man, were it not for the face.

Watching him moving among his friends in high good humor, his whooping laugh ringing out as he greeted his dear friend, Lady Charlotte Greville, Charis could not take her eyes from his face. She longed for pencil and paper so that she might capture its changing moods— the eyes, piercingly blue, that could turn suddenly chilly beneath shaggy brows; the mouth, now pursed in reflection, now open in laughter; and dominating all else, that most famous, majestic, autocratically bony nose, whose high-bridged propensities could transform a mere frown into awesome displeasure.

Lady Rowby had been a little nervous as to how he would react to the Comte de Mallon's presence, but beyond a certain snapping of his eyes, the moment passed off without incident.

By suppertime the atmosphere was pleasantly relaxed, and Charis, laughing over her shoulder at some witty observation of the count's, found her glance drawn toward the supper room doorway. A figure stood outlined there, tall, loose-limbed, motionless, his long face in shadow. But Charis, her heart turning over, did not need to see his face. After a moment's pause, he stepped into the room and came unerringly toward her.

"Good evening, Miss Winslade," said Major Hammond.

ᕙᕦ 8 ᕤᕗ

Dan had come to Brussels with high hopes, appointed, with the Duke of Wellington's connivance, to Slender Billy's staff.

"The prince is a good, enthusiastic fellow," the duke had confided to close colleagues, "but he hasn't the advantage of years, let alone experience of command. I have it in mind to suggest Major Hammond to him as an aide-de-camp. Hammond is not unknown to him. He is young enough and lively enough to please the prince, and that should allay any suspicion that he is being guided. And Hammond is a damned fine soldier into the bargain—has a positive genius for scenting trouble—a talent that served me well in the Peninsular on more than one occasion. Who knows when we may again have need of his particular skills."

With Bonaparte safe on Elba, the likelihood of trouble seemed remote during that victorious summer, but such was the duke's reputation that no one presumed to question his opinion.

Dan certainly did not cavil at the appointment. Brussels held infinitely more attractions for him than the 95th's camp at Dover where he had seemed doomed to spend the next few months kicking his heels. Brussels, after all, held Charis Winslade.

It was evening when he arrived in the Rue Ducale to find the reception in full swing. A brief word with his uncle's butler and he was shown to a bedchamber where it took but a short time to wash away the grime of his journey and change into his dress uniform, hastily unpacked and pressed by his inestimable servant, Parker, who had served him with taciturn devotion as both batman and groom for more than ten years, and would let no one else near what he referred to grandiosely as "the major's accoutrements."

Dan had little doubt that Charis would be at the party; what he hadn't expected, and what shook him to the soles of his gleaming Hessian boots, was to find her taking so much pleasure in the company of a flamboyantly handsome brute of a fellow at least ten years his senior.

At that moment, nothing would have afforded him so much pleasure as to ram the smiling stranger's gleaming white teeth down his throat. But the polite amiability of his greeting betrayed no hint of such base thoughts. He derived some small comfort from the fleeting moment of leaping awareness which preceded the blankness of shock in Miss Winslade's eyes; it was further confirmed in the betraying flood of color that followed, but he had been disconcerted nonetheless to discover that she was not visibly pining away for love of him.

If only he could have known what a tumult was raging inside Charis as she calmly introduced the two men to one another, and chidingly queried the major's unexpected presence among them.

He explained. "I had thought to surprise my uncle and aunt." That look of wry amusement she knew so well lit his eyes. "I only hope I have not succeeded too well!"

Lady Rowby, hurrying up that moment, hands outstretched in delighted greeting, dismissed any such ideas, and presently carried him off to renew acquaintance with his new commander, and Charis, watching between the drifting throng of people, saw the Prince of Orange take him warmly by the hand, an affable smile in his rather protuberant eyes, before a cloud of pretty skirts closed around them. It was some moments before she became aware that the count was speaking to her.

"He is a very taking young man, the nephew of Lord

Rowby," he repeated as she looked blankly at him. "Have you known him long?"

"No," she said, almost too quickly, too positively. "Hardly any time at all, really."

"Strange," he mused. "I had quite thought . . . but, no matter." He offered his arm. "Shall we take supper, Miss Winslade?"

She ate and drank, laughed and talked, with one ear constantly attuned for the sound of *his* voice, her eyes roving apparently casually over the guests in search of that coat of distinctive Rifle green, the brilliant slash of the red sash. The count, having been many times on the receiving end of just such an obsessive infatuation, recognized the signs at once. A less experienced man might have been tempted to bridle, to take issue with her, but Mallon simply smiled and bided his time, knowing exactly how to distract her thoughts when it became clear that the good major would not seek her out during the remainder of the evening.

Lady Rowby embraced Charis as she prepared to leave, drawing her a little to one side.

"My dear child, I have seen scarcely anything of you! But the evening has gone well, I think, don't you? Rowby is well satisfied, I know. And as for that graceless nephew of ours, turning up like that without so much as a hint, and with such news!" She paused, looked a little closer. Was it the candlelight that made Charis seem rather paler than usual? "Are you quite well, my dear? Dan's coming like that without warning has not . . . ? Oh, forgive me, but I have not been entirely unaware that you and he . . . that in London there was a certain something . . . But there, I can see that I am being odiously inquisitive, and you may tell me to go to the devil!"

"As if I would!" Charis gave her a fierce hug and smiled valiantly as she let go. "There was never much to tell, dear ma'am. A few moments of silliness born of propinquity. If I seem a little flat, you must blame the splendor of your hospitality. I am simply tired."

She tried hard to make herself believe her own fabrication, with little success. Throughout the journey home, she was painfully aware of Tristram and Celestine sitting opposite her, their shadowy figures intimately close in a communion that had no need of words. The count, to her immense relief, made no attempt to break the silence, nor did he linger over his leavetaking, though there was nothing in the manner of it to suggest that he found anything amiss.

But in the privacy of her room, with all hope of sleep abandoned, and every nerve and fiber still quivering from the impact of seeing Major Hammond again so unexpectedly, Charis recognized with dismay the futility of supposing that what she had felt for him, what she still felt for him, would simply go away. She loved him deeply, irrevocably, and through cowardice, she had driven him away. What was it he had said to her? *"I could have sworn that you were the kind who would fling herself into love headfirst, and not care about getting hurt!"*

And I am! she cried inwardly. I would, if only I could have another chance! He said he loved me. Surely, if he meant it at all, he cannot have changed so soon?

But he made no attempt to seek her out. Oh, he was his usual engaging self when they met in the park on the following afternoon, but he had a charming Bruxelloise clinging possessively to his arm and he showed no particular inclination to relinquish her for the favor of Charis's company.

Her hopes must now be pinned on the grand birthday ball in honor of the Prince Regent. He would surely be there, and if she was to have any chance of winning him back, that must be as good an occasion as any. She had taken the greatest pains with her gown; the current vogue for wearing the flimsiest, most daring of styles was not wholly to her taste, but she had managed a compromise between fashion and elegance that did not displease her.

Emily MacGrath was less impressed.

"You're never thinking of going among decent folk dressed like that! Downright indecent, that's what it is!" was her verdict as she grimly surveyed the clinging amber silk, prettily scattered around the discreetly plunging neck and hem with butterflies embroidered in silver thread.

"Really Em! This is positively demure, I promise you. You should see what some of the more dashing young beauties are wearing!"

"Not I! I've no wish to have me sensibilities outraged any further! And don't be looking to me to nurse you when you come down with an inflammation of the lungs, which you will—and it no more than you deserve!" she muttered darkly.

Tristram's obvious approval, however, did much to reassure her, and when Lady Rowby told her that she looked "quite delightfully," her confidence was once more restored.

There could not have been a more romantic setting than the lavishly appointed ballroom, its decorative theme coming to a glorious conclusion in the form of a dais at the far end, completely swathed in blue and silver, and presided over by the Goddess of Peace. The company was distinguished and varied, including as it did many Dutch and Belgian notables among the great number of English visitors to Brussels. The Duke and Duchess of Richmond were much in evidence with their party, also Lady Charlotte Greville and her husband, Colonel Charles Greville, and the Earl and Countess of Mountnorris and their daughters, who were cousins of the Duke of Wellington, on a visit of indefinite length from Ireland.

It was a brilliant affair, and so crowded that, at times, it was difficult to move about, let alone find any one particular person.

Charis did not want for partners. The Comte de Mallon, as usual, was never far away, so that she was glad of Ned's company together with Tristram and some of their friends.

"I don't dislike the count, precisely," she confided to Ned. "It's just that I would as lief not encourage him too far."

"Very wise, m'dear. You just give me the nod and I'll do the necessary," Ned said earnestly. "Can't say I care for the fellow m-myself—bit of a loose fish, don't y'know."

Charis was obliged to smother a giggle at Ned's conviction that he could see off the dashing count, but she was grateful nonetheless for his solicitude.

It was well into the evening when Dan Hammond arrived, and later still when Charis had her first glimpse of him among the Duke of Wellington's party, his head bent in that absorbed, amiable way toward Lady Catherine Annesley, the younger of Mountnorris's daughters, who was etherially fair with an appealing air of fragility. The demon jealousy stirred in her breast and had to be firmly quelled.

She had all but made up her mind that he meant to give her the go-by once again when he left Lady Catherine's side, stopped for a word with his aunt, and then, as the musicians struck up for a waltz, came purposefully toward her. Instinctively her chin lifted a fraction.

"Miss Winslade?" He held out a hand, and after a moment's hesitation she put her own into it.

They danced at first without speaking, Charis being very conscious that his touch lacked that former hint of intimacy.

"Did Lady Rowby persuade you to ask me?" she said at last, unable to bear the silence any longer.

"No. Is that what you think?" To her overly sensitive ears, his voice sounded amused.

"I . . . wondered." Charis kept her gaze fixed firmly

on one of the silver buttons of his coat. "After our last meeting, I had not expected . . ."

"Oh, that!" he said, his voice gently rallying. "My dear Miss Winslade, I beg you will put that unfortunate incident out of your mind. I should not have spoken as I did—it was ill-judged, presumptuous, and quite odiously selfish of me to treat you in that ramshackle way! I should not wonder if it has given you a lasting disgust of me!"

"Oh no!" The exclamation was out before she could prevent it. She added lamely, "I, too, said things which . . . which I could wish unsaid!"

His arm tightened a little. "Well then, do you suppose that we might both forget that it ever happened and return to our former happy relationship?"

This was not in the least what she had wanted him to say, but perhaps it was as much as she deserved. Her voice subdued, she assented.

It was all the encouragement he needed. With a low exultant laugh he drew her close and whirled her around dizzily toward the end of the ballroom where, as the music drew to a close, he waltzed her straight out through one of the long open windows leading onto a terrace, and beyond into the shelter of a small clump of trees. Against the black, star-strewn night the face she lifted wonderingly to him was a pale blur.

"Did you really imagine that I would give up so easily?" he demanded, soft-voiced.

Charis felt very strange—all tremulous and melting, not at all like herself.

"I thought," she said shakily, "that you would by now have dismissed me as a silly, inexperienced girl."

She heard his breath drawn sharply in. "Inexperienced, perhaps . . . it was one of the qualities that most endeared you to me, but never silly, my lovely Charis! Mine was the only folly in attempting to rush you!"

His kisses explored her mouth gently at first until, as she responded with a sweet ardor, he caught her closer and passion leaped between them, sending the blood coursing riotously along her veins.

At last, reluctantly, he raised his head and, by now grown accustomed to the darkness, saw her deep-shadowed eyes languorous with desire, her quivering mouth full and soft.

"Oh, dear God!" he exclaimed unsteadily. "I can't possibly take you back in there looking like that, and if we stay here, I won't be answerable for the consequences!"

She disengaged herself. "Then we must be sensible," she said shakily.

"Sensible!" He caught her hands as she would have moved away and held on to them. "I don't feel at all sensible! I want to run away with you this minute! I want to rush into the ballroom and shout my love aloud. . . ."

"Oh, but you won't?" Her laughter was tinged with alarm. "You mustn't! I should die of embarrassment . . . and besides, we must first tell your uncle and aunt, and Tristram, too!"

Dan frowned. "Will he object, do you suppose?"

"Not if he is satisfied that I'll be happy."

"That's all right, then—because you will be, I promise! Ecstatically!"

His sublime confidence infected her, too, so that she felt almost light-headed with joy.

"I came here with all kinds of good intentions, re-solved to woo you most circumspectly, to gain your trust—" a note of belligerence entered the gentle, self-mocking recital— "and then I saw you enjoying the attentions of that middle-aged roue—"

"The Comte de Mallon?" Charis gurgled with laughter. "Oh, how mortified he would be to hear himself so described! Were you really jealous of him?"

"Damnably!" he said grimly.

"Oh Dan," she admitted. "So was I . . . of that beautiful creature you had on your arm in the park!"

He groaned and pulled her close, kissing her fiercely. "To my shame, I meant you to be! I wanted you to feel exactly as I felt. You see what a despicable fellow I am?" She denied it vigorously and he kissed her again. "Even tonight, I meant to pursue the same devious strategy . . . until I held you in my arms. Then I knew that there was no need for further skirmishing . . . the prize was already mine!"

"Was I so transparent?" she exclaimed weakly.

"Only to me, darling girl," he said, soothing her fears. Then he chuckled. "You'll have to marry me now, of course. I have compromised you beyond all decency, keeping you so long out here alone with me!"

"It is what I have been wishing for more than anything ever since I feared that I had thrown away my chance," she said simply.

He squeezed her hands very tight. "How soon?"

A part of her wanted to cry "Tomorrow," but that would be quite impractical.

"Oh, good heavens! I don't know. You must give me time to get used to the idea! There will be all kinds of arrangements to be made . . ."

"That's women's talk! I could make all the necessary arrangements, and we could be married within the week." He peered at her in sudden alarm. "You don't want a grand society wedding?"

"No, of course not!" she said, half-laughing. "But I won't be stampeded into a skimble-skamble affair either!" Her voice grew pleading. "Just a little time. Apart from anything else, Em would never forgive me if I didn't do the thing properly!"

He gave an exaggerated sigh, and agreed. There was hardly a breath of wind stirring the trees as they turned, fingers entwined, and walked slowly back toward the ballroom. Above them, the slim silver crescent of a new moon rode high among the trembling stars, its beauty so in keeping with her mood that Charis felt that her heart would burst with sheer happiness.

"You will come with me on campaigns? I don't think I could face leaving you at home."

"You won't have to!" Charis stopped and turned impulsively, reaching up to touch his face, which seemed almost luminous, disembodied—its clean-cut lines fading into the silver misted darkness.

Dan drew her hand from his cheek and the kiss he buried in its palm was like an obeisance. "You are an extraordinary girl—" his voice was oddly husky— "and I fear that I shall prove quite unworthy of you." She moved to protest, but he would not let her. "If I ever hurt you, ever disappoint you, remember that I *do* love you!"

In the days and weeks that followed, there was a radiance about Charis that could hardly escape the notice of those who knew her well; to her natural ebullience was added a smiling, dreamlike quality which carried her through the balls and receptions and visits to the theater that proliferated throughout the duke's visit and beyond.

There was never any question of hiding her newfound happiness from Tristram; even had she wished to, it would have been impossible, for they were so close that whatever deeply affected the one inevitably communicated itself to the other. And now, with Tristram more than halfway in love himself, he saw immediately how it was with her.

"So it's to be Hammond, is it?" he mused on the way home from the ball. "I knew there had to be someone at the back of your odd humors a while back. Well, it was bound to happen one day, and he's a decent enough fellow, I suppose, if you must marry!"

There was a wistful note in his voice that smote Charis. She linked her arm through his and laid her head on his shoulder. "Oh Tris! Shall you mind dreadfully? I'm not rushing off tomorrow, or anything like that . . . in fact, you must know that I wouldn't dream of leaving until you are firmly established, and that cannot be long, for I know how pleased Lord Rowby is with you."

There was a deep sigh in the darkness. "You mustn't worry about me, love. I shall do well enough with Em to bully me."

But this was awful! She had no idea he would mind so much. She lifted her head to peer into his face, and he chuckled.

"*Stoopid!*" Tris removed his arm from hers and hugged her. "I am delighted for you . . . couldn't wish for a finer addition to the family than Hammond." And as she found relief in laughter, he said off-handedly, "Who knows? I might yet follow your example."

"Celestine?" Her heart hollowed with unease. "You are that serious about her?"

"Oh, I'm serious, right enough."

Charis hadn't heard quite that note in his voice before—a sureness that had nothing of his usual impetuosity when in love. She felt impelled to warn him that Celestine was little more than a babe, that, in her father's eyes he would have little to commend him, for surely in their present circumstances, he would be looking for a more advantageous match.

"You are very quiet of a sudden," Tristram said. "You think I'm air-dreaming, don't you? But you'll see!" As the carriage drew to a swaying halt, he gave her a last quick hug. "Be happy, love. Don't let my problems fret you. I shan't do anything rash or precipitate, I promise you."

Emily's inquisition was thorough to the point of embarrassment. Who was this Major Hammond? How and when had Charis met him? And why had there been neither sight nor mention of him until now? The former could be explained away by a precariously fabricated string of military duties, which were acknowledged with one of Emily's sniffs, but as to why Charis had never mentioned him? In the end, she took refuge in hauteur, declared that it was none of Emily's business if she chose not to do so . . . and ran before the old lady could draw fresh breath, knowing full well that Dan would be well able to charm her out of her sulks within moments of their meeting.

Lady Rowby greeted the news with unfeigned delight. Nothing, she said, could please them more than to have Charis for a daughter. When all the fuss of the duke's visit had died down, they would give a celebration dinner to mark the engagement—"Just a small affair," she promised.

After some opposition from Dan, who wanted it next week, the wedding was fixed for early spring.

"The prince would not thank you for falling into marriage within days of being appointed to his staff," Charis said.

"Nonsense! The prince is a most amiable fellow. Likes to enjoy life, so I doubt my duties will prove arduous. In fact," Dan said in that softly persuasive way she found so difficult to resist, "I begin to wonder how I am to pass my time, so you see . . ."

She fended him off, laughing. "No, I won't be coerced, however agreeably. *My* time, I may tell you, is fully accounted for. There are bride clothes to be made—"

"You look delightful just as you are."

"Sheer flummery!" she exclaimed, with a rueful glance at her much worn muslin gown spread out on the grass. "However, if you are prepared to explain to Em that I have no need of bride clothes . . ."

"I would as soon face a charge of cavalry," he retorted with feeling. "Sooner, in fact. Your Mrs. MacGrath fills me with terror!"

"For shame!" she chuckled. "What price the Conquering Hero now?"

"Every man's courage has a breaking point," he avowed valiantly. "It just so happens that your Emily is mine!"

It was late September, and unseasonably warm. Dan had borrowed a phaeton from a friend and they had

driven out for a day in the country. They had left the
carriage at a small inn, and had walked some way until
they found their present vantage point in the lee of a
hedge, with the remains of their picnic tumbled on a
cloth nearby, the Chateau de Hougoumont behind them,
and a patchwork of fields as far as they could see, some
ploughed up, some still bearing the untidy scars of
harvest. Autumn sunshine picked out the gray stone
walls that divided the plain and winked occasionally
from the windows of a little farmhouse which Charis
knew as La Belle Alliance. "Such lovely names they
give to their farms and villages around here," she said
dreamily. "I really must come out one day with my
paints before the weather closes in."

They would come next week, he promised. She could
paint and he would sit back and watch her. This presented an idyllic picture, but Charis suspected that he
would be incapable of being inactive for so long at a
stretch, and his being there, so close, would make it
equally impossible for her to concentrate. But the day
was too perfect to mar with argument; so perfect, in
fact, that they were loath for it to end.

When they finally, regretfully, packed up to leave,
the afternoon was well advanced, and as they drove
past the little village of Waterloo and into the Forest of
Soignes, where the massive beech trees stood in serried
ranks, the sun was already beginning to set. It turned
the leaves above them to molten gold and now and
then, as a faint breeze disturbed the still, warm air, a
few came floating soundlessly down to join the thick
red-brown carpet that crunched beneath the carriage
wheels.

Charis had thrown her bonnet carelessly in with the
picnic things and her hair, tumbled by a day in the
open air, was likewise burnished to a rich auburn. She
stretched like a contented cat, and Dan, leaving the
horse to pick its way with only the minimum of

guideance, watched her from under sleepy eyelids, his eyes crinkled with love.

"If you arrive back in Brussels looking like that," he said huskily, "everyone will infer that I have seduced you."

She turned to meet his eyes, her breath catching on a laugh, the color deepening in her face. "Will they?"

"And don't think for one moment that I am finding it easy to resist the temptation!"

⚜️ 9 ⚜️

The Duke of Wellington left Brussels late in August, and in his wake went a few of the more restless of the pleasure seekers, some bound for Paris and some for Vienna, where the Great Peace Congress was shortly to be held.

Brussels retained much of its gaiety, but the pace of life grew less frenetic and Charis, when not busy sewing, found herself more at liberty to explore the quaint and beautiful corners of the city, sketchbook in hand, so that before long it was not simply her portraits that were in demand. She purchsed a smart little gig and a nicely mannered pony, and was soon to be seen taking the air, often unaccompanied, in this modest equipage.

Such forwardness scandalized one or two of the more staid society matrons, but Lady Rowby could see little harm in the venture and Dan, amused by her enterprise, merely teased her about becoming "a woman of property."

Tristram was the only member of her close circle to make adverse comment, apart from Em, and her brother's argument was not against the purchase as such, but rather that she should have chosen so tame a turn-out: "If you had only said, love, I could have put you in the way of the most bang-up rig you ever saw . . . a perch phaeton with the finest little blood mare, and all going for next to nothing! Fellow got himself badly into debt. This—" he had gestured scornfully— "don't hold a candle to it!"

Her pony turned a lugubrious eye upon him, and Charis, knowing full well that anything advocated by Tris would be designed for speed rather than comfort, thanked him kindly, but insisted that she was well satisfied with her purchase. He looked so crestfallen that she added impulsively that if he really wanted the phaeton, and if it really was such a bargain, they might just be able to afford it.

"We are living much more cheaply here than I had anticipated," she said, the look on his face making it impossible for her to retract. "And with my painting, and that nice Mr. Todd, who manages our affairs so admirably back home, writing only last week to say that he has let the London house—" The rest of what she had been going to say was smothered in an affectionate hug.

"And we shouldn't have any difficulty with stabling," she concluded when at last she could draw breath. "Madame Latour has already offered to put the stables here at our disposal, and since they keep but one shabby barouche at present, there would be ample room."

Madame's condition was continuing to trouble Charis. The Comte de Mallon had departed for Vienna, via Paris, soon after the announcement of her engagement.

"I have resigned my commission and there is little point now to my remaining here," he had sighed regretfully, holding her hand reverently in both of his. "This little member is bestowed elsewhere, and can never be mine!"

She could not quite suppress her mirth at the absurdity of this highflown speech, convinced as she was that the sentiments it expressed sprang solely from the head, not from the heart. She said everything that was proper but although he accepted her commiserations with a certain arrogance, Charis suspected that he did not care to be ridiculed. Altogether, she was not sorry to see him go; his attentions, at first flattering, had become vaguely disturbing and only the beneficial effect his visits exercised upon Madame Latour had made her tolerate them with any degree of equanimity.

Her only fear was that his going would prove doubly unsettling to Madame, and indeed, so it was found to be. Apart from a personal maid of immense age, there seemed to be no one—servant or acquaintance—willing to bear her company. Celestine did try, but her character was not sufficiently outgoing and positive to lift the older woman's spirits, and her mama's bouts of vagueness clearly upset her. In the end it was Celestine's governess, Mrs. Grant, who stepped in to take responsibility, her official role having become somewhat anomolous. She proved to be an excellent companion for Madame, and Celestine took to spending more and more time with the Winslades.

Charis grew quite fond of the girl, though she occasionally worried about the excessive nature of her feelings for Tris; as for him—she had never known him to have such a care for anyone, except perhaps herself. She felt quite powerless to intervene, nor for that matter could she feel that it was her place to question Tris's right to the same degree of happiness that she had found. And Dan agreed with her.

"I know that you've always made a point of trying to solve your brother's problems for him . . ."

"How odious that makes me sound!" she exclaimed indignantly.

"But this is something he must work out for himself," Dan concluded inexorably, and then set himself to dispel her vexation, though not before she had demanded in pained tones to be told whether he truly found her to be a managing female.

"Not in the least," he said soothingly. "You just like to take the initiative—get things done." He punctuated the words with kisses until her irritation had very nearly melted away. "Excellent qualities in a soldier's wife, I may say."

Charis swayed a little toward him, much mollified. "A soldier's wife. I like the sound of that."

He grinned lazily. "So do I, by God! One day I must

introduce you to Harry Smith's wife, little Juana. She's
something of a legend among the Light Bobs. Married
Harry at sixteen . . . a mere babe! A drumhead wedding,
it was, after Bajados, and she's hardly left his side since
. . . until now. Lucky dog's gone off to America and she
is at present immured in England among strangers."
There was an affectionate, oddly possessive note in his
voice that almost made Charis jealous. "I ran into her
briefly just before I left London—being very brave,
trying desperately to learn English, and hating every
minute that separates her from her beloved Enrique!"

"Ah, the poor girl!" Charis said, and then half-
diffidently: "You seem very fond of her?"

He laughed. "We all adored her to a man from the
first! You'll see why when you meet her. There's nothing *poor* about Juana Smith. She's the perfect soldier's
wife . . . bears all stoically, insists that the war in
America will soon be at an end, and that her Enrique
will then be back with her, restless as ever and full of
his exploits!"

This was a Dan she seldom saw—the daredevil behind that languid pose. He sounded envious. Charis
knew that he found his duties with the Prince of Orange less than demanding; knew also that, agreeable as
it was to be close to her, he too was restless and longing
for excitement, action, danger.

For the first time she had some inkling of how her
life would be, married to a man whose aim must always
be to go where the fighting was at its thickest; living
constantly with the dread of learning that he had been
killed in action. Would she be able to bear all stoically?
She shivered slightly.

Dan looked down at her. "Cold, sweetheart?" He put
an arm around her and she leaned against him, pressing
her face into his coat to hide the sudden panic.
"Heh!" His fingers felt for her chin, lifted it. "What's
wrong?"

Oh, this would never do! Such shameful weakness—
and before her nerve had even been tested!

"Nothing," she said with a bright, determined smile.

As September slipped into October, news began to
filter back from Paris that all was not well.

A fellow diplomat, writing to Lord Rowby, confessed
that "a discernable atmosphere of disquiet is developing
among our people here. Wellington is lionized everywhere—also, he has been well received at court and is
applying himself with considerable skill to the delicate
task of persuading the king to abolish the slave trade in
the French colonies, though there is much general
opposition to such a policy. He is much with the royal
family, gaining their confidence, hunting with them
(upon one special occasion he even submitted to being
decked out in all the trappings of gold lace, jackboots,
and hunting knife! But once only!). Clearly he is enjoying the concerts, theaters, balls, etc., and delights in
paying court to the reigning doyennes of the old world
and the beauties of the new! But at the back of all the
socializing there lurks an air of menace. The Bonapartists plot, and the returning royalists fret and fume as
the government of Louis XVIII degenerates already
into a muddled kind of paternal anarchy. I find myself
fearing for the future!"

"Is there anything in it, do you suppose?" Lady Rowby
asked with a frown.

His lordship shrugged. "You know Hetherington—bit
of an old woman. Still, it's to be hoped King Louis don't
make a sad botch of things, or his subjects may be
wishing him fair and far away! After all, give Napoleon
his due, whatever his shortcomings, he was deuced
efficient!"

"But the man was a tyrant!" exclaimed his shocked
wife.

"Aye, m'dear, but sometimes even tyranny can seem

preferable to the blunderings of a benevolent despot who succeeds in pleasing no one!"

Toward the end of October, there was an alarming report of bullets narrowly missing the Duke of Wellington as he attended a review with the Duc d'Angouleme on the Champ de Mars, and shortly afterward the Prince of Orange received a missive from the duke requesting the services, temporarily, of his new A.D.C. "Things grow a little uncomfortable for us here," wrote the Great Man with his usual phlegm, "but I do not attach too much importance to these matters. . . ."

"So?" The prince's erratic features quirked into a wry grin. "You are honored, my friend. What qualities do you have, I wonder, that make you of such value all of a sudden?"

"As to that, sir," Dan murmured, "I really cannot say."

"Can you not?" mocked the prince. "Well, I will tell you something. It is true that our paths seldom crossed in Spain, but there was a most interesting story circulating among the esteemed Commander-in-Chief's family—I had it from Fitzroy—it concerned a crazy young major of the 95th, one of Cameron's lot, who was not above venturing into enemy territory whenever there was a need for vital information."

He smiled disarmingly, inviting comment.

Dan obliged, at his most bland. "Some men," he said, "will do anything to alleviate boredom."

The prince chuckled. "Quite so, Daniel." He sobered almost at once. "However, I think perhaps that you had better make all speed to Paris. In view of the latest rumors of Bonapartist plots against the duke's life, he may have need of just such a crazy man!"

Charis was less generously disposed toward Wellington's needs. "He has any number of people to call upon," she complained when initially faced with Dan's imminent departure. "Why must it be you?"

"Perhaps the duke wished to avail himself of my

superior experience of all the best Paris hells," he suggested whimsically.

"Don't try to humor me!" she snapped

The major regarded his beloved with all the natural reluctance of a man forced to part, however briefly, from all he holds most dear. Had indignation lent that added sparkle to her eyes, or could it be a film of tears? He took her in his arms and felt every nerve resist him.

"I confess I had hoped for a warmer leave-taking," he said against her hair, and though there was amusement in his voice, there was also a hint of exasperation, of steel beneath the surface, as he added, "It isn't of my choosing, either, my dear."

Charis was at once filled with remorse, furious with herself for behaving in a way that she most despised, and spent the next few moments being most agreeably reassured that it didn't matter.

"I shouldn't be away too long. . . ."

"Of course not. But you will be careful, won't you?" A terrible thought had seized her, for she remembered suddenly a conversation with Lady Rowby—oh, a long time ago—about Dan's having executed some very unorthodox missions while in Spain. It had all been very vague at the time, and the word *spy* seemed much too melodramatic, but her breath caught in her throat for all that. "I mean, if there *should* be trouble—"

"There won't be, sweetheart," he said, so calmly that she immediately adjured herself not to be so foolish. "You know the French—all bombast and bluster, but very little that's to the point!"

"I just wish I might go with you!"

"No more than I do," he said softly. "There is a little restaurant just off the Boulevard St. Germain . . . but that will have to wait." He broke off and kissed her with lingering fervor. "I must go!"

Charis felt his absence greatly at first. Then she decided that this was an excellent opportunity to practice the art of learning to be a good soldier's wife. The secret, she found, was to keep busy. She had formed the habit of driving out early each morning while the smart and the fashionable were still fast asleep to sketch the Flemish peasants coming into town with their wares.

A favorite spot was the bridge at the end of the Allée Verte. Although it was so late in the year, there were usually one or two painted barges to be found playing their way up the canal. But it was the peasants who were a constant source of joy and inspiration to her; in their blue embroidered smocks and bright red woolen caps, and their striped stockings, they came plodding over the bridge, the clatter of their wooden sabots mingling with the creak and rumble of the wagons as they dismounted to guide across the teams of horses that drew them—huge fat, horses that were equally colorful, their harnesses bedecked with brasses and all manner of bright tassels and fringes.

At first the faces of these rather stolid country folk seemed to be lacking in character, the eyes that glanced at her in passing holding no perceptible degree of interest. In a country that had been ruled successively by the Spanish, the Austrians, and now the Dutch, they had long since grown used to the presence of foreigners. Now, they kept themselves to themselves and so long as no one pillaged their land or commandeered their crops for forage, they were reasonably content.

But as Charis became a familiar sight, sitting at the side of the road wrapped in a warm cloak, sketchbook in hand, while her pony grazed contentedly between the shafts of the gig, she began to receive the occasional nod of the head, an irregular toothy grin, a muttered greeting; indifference was gradually replaced by a curiosity to know what she was doing, this strange young woman who seemed oblivious of the dank autumnal mists of early morning as the pencil in her hand moved swiftly, unerringly across the paper.

One or two paused on their way, and when she beckoned, came closer to look and, recognizing themselves or a companion, hailed others to come and see. Soon Charis had a whole new collection of friends and began to arrive home laden with presents pressed upon her by these good folk in exchange for one of her sketches of themselves.

"It really is quite impossible to refuse," she said by way of explanation when presenting Emily with yet another chicken—the third in almost as many days. "They would be most offended. Perhaps Madame Latour's chef could make use of it?"

Emily's sniff was louder than usual. "He might, but it's not me as'll be asking him!"

"Oh dear! You haven't had words again?"

Charis had long been aware of the running feud between Mrs. MacGrath and the sharp-faced little man who ruled over the Latour's kitchen; his ready flood of Gallic invective did not impress the redoubtable Emily, who usually allowed him to proceed until he ran out of breath before demolishing him with a few well-chosen epithets of her own. Since neither understood one quarter of the other's insults, it was difficult to decide who ran out the winner, but Tris had no doubts—"I'd back Em against the Frenchie any day!"

"Words?" Emily said now with ominous calm. "I wouldn't stoop to address myself to that creature after what he did yesterday!"

Charis's curiosity almost overcame her, but the thought of one of Emily's lengthy diatribes before breakfast was more than she could face, so she refrained from asking for the usual blow-by-blow account, flung her cloak over a chair back, and said cheerfully that she would take the chicken around to Lady Rowby's later that morning. "Her Mrs. Dalgleish will doubtless find a use for it."

Mrs. MacGrath, deprived of her dramatic rendition, eyed the carelessly deposited cloak with a jaundiced eye. "Is that mud you have on the hem of that garment? It's time you gave up this mad ploy of going out at the

crack of dawn. Look now, if the whole thing isn't damp?"
She took hold of the cloak and draped it over her arm,
calling over her shoulder as she marched to the door,
"If you're not set on by vagrants, you'll be carried off by
a chill before ever you get to the altar, and what Major
Hammond will say to me then, I don't care to think!"

Charis's laughter followed her out of the room, but it
was true, she reflected, that the mornings were becoming too inclement for many more excursions, and when
Lady Rowby said very much the same thing in her
gentle way, she decided to give them up for the time
being.

To her great delight, there was a letter for her from
Dan which had been enclosed with his lordship's diplomatic correspondence from Paris. She took it eagerly,
her very first letter from him, her fingers about to
break the seal when she realized how impolite she was
being, and looked up.

"Do you mind?"

Lady Rowby patted her hand and with great understanding remembered something she simply must tell
Lord Rowby at once, before she forgot, thus leaving her
young friend to peruse the contents of her letter in
private.

It was amusingly written, but subtly underscored
with love so that Charis could almost hear his voice
speaking the words. He touched but lightly upon the
prevailing conditions in Paris, confining his anecdotes
to the superficial delights which people seemed to be
pursuing with a hectic, shameless gaiety, and which he
might feel a great deal more ready to enjoy if only she
were there to share them with him. There was more in
this vein, enough to bring a blush to her cheek so that
it was as well she were alone.

One evening, well into November, Tristram came
home early and found his sister and Celestine comfortably settled upon the sofa close to the fire, giggling
companionably over a collection of caricatures that Charis

had compiled some weeks previously portraying with cruel perception the rather grandiose coterie of fashionables who had been present in Brussels at that time.

The two girls could not have been more opposite in appearance—Charis, with her short, crisply springing auburn hair, lively green eyes, and that straight-backed, curiously boyish elegance, and Celestine, all soft femininity, a hint of childishness still clinging to her curves, and as good as she was fair, with those amazing eyes that sometimes seemed to turn to deep violet when they gazed on him. The sight of them together, these two who meant the most in all the world to him, moved Tristram profoundly, and as always when he was moved, he took refuge in mockery.

"What a very domestic scene!" He strolled across to look over their shoulders. "Shame on you, sister dear—corrupting such a pure young mind!"

Celestine sprang to her feet, her cheeks, already flushed from the heat of the fire, glowing deeper at the sight of him. "Oh, but no!" she cried, laughter still lingering in her beautiful eyes. "Me—I am not corrupted at all, I promise you!"

He came around the sofa and stood very close, not attempting to touch her.

"No, indeed you are not!" he said, his voice not quite steady.

Charis, watching them, sat very still, hardly daring even to breathe, feeling her mere presence to be an intrusion.

Then Tristram gave his head a shake, as though to clear it. "Dearest little Celestine, do you think you will manage to go on without us for just a short while?"

"W-without you?" The young girl's voice faltered, the light slowly dying out of her face.

Charis found her voice, too. "Tris, whatever *do* you mean? Must you talk in riddles?"

He turned to her, a half-dazed look still in his eyes. "Sorry, love! It's what I came to tell you." With a faint smile, he added, "We are off to Paris for a few weeks!"

◄◖ 10 ◗►

It was nearly evening when the Winslades reached the outskirts of Paris, and their first impressions made them more than thankful that Lord Rowby had insisted upon their using his private traveling coach.

"Do it good to be used," he had said gruffly. "Do that coachman of mine good, too. He's growing idle, never going more than a mile or so at a stretch! Anyhow, public travel in France ain't what you're used to in England. Nasty, lumbering *diligences* . . . none too clean, most of the time, and devilish ill-sprung!"

The entrance to the city, as they came upon it suddenly out of a gray swirling mist, was not prepossessing—a wooden pallisade with a high, uninviting gateway guarded by idle louts who looked more like brigands than soldiers as they sullenly passed them through. The coach then rattled and jarred its way along narrow, villainously paved *allées* where ancient crumbling houses with pointed roofs and extraordinary gables almost shut out the sky, and the only light came from a few creaking lanterns swaying back and forth on ropes.

With a kind of aweful fascination, Charis let down the window and leaned out to find the stench overpowering, the center of the roadway running with a trickle of fetid water, and mud everywhere, through which an excitable rabble tramped unconcernedly. As one of their number, a grimacing blackguard with giant earrings, pushed his face toward her, she drew back, hastily closing the window on his raucous laughter.

"Oh, Tris!"

He laughed. "Cheer up, love. It can't all be like this!"

And sure enough, the streets by degrees became less oppressive, until finally, as they came closer to the heart of the city, the aspect began to change dramatically. They found wide boulevards lined with trees, whose leafless branches laced the sky, illuminated by the haze of light streaming out from innumerable restaurants and salons, their misted windows occasionally clearing to reveal huge gilded mirrors that reflected back the brilliant prisms of crystal chandeliers. And everywhere, people—indolent, stylish people.

Charis felt a tremor of excitement and turned eagerly to Tristram, the tedium of the journey already consigned to memory.

The coach at last reached a quiet tree-lined street where it was just possible to discern the vague shapes of lofty mansions set discreetly behind high walls. Presently it stopped, a pair of gates swung open, and they drove into a courtyard and drew up before an elegant pillared portico.

Sir Thomas Hetherington, with whom they were to stay, and who had been a great friend of their father, was waiting to greet them in a spacious salon that had about it the same uncluttered air of restrained elegance that epitomized its present incumbent. Sir Thomas was a tall, distinguished man, his hair grown prematurely white. He had about him a fastidiousness which perhaps explained why he had never married.

"Come along in, my dear young friends," he exclaimed, a long, slim hand extended to each in welcome. "This is the most tremendous pleasure for me, you know. My guests on the whole tend to be tedious government officials who wish only to talk business!"

As he begged them to be seated, one eyebrow quirked at Tristram. "You have a diplomatic bag, I see. Nothing too tiresome, I trust?"

Tristram grinned. "Only some papers from Lord

Rowby, and a letter. He said he wished me to have some experience of how things are done here, but *I* think—" he cast a roguish glance at his sister— "that his lordship's motives were rather more altruistic!"

"Ah yes!" Sir Thomas turned to Charis with twinkling eyes. "The young man who has been haunting my doorstep for the past two days, eager for news of your arrival."

Charis blushed, but the corners of her mouth curved upward. "Is Major Hammond quite well, Sir Thomas?" she asked with commendable composure.

"Oh, fit as a flea, my dear, though he'll doubtless be all the better for seeing you! But there—" he stood up— "I must not keep you talking when you are probably longing to rest and refresh yourselves after the exigencies of your journey. I thought perhaps a light supper later?"

They expressed their willingness to fit in with anything he might suggest.

"Good. We can then discuss how we are to make your visit as agreeable as possible."

At around the time the Windslades arrived in Paris, Dan was lounging at a table in an ill-lit corner of a café tucked away behind the Palais Royale, unshaven, the brim of a shabby beaver hat tipped forward to shield his eyes while one, none too clean hand, was idly outstretched, fingering a wine glass.

The café was empty but for a group of three men hunched together on a settle near the fire, talking, low-voiced. There was a tenseness in their attitude amounting almost to furtiveness, but although every now and then a few words broke out impatiently, Dan could make no sense of them. First one head and then another kept turning toward the door, which seemed to indicate that their number was incomplete, and this was borne out when the jangle of the doorbell and a quick inrush of air proclaimed a new arrival.

He was thick-chested, well and above medium height—a square-jawed man with eyes like cold, wet pebbles. His dress was neat, but unremarkable. He had come into the reckoning several days ago—and instinct, and an unerring ability to detect one of his own kind, told Dan that the man was, or had been, a soldier, almost certainly an officer. It was no secret that the army was pro-Bonapartist almost to a man, so that his presence here now, and the way the others shuffled into some kind of order as he approached their table and sat down, made the situation reek of conspiracy.

Dan sipped his drink and watched, narrow-eyed, over the rim of the glass. The man sat down and nodded curtly to the patron, who poured a generous measure of brandy and carried it across, setting it down carefully out of reach of his moving hand. He seemed to be sketching something, explaining it minutely to his companions. Dan heard him say "We'll know tonight," but it was all tiresomely vague.

And then the door opened again, and a gentleman stood on the threshold, eyeing with unconcealed distaste the general shabbiness and the candles guttering in crude jars that served for light. Dan's interest quickened. The bored, ascetic features were not unknown to him, but in this present setting they were as incongruously out of place as it was possible to be.

A silk handkerchief held fastidiously to his nose, he minced his way across to the table near the fire, his greatcoat falling carelessly open to reveal a quantity of gold embroidery and rich ruffles of lace. He did not deign to sit; indeed, though his movements were quite markedly languid, it was evident that he was desirous of completing his business with all possible speed. Reaching into his coat he brought out a leather pouch which chinked with coin as he set it down in front of the group's leader, uttered a few carefully chosen words, and left as he had come.

The outburst of excited comment as the door closed behind him was cut short on a kind of concerted gasp as the leader counted out two or three coins into each outstretched palm and pocketed the remainder.

"The rest when it's done," Dan heard him say curtly.

But when what was done? Dan mused furiously. What was so important that it could bring together the Marquis de St. Cloud, a royalist of the first water—close to the king's brother, if not the king himself—and the Bonapartist scum he had been keeping under surveillance for the past few days?

The argument at the table near the fire still went on, though now subsided into sullen mutterings, but so incensed were the men that they accorded Dan no more than a passing glance as he rose from his place and slouched across the door, chin sunk into his collar, his gait unsteady.

The night air was bitingly cold and dank with mist, the road deserted. Then, from the deep shadow of an adjoining doorway, came the faint sound of a heel scraping on stone.

Dan stiffened imperceptibly, and then relaxed as Parker's voice rasped low: "All right and tight, major?"

"I'm not sure. Something devilish queer going on—needs thinking about."

"Want me to carry on watching our Froggie friends, do you, sir?"

"Yes." The major's voice was thoughtful, as though his mind was half-occupied elsewhere. "I'd dearly like to know how it all ties up, Parker."

"Look a right skimble-skamble lot to me, beggin' your pardon, major—all but that sadistic cove you was so interested in. Got 'is measure now, I have." Parker spoke with a certain pride, and was rewarded when the major looked up, all attention. "Name of Dubois . . . captain, late of the Grenadiers and said to be bitter as hell at being defeated . . . a Bonapartist to his rotten soul, sir."

"Well, keep him in your sights, Parker—but if he rumbles you, for God's sake, cut and run! I want no heroics!"

Little more than an hour later, shaved and eminently presentable once more, Dan stood beneath the portico of the house in the Rue de Columbine—and was presently admitted by an obsequious lackey, who in turn relinquished him into the safekeeping of Sir Thomas's major domo.

The major domo did not by so much as a flicker convey his approval of such constancy in a young man in love. Yes, he murmured, Monsieur Winslade and his sister, the mademoiselle, had indeed arrived, and were even now about to partake of a light repast. If Major Hammond would care to step upstairs . . . ?

Major Hammond would—and did, to the great delight of his beloved. Nor did he need much persuading to take supper with Sir Thomas and his young guests.

Sir Thomas, presiding graciously at table, was amused to see the lovers so wrapt in each other that they occasionally lost the thread of the conversation. However, Tristram Winslade covered admirably for them, and in so doing acquitted himself well in the older man's estimation by indulging Sir Thomas in his fond and ofttimes witty reminiscences of their late father. It was, he hazarded, a promising start.

Lord Rowby's letter, which had preceded the visit of the two young people, had begged him to test the young man out in the present unsettled conditions which prevailed in Paris at that time, and to report to him upon Winslade's handling of both himself and events. "There has been until recently in his attitude to his duties a degree of irresponsibility which would give me pause were I not almost certain that it arose from youthful high spirits rather than a basic weakness of character and is now hopefully at an end. I would be more than happy to have my judgment endorsed, should you feel able to do so."

Well, thought Sir Thomas, there was little evidence of wildness apparent in young Winslade's present demeanor; in fact, if one discounted his innate charm and good manners, one might be tempted to think him a shade subdued, though it was early days and there had been glimpses of an engaging will to please which augered well.

Charis was deeply conscious of the effort her brother was making to overcome an inclination to sink into melancholy. Attuned as they were to each other's changes of mood, it was not difficult to sense his lowness of spirit, or to find its cause.

"Poor Tris!" she said as they retired for the night. "It must have been quite wretched for you, seeing me and Dan so happy together when your little Celestine is so far away."

"I had not thought to miss her so much," he acknowledged with a wry grin. "However, the time will soon pass." His grin broadened. "Between Sir Thomas and your Dan, we are like to be kept so busy that I'll have little time to pine!"

And so it proved. After some early morning rain, the sun shone—a weak wintry sun, but it was sufficient to gild their first sight of Paris by day. And how different a Paris! Full of space and light—its massive public buildings, unstained by smoke; wide boulevards whose trees, now bare of leaf, had a grandeur of their own; the venerable walls of the Tuileries rising into the hazy sunshine, the banner of ancient France flying above its formal gardens; and by no means least, Napoleon's splendid triumphal arch topped by great bronze horses.

"Stolen fruits, of course," murmured Sir Thomas in his droll way. "They are Venetian, and will no doubt be reclaimed in time. Bonaparte had an unerring eye for a masterpiece—you will see many more in the next few days!"

Charis thought it a curious anomaly that this scourge, this tyrant of Europe, should have possessed such a capacity for recognizing and enjoying beauty. She even, to her acute embarrassment, found herself owning to a fleeting admiration for the late Emperor's vision.

"You are not alone, my dear young lady! The man was a tyrant, but a tyrant of taste!" Sir Thomas's eyes twinkled. "His admirers will tell you that had he reigned some years longer, the Emperor would have made Paris the finest city in the world!"

She had further evidence of this some afternoons later when Dan took her to the palace of the Louvre, where the artistic wealth of many nations, commandeered as spoils of war, had been assembled. She stood in the statuary hall lost in admiration of the Apollo Belevedere, glorying in the perfection of its sulpture—a Grecian god fashioned in glowing marble, untouched by time.

"I know one ought to be horrified . . . and of course I *am* to think that any country should be plundered of such treasures, but at this moment—" her voice was softly passionate— "I can only feel a deep gratitude at being vouchsafed a chance to see so many beautiful things that I could never otherwise have hoped for a glimpse of!"

Dan was silent and she glanced up at him, a little shamefaced. "Does that make me sound hideously selfish?"

"H'm?" He returned her look with a kind of absent-minded indulgence. "No, certainly not, sweetheart. Why waste time feeling guilty? There're here. Enjoy them." He shrugged carelessly. "For my part, I don't envy whoever is eventually appointed as arbitrator in the inevitable tug-of-war over their return. Imagine trying to remain calm while irate governments haggle over who owns what!"

His off-handedness seemed to display a want of sensitivity quite out of character with his normal behavior. Charis found her pleasure correspondingly diminished. He had, now she thought about it, been something less than his usual attentive self throughout the afternoon, and the suspicion that he might be bored and be wishing himself elsewhere made her rush through the remaining rooms almost without comment.

Dan, his mind obsessed with trying to anticipate Captain Dubois's next move, scarcely noticed how quiet Charis had become. He had received a message from Parker, who had finally come up with a day—Wednesday. But which Wednesday? There had to be a way of finding out, also, the "what, where, and how." If Wellington's life was in danger, which on the present evidence seemed a distinct possibility, he would have to be informed of it. Not that his lordship would deviate one iota from his accepted list of engagements; to suggest that he might consider doing so would be to invite one of the duke's chilling reproofs, which inevitably left one with the curious sensation of having been plunged into cold water.

There was also a small niggle at the back of Dan's mind that there might be more to it than a straightforward attempt on the duke's life. The Marquis de St. Cloud's involvement still needed explanation; Wellington had certainly made enemies among royalists like St. Cloud—ambitious men whose expectations of a new golden age of wealth and power were not likely to be realized while the British ambassador wielded so much influence over the king.

But as to whether St. Cloud was sufficiently desperate to throw in his lot with embittered Bonapartists? After all, the removal of Wellington would only partially heal the canker of grievance that was eating into him; it was the king himself surely—gross, indecisive, and seemingly lacking in either motivation or inspiration—whom St. Cloud and his like saw as the real obstacle to the restoration of national pride and power.

To them, he was an imbecile, content merely to lick the boots of his conquerors.

Belatedly, Dan recalled himself to the present. A glance at Charis showed him a rigid profile beneath her bonnet.

"Forgive me, dearest," he exclaimed with endearing repentance. "I have been neglecting you most shamefully. Come, if you've seen all you wish to see, I'll make it up to you. Let us walk in the Tuileries gardens."

"Pray, do not feel that you have to entertain me," she replied distantly, resisting the impulse to look into his eyes. "I am sure you must have far more important matters to claim your attention!"

"A hit!" He chuckled and took her arm. "And well deserved! I do have things on my mind, but it was unforgivable of me to allow them to intrude upon my precious time with you."

"Oh Dan!" She was instantly ashamed. "I forget that you are not here simply for pleasure. It is I who should be forgiven for being so cattish!"

He chuckled again, his fingers tightening possessively on her arm as he guided her past a group of people on their way into the palace, and out into the November afternoon. The best of the day had gone and damp wisps of mist were already curling about them as Dan fastened the collar of her pelisse, with its swansdown edging, tight about her neck.

"You won't find it too cold for walking?"

Charis shook her head.

The gardens were deserted and they were able to stroll at will, and with more intimacy than would otherwise have been allowable.

"Would it help to talk about what is troubling you?" she asked. "I shan't be the least offended if you cannot, but speaking one's thoughts aloud does sometimes help to clear one's mind."

Dan glanced down teasingly at her. "Wise as well as beautiful!" And then, sobering, he explained the gist of his problem. "I can't help feeling that I am missing something. Not where the duke is concerned . . . there is little doubt, I think, that a plot does exist to assassinate him. And I'm more or less certain that Dubois is concerned in it. In fact, until recently, I had assumed that he was its main instigator. He is a fanatical supporter of Bonaparte and won't shrink from anything that might open the way for him to return."

"But . . . there's no chance of that, surely?"

Dan's voice was laconic. "Oh, there's a chance, all right. Napolen may appear to be safely contained on Elba, but I would be very much surprised if he is not this minute devising some ingenious ploy to escape and regain his crown! And the one man, more than any other, who may be relied upon to thwart any such attempt . . ."

"The Duke of Wellington!" Charis concluded. "But . . . does *he* know? Is the government not aware of events? Surely he ought to be removed from danger as soon as possible?"

Dan smiled at her indignant concern. "Clearly you are not acquainted with his lordship! Of course he knows the risk. I believe Lord Liverpool writes almost daily urging him to arrange matters so that he may slip away quietly, but the duke's phlegm is such that he will not be panicked, and I may have to be devious if I am to protect him. I'll have a quiet word with Lord Fitzroy Somerset. He'll know Wellington's movements. If I can find out where he is to be the next few Wednesdays, I may be able to pinpoint the most likely source of danger."

"You *will* be careful?" Charis said quickly.

Dan stopped in his tracks and pulled her to him, crushing her mouth beneath his. She emerged breathless, her bonnet askew and her cheeks delightfully pink.

"The devil take Dubois!" he said a little unsteadily. "And the Duke of Wellington . . . and Bonaparte, and anyone else who keeps my thoughts from you for even a moment!"

Charis professed to be shocked by these sentiments, but her protest lacked conviction and she was not sorry when Dan refused to waste any more time in fruitless conjecture, and instead vowed that he would devote himself solely to her pleasure.

Except that, in a tiny corner of his mind, the problem of St. Cloud still lingered unresolved.

৽৹(11)৹৽

Charis was delighted to see how well Tristram was acquitting himself in Sir Thomas's eyes. He had formed an immediate friendship with the diplomat's junior secretary—a young man not unlike Tristram, and with a similar taste for speed. The young secretary had recently acquired a spanking new racing curricle, together with a pair of sleek thoroughbreds mettlesome enough to meet even Tristram's exacting standards, and every moment not claimed by Sir Thomas was devoted to trying their paces.

"Adam can drive to a feather!" Tristram was ungrudging in his praise. "Hands as gentle as a babe! Knows his way around Paris, too!"

This somewhat oblique observation confirmed Charis in her suspicion that her brother and his new friend were exploring other, quite different avenues of pleasure, and while it might be no bad thing if it took his mind off Celestine a little . . .

"I'm not sure whether Sir Thomas is aware of how late Tris is staying out," she confessed her troubled thoughts aloud to Dan. "Sometimes well into the morning hours! Thank God, he has not yet taken to singing bawdy songs when he comes home!"

"I think," said Dan dryly, his eyes crinkling with laughter, "that Sir Thomas knows exactly what goes on in his own house. He also, no doubt, remembers from past experience what it's like to be a young man let loose in Paris."

"And if he didn't, I daresay you could enlighten

him? You may take me for a great looby, Daniel Hammond . . ."

He protested that he did nothing of the kind.

"But," she swept on, "I cut my eye teeth a long time ago, let me tell you!" Her nose wrinkled in mock displeasure. "All those disreputable cafés, full of painted hussies, who, to quote Emily, 'are no better than they should be'—flaunting their ankles, and goodness knows what else! You wouldn't know about those, I suppose?"

They were alone in Sir Thomas's *petit salon*, and Dan made the most of his opportunity by nibbling her ear as he besought her in his most persuasive tones to believe that all pursuits of that nature were a thing of the past.

"So I should hope!" she retorted, fighting a losing battle with her aroused senses. "If that is how gentlemen must seek their amusement, then I'm very glad that I am not a man!"

He laughed aloud in his delight, and caught her to him. "So am I, my dear idiotish love! *Very, very glad.*" His sleepy eyes roved her face. "But take care that your impetuously hurled stones don't rebound upon you, for I suspect that you are not above enjoying a little gratuitous flirtation yourself. Don't imagine for one moment that I've forgotten Mallon." It was her turn now to make vain protestations. He concluded piously, "I may show a brave face, but I live in almost hourly dread that you will cast me aside in favor of one of those charming high-born gentlemen that Sir Thomas keeps putting in your way. I've seen them, whispering their seductive Gallic compliments into your not unreceptive ear!"

"You're jealous!"

"Of course, I am—madly!"

"Good!" Charis chuckled. "It will be a very salutary experience for you," she declared, omitting to add that she was not greatly enamored of any of her would-be suitors.

In fact, as she was beginning to realize, she did not

greatly care for the French as a race; with a few exceptions, she found them to be arrogant, cynical, and totally amoral, especially with regard to their amorous intrigues; also, they seemed quite impenitent about the suffering they had caused, and could occasionally be capable of flagrant duplicity.

Charis had been afforded evidence of this latter quite early on in their stay, when she and Tris and Dan had set out on foot to walk the length of the Champs Elysees, and found throngs of people lining the road, and the traffic halted.

She turned to Dan with a question already framed, but before she could speak there came a great thunder of hooves and of wheels rattling over the ground.

"His royal majesty," murmured Dan. "He always travels at that pace."

"On the premise that a moving target is harder to hit, I suppose," said Tris with a chuckle.

"Oh, surely not!" Charis exclaimed.

It was true that Sir Thomas's newspaper had, that very morning, carried an extremely hostile and outspoken article, expressing the view that if the king did not soon act positively to improve the lot of his less fortunate subjects, many of them half-starving ex-servicemen, they would lose patience, and his own position might be seriously threatened.

And yet here were those very people looking anything but intimidating, waving and cheering as the royal coach dashed past amid shouts of "Vive le Roi!"

"It only goes to show how uninformed newspapers can sometimes be," she said.

"You think so?" Dan shot her a laconic glance and, without raising his voice, said clearly, "Vive l'Empereur!"

"Are you mad?" Charis whispered.

But already several heads had turned; bright, inquisitive eyes were surveying them, and then the sly grins appeared.

"Mais oui, monsieur," came the reply, "Vive l'Em pereur—vive Napoleon!"

"Well really!" Charis exclaimed in disgust.

But nothing could spoil her appreciation of Paris itself. There was so much to take the eyes, enough to keep her pencil busy during every spare moment between balls and soirees and visits to the opera, all following upon the reception which Sir Thomas had given soon after their arrival. This, the Duke of Wellington had been pleased to attend. He remembered them well from his short stay in Brussels, asked kindly after Lord and Lady Rowby, and expressed himself delighted to meet again "Lady Rowby's artistic young friend."

"The portrait you painted of Georgiana Lennox impressed me greatly," he told her, his blue eyes lighting up. "Splendid likeness! It pleased the Duchess of Richmond no end to have so excellent a remembrance of her daughter!"

Charis scarcely knew how to respond to his kind praise, but he dismissed her murmured thanks with one of his neighing laughs, and moved on to talk to someone else.

"I never before saw you *so* lost for words!" Tris said teasingly.

"Masterly, wasn't it?" Dan lifted a quizzical eyebrow. "Do you suppose he would teach me the way of it?"

"You can both scoff," she retorted loftily, her cheeks pink. "But it may interest you to know that, quite apart from our being invited to dine at the embassy later in the week, his grace has been pleased to ask me if I will sketch his likeness while we are here!"

Her brother and her fiancé exchanged glances.

"Oh lor!" Tristram groaned. "There'll be no living with her now! You just wait, Daniel, my poor friend . . . the next thing you know, she'll be boasting of having become one of Wellington's flirts!"

"Not if I have anything to say to it, she won't!" declared her beloved with a martial glint in his eye.

Tris hooted with laughter. "Damn me, if it wouldn't

be the greatest diversion ever! What would you do, Dan—call the duke out?"

"Very likely . . . but not before I'd wrung your neck, you miserable young toad!"

But Charis had already been reduced to helpless mirth by a sudden vision of Dan and the duke facing one another in the cold dawn, pistols primed and cocked, and all for love of her. Weakly she begged them to desist.

It had been a carefree beginning, but the time went almost too quickly and by the time they went to dine at the British Embassy, Charis found her thoughts dwelling more and more often upon the degree of danger that Dan might be courting.

During the informal reception her eyes strayed constantly to the far side of the room where he stood deep in conversation with Lord Fitzroy Somerset. His lordship's handsome, rather square features in general mirrored a quiet, serious disposition, but it seemed to Charis, watching him now, that he was looking more than usually grave and her heart lurched uncomfortably.

"Come now, Miss Winslade, we cannot have you looking so pensive!" The duke's jovial voice boomed in her ears and she dragged her thoughts away from Dan to smile at him. "That's better. Capital!"

His eyes were very blue, very appreciative of her gown, not made by her for once, but bought from a talented little modiste in the Rue de la Paix, and Charis, remembering Tris's nonsense about becoming one of the duke's flirts, was obliged to suppress a giggle. There could be little doubt that he received much female adulation or that in Restoration Paris, where everybody gossiped, his name was linked with more than one beautiful woman, most notably at present the Italian singer, Grassini, who had previously bestowed her favors with equal graciousness upon Napoleon.

Charis could not but feel for the Duchess of Wellington; to be sure, her grace was too gentle, was perhaps possessed of too colorless a personality to match her husband's brilliance and exuberance. But she had received them so kindly that Charis had quite warmed to her.

"You must tell me what you think of our embassy, Miss Winslade—seen through the artist's eyes. Eh?" said the duke at dinner, as one sumptuous course followed another. "It belonged to Napoleon's sister, you know—the Princess Pauline Borgese." His voice took on a curious inflection as he spoke the name, but the moment was too fleeting for Charis to determine if it was admiration or something less flattering. "I believe I have done our government a great service in acquiring such a rare treasure."

Charis, knowing from Sir Thomas how much the "treasure" had cost, hoped the government would share his enthusiasm.

"It is a most beautiful residence, your grace," she said with perfect sincerity. "If the rest is in keeping with what I have been privileged to see, then you have indeed been fortunate in your choice."

The duke beamed with pleasure. "I shall make a point of conducting you over it myself—either this evening, or when you come to sketch my portrait. You have not forgotten?"

She murmured that she had not, took a recruiting sip of wine to cover her confusion, and, catching Tris's eyes across the table, almost choked.

The gentlemen lingered so long in the dining room that by the time they appeared she was in a state of agitation from listening to inconsequential gossip, so that she was scarcely able to restrain her urge to rush across to Dan's side the moment he entered the room.

"Was Lord Somerset able to help you?" she murmured when finally they could draw aside a little.

The fine strong lines of his face seemed to her to be more pronounced than usual. "I doubt that help is the right word," he said dryly, "but at least I know where Wellington will be on Wednesday week."

Charis waited impatiently for him to finish.

"A close friend of the king has a chateau just north of Paris, to which his majesty, most of the royal family, and the Duke of Wellington have been invited for a day's hunting, culminating in the evening in a grand display of fireworks—"

"Oh no!" breathed Charis.

"Oh yes." A wry smile twisted his mouth. "Damnable, isn't it? An assassin could hardly hope for occasion more suited to his needs. He may virtually choose his own moment!"

"What will you do?"

Dan shrugged. "Fitzroy will try to persuade his grace not to go, but he holds out little hope of succeeding." His sleepy eyes were rueful. "A few prayers might not come amiss! With any luck, perhaps we can stop them before then."

"Kill them, you mean?" Charis's voice was hardly above a whisper as her breath caught in her throat. Just for an instant she had glimpsed a ruthlessness in his eyes that reminded her of his calling, then it was gone and he was smiling again.

But the quarry had gone to earth. Their plans laid, they had nothing to do but wait. And Dan, fretting in the knowledge that he was helpless, set the few men he had at his disposal to scour Paris yet again and the area around Raincy where the *chasse* was to be held.

Meanwhile, life went on much as usual. No one but Charis, not even Sir Thomas, had the least inkling of Dan's real purpose in coming to Paris, so the facade of his being some kind of aide to Wellington—a mainly pleasurable pastime—had to be kept up. As time grew shorter, so did his temper, and a visit to the theater was the last thing he wanted.

But Sir Thomas was insistent and chided him humorously for neglecting his bride-to-be, so he subdued his restlessness and joined Sir Thomas's party in his box at the Comédie Française.

"You didn't have to . . . not for my sake!" Charis whispered as they settled in their seats.

He took her hand, his thumb smoothing it gently. He lifted it, closed a kiss within its palm, and spoke without looking at her in a low, husky voice.

"Have I ever told you what an incredibly lucky fellow I am? There is this very beautiful, very talented, amazingly understanding young lady, you see. I met her in a rainstorm and fell in love with her on the instant, and she, to my great good fortune, was similarly afflicted—"

"Oh, please stop!" she begged him, her throat constricting painfully. "You'll make me cry, and if I once start I won't be able to stop, and then Tris and Sir Thomas and everyone will want to know why, and I shan't be able to tell them that I am nearly out of my mind with worry! If anything should happen to you. . . ."

He gave a muffled exclamation, his fingers tightening almost unbearably on hers. "It won't, sweetheart, I promise!" And then, on the ghost of a husky laugh. "After all, I came through nine years of war with nothing worse than a bad case of boils in a very uncomfortable region of my anatomy, so why should now be any different?"

Her own laugh was a rather hiccuping affair, but it brought her a final comforting squeeze before he released her hand, and an approving, "That's more like it!"

Sir Thomas's box was situated near the royal box, and as the occasion was graced by his majesty and most of his immediate family, Charis was afforded the closest view she had yet had of the French royal family as they arrived to cheers and the singing of patriotic songs.

She had no difficulty in recognizing the king, who was so gross that he had to be helped to his chair by two strong lackeys. And under cover of the formalities, Sir Thomas pointed the others out to her—"the Duc d'Angouleme and his Duchesse . . . she is the only surviving daughter of Louis XVI and poor Marie Antoinette," the diplomat's voice intoned, and Charis thought how sad and regal she looked, "and the Duc and Duchesse de Berri . . ."

A tall, austere-looking gentleman had followed the king into the box and stood a little behind and to one side of him.

"And who is he?" she asked.

"Ah!" Sir Thomas was curiously unenthusiastic. "That is Monsieur—the king's brother. A cold fish, or so I've always found him . . . don't encourage one to put oneself forward, if you know what I mean. Isn't that so, Hammond?"

"H'm?" Dan, too, was looking at Monsieur—and at the man who stood beside him, and who at that moment turned to speak to him with more than a hint of familiarity; an elegant man, with more than a touch of the dandy in his dress. As they both turned briefly to regard the king, a great dawning of light rushed in on Dan. Of course! What a blind fool he had been!

For Monsieur's companion was St. Cloud.

❦ 12 ❧

Dan spent a restless night. The look that St. Cloud had directed at the king was as illuminating as it had been malevolent; the last piece of the puzzle had instantly slipped into place, and the nature of his collusion with Dubois stood revealed.

A double assassination! It was really so obvious that he could have kicked himself for missing it. St. Cloud wasn't really interested in Wellington; his target was the king. But how much simpler for him to make use of a Bonapartist to do his work for him—a fanatic so eaten up with the desire to see his emperor back on the throne of France that he could be persuaded without too much trouble to believe that removing both men at a stroke was the quickest way to achieve his ambition. It would be relatively easy to ensure that Dubois did not long survive to point the finger at him, and with the king gone and Monsieur, on the throne, St. Cloud as his close friend would be in a position of power.

Dan did not suppose for one moment that Monsieur was concerned in the conspiracy; it was no secret that he was growing increasingly impatient of his brother's muddling ways, and that he would not be above intriguing to force the king to abdicate. But murder—and fratricide at that—would be abhorrent to him.

The dilemma now facing Dan was how best to thwart the Marquis de St. Cloud's plans without causing a great national furor, so that by comparison all his previous problems seemed trite. By morning the germ of an idea had taken hold; it was amazingly simple, but relied for its success almost entirely upon an ability to time events to an inch. He felt the old excitement stirring in him. Outwitting an enemy was one of the things he was best at, and he suddenly realized how tame life had become of late. Nothing, however, could be done without the Duke of Wellington's approval.

Charis was puzzled, and not a little put out. It was clear to her that something had happened while they were at the theater—something that had the oddest effect on Dan, leaving him preoccupied for almost the whole of the evening. When she had attempted to quiz him about it, he had been almost brusque. Coming, as it had, so soon after that moving evocation of his love for her, it was doubly puzzling and doubly confusing almost, she thought in sudden panic, as though he wanted her to know . . . in case . . . Oh no, surely not! She was being overfanciful.

But when no word came from Dan on the following day, all her perturbation returned. In her imagination she saw him lying mangled in some dark back alley, and was obliged to take herself severely to task. Dan knew exactly what he was about. Tomorrow was Wednesday, and he would have far too much on his mind to be considering her. What kind of a soldier's wife would she make if every time he was out of her sight, she worried herself into a quake?

Several times she caught Sir Thomas looking at her, until finally he asked with gentle diffidence if she was quite well.

Charis gave him a wan smile. "I'm not very good company today, am I? I fear I may be sickening for a cold."

It was only a small untruth, but Sir Thomas was more acute than she gave him credit for. It had not escaped his notice that there had been no sign of Major Hammond all day, not so much as a note. A lover's tiff, perhaps? Ah, well, no business of his. With great tact he said kindly, "A cold? How very distressing for you. I do hope you may be mistaken. Still, perhaps you would rather not go to Madame Recamier's evening salon?"

For a moment Charis wondered which would be worse—to go through the pretense of enjoying herself, or to remain at home with only her thoughts for company. But the chance that Dan might come, or send word decided her.

"If Madame would not be offended . . . ?"

"Nothing of the kind, my dear Miss Winslade," said Sir Thomas with great courtesy. "I will explain and give her your deepest apologies. You will do much better to retire early."

Charis was at once riddled with guilt. She could only be thankful that Tris was away overnight with Adam, executing a small commission for Sir Thomas. He would have seen through her deception in an instant, and would have quizzed her with far more persistence.

She had already retired to her room when Dan's note came. She tore it open with fingers that were not quite steady. It had clearly been penned in haste and was full of remorse for his neglect of her. *Matters have rather run away with me, sweetheart,* it ran. *I cannot explain, but all is now changed. Do you think Tris would oblige me with a trifling favor? I'd be everlastingly grateful, and swear to you that he will be in no danger! I shall send Parker to wait outside Sir Thomas's house at six o'clock in the morning on the off chance. . . .* The note ended with his dearest love to her.

For some minutes Charis sat unmoving, wondering what it all meant; then she gave up and fell to deciding instead what could be done. There was no way of letting Dan know that Tris was away. She would have to get up early herself, to slip out and explain to Parker. But overriding all other considerations was the dismal reflection that she was, albeit unavoidably, letting Dan down.

Perhaps the answer had been there from the beginning, at the back of her mind, but it was some time before she gave it conscious thought. She and Tris were so nearly of a size that she could wear his clothes with the greatest ease, and they were sufficiently alike to pass all but the closest scrutiny, so why should she not go in her brother's place? No danger, Dan had said, and she would be near him and perhaps be of some help.

A swift search through Tris's closet and Charis emerged triumphant, bearing his second best pair of buff riding breeches and his olive green coat, a shirt and neckcloth, a greatcoat of enormous bulk, and a hat with a brim of sufficient width to mask her face a little. Boots were something of a problem—her own would be an immediate giveaway. She would have to pack the toes of Tris's old ones, and hope for the best.

She hardly slept for fear of not waking in time, and only remembered at the last moment to leave a brief note, pleading an overlooked invitation begging Sir Thomas not to worry about her and promising in a spirit of reckless optimism that she would be back later in the day.

Then she crept down the stairs, praying that she wouldn't bump into any of the servants whom she could hear already moving about.

Just beyond the gate there was a shadowy mass, blacker than the darkness that surrounded it; only the occasional wheeze and shuffle and jingle of harness betrayed the presence of horses.

"Parker?" she whispered, her voice hoarse with nerves.

Until that moment, Charis had been thinking in terms of a carriage, but as her eyes grew accustomed to the light, she realized to her horror that the groom was riding and leading a second horse.

"That you, Mr. Winslade? Do you want a leg up, sir?"

A good question! She had ridden astride often enough as a child, but now she doubted if she could mount a horse clad as she was without falling flat on her face. Still, better to try than have him coming to help. With a distinct feeling of fatalism she held out her hand imperiously for the reins and, impeded by the flapping folds of the caped greatcoat, she anchored one foot firmly in the stirrup, grasped the pommel with both hands, and hauled herself inelegantly upward, thanking heaven for the all-enveloping darkness. More by luck than skill, and with Parker holding firmly to the horse, she got her leg over and presently found herself sitting in the saddle, the coat uncomfortably bunched round her legs, but still in one piece.

"That's the barber! Now, before we set off . . . know how to use one of these, do you, sir?"

Something heavy and cold was being thrust into her hand, and as her fingers closed on the smooth barrel and fumbled their way along to grip the butt, she felt the first stomach-lurching twinge of unease. No danger, Dan had said!

"It's loaded, so for Gawd's sake handle it easy!"

She slid the gun gingerly into the greatcoat pocket and cleared her throat, all too aware from Parker's disapproving tones that he thought such a frippery young man unfitted to be in charge of dangerous weapons. She wondered briefly how he would feel if he knew who, in truth, he had at his side—but found it too unsettling a train of thought to pursue. Deepening her voice, she spoke briskly.

"Thank you, Parker—I do know what I'm about."

It was true that she could handle a pistol with reasonable competence; in fact, in her more confident moments she was wont to assert her superiority over Tris in terms of accuracy, but she could not help feeling that an aptitude for nicking a playing card at twenty paces in a spirit of friendly rivalry fell some way short of equipping one for combat of a more deadly nature.

But it was already too late to draw back. With a noncommittal "Yes, well . . ." Parker had set off, and there was nothing for it but to follow.

"Where are we going?" she asked when he showed no inclination to enlighten her.

"Raincy."

Silly of me to ask, she thought, feeling a strong inclination to go off into hysterics. She wondered if she might venture a further question as to where Raincy was, and immediately thought better of it; they traversed the back streets at a circumspect trot until they were beyond the city walls. Then, after a few more moments of what Tris would have called "glumpish silence," Parker suggested they let the horses out and he become marginally more approachable.

"Shouldn't take us too long if we keep a steady pace. The major wants us there before daylight. He's a deal to organize. All must be timed to a T, d'ye see, sir."

"Well, no . . . I don't see," said Charis, striving to appear nonchalant. "I'm not really sure what D—what the major is planning, or where I come into it."

But with maddening calm, the groom replied, "Better if he tells you that himself, Mr. Winslade. All I know is he's got it all worked out."

With that, Charis had to be content. In any case, with every moment that passed she grew increasingly uncomfortable, and disinclined to talk. The wind, rushing past her face, had very quickly reduced it to a state of total numbness which was gradually spreading to her other extremities. She now had cause to bless that streak of the dandy in Tris which she had so often teased him about, for without it he would not have succumbed to the purchase of a stylish new greatcoat trimmed with astraken; inconveniently bulky though she found his discarded one, it had almost certainly saved her from total petrification.

By the time Parker observed with satisfaction that they were within striking distance of their destination, she was beyond coherent thought. The sky had begun to pale, revealing an uninviting gray-white world, but Charis rode on, heedless of her surroundings, her teeth gritted in grim concentration, her eyelashes rimed with frost.

When Dan's voice finally penetrated her misery, she thought at first that she must be dreaming. But there he was, having apparently brought the horse to a halt (for she had no recollection of doing so herself), standing at the animal's head, the bridle in one gloved hand, running the other gently down its sweating neck, and teasing her about being half asleep.

"Poor Tris! I'll wager you haven't been abroad at this hour since you were in short coats, if then!"

Charis felt that any reply other than a kind of grunt was beyond her for the moment, but he didn't seem to expect one.

"Frozen, are you?" He grinned sympathetically. "Well, come on down and I'll find you a drop of something guaranteed to warm you up a bit!"

Mercifully, he didn't wait for her to dismount, but strode off to where a small group of men was gathered. She turned her head stiffly and saw that she was in a small beech copse. Now—if she could only, by some miracle, swing her leg over the saddle . . . The sight of Parker, having dismounted himself, on his way toward her, galvanized her into painful action; she slid to the ground with a muffled skirl of agony and half-fell, half-hobbled across to lean against the massive, blessedly solid trunk of a tree.

"I'll take Jupiter away and see to him, shall I, sir?" Parker's glance at her, sagging miserably against the tree with her arms wrapped convulsively about her body and her teeth chattering, said more clearly than words that the major must be desperate to be enlisting the help of such a one! "I'd go across to the others, Mr. Winslade, if I were you. Beggin' your pardon, but you'll not get any warmer standing there."

Charis watched him walk away with something almost akin to loathing in her heart. How dare he be so smug . . . so superior! As if he knew that she would crumple into an ignominious heap the moment she abandoned the safe haven of her precious tree trunk.

Only one way to find out.

The first few tentative steps were sheer hell, but she clenched her jaw and went on putting one numbed foot in front of the other until the voices, faint at first, grew louder.

"Over here, Tris." Dan's voice sounded unbearably cheerful. "This should make you feel a bit more the thing."

He thrust a flask into her hand and bade her make full use of it while he explained what he wanted her to do. The whiff of brandy fumes caught in her throat, making her cough; but the first few reluctant sips, though they made her gasp, had such a glowingly beneficial effect upon her that she gulped more greedily and almost choked on the fiery liquid.

"Hey! Go easy, lad!" someone called amicably. "I doubt you've broken y'r fast, and we don't want you too foxed to sight the enemy."

The sense of this did not immediately sink in, for Charis was still preoccupied with the happy discovery that brandy, after its initial tendency to set one's throat on fire had been overcome, could induce the most agreeable sensations of well-being, which even the stabbing agony of sensation returning remorselessly to her feet could not quite dispel.

"I don't know how much Charis told you," Dan was saying, and she dragged her mind back to an acknowledgment of the fact that he really did think she was Tris—and that now did not seem to be a good moment to disabuse him.

So, "Nothing really," she muttered. "Said it would be better coming from you." And then, feeling that something more Tris-like might be expected of her, "Deuced mysterious she was, in point of fact. Hinted that I'd find it the greatest adventure ever!"

"I don't know about that," said Dan dryly. "But if we pull it off, it will be quite something!"

He launched into a brief explanation of what had led

to their all being here in the freezing cold in the middle of nowhere. Since she had heard most of it before, her mind began to wander once more. . . .

It really was quite extraordinary that Dan did not know her. The light was not good, of course, but somehow she had been convinced that he would have penetrated her disguise at once. But he hadn't. At this moment, his enthusiasms and powers of observation all being concentrated upon the schemes he was scheming—and so like Tris did she appear—that he saw exactly what he expected to see.

The knowledge piqued her. And common sense, which dictated that she should own up here and now, and bear what she was sure would be his certain displeasure, was firmly squashed. With an amazing clarity induced by the brandy she reasoned that anything Tris could do, she was quite capable of matching! Had she not proved as much many times in the past?

"Tris, are you attending me?" Dan's voice was sharp, and instinctively she straightened up and strove to look alert.

"I was saying that, with the king become involved, this whole matter has had to be handled as discreetly as possible."

"The king?" Charis groped for understanding. "I thought we were concerned with the Duke of Wellington?"

"I knew you weren't listening! Do try, there's a good fellow. The success of this operation is dependent upon every man here performing his appointed task, however slight it may seem, to the best of his ability."

"I'm sorry," she muttered, aggrieved as much by her own carelessness, as by the implied reprimand. "If you could just explain again—about the king?"

He did so with ill-concealed exasperation. "Of course, I had no proof of St. Cloud's treachery, but the evidence was too marked to be ignored. I consulted with the duke and he agreed that there could be no question of exposing the king to such danger, and that in any case he would have to be informed."

Charis was by now so interested that she almost forgot to maintain her assumed identity. "And how did poor old 'Louis Gros' take the news?" It was how Tris invariably referred to the king.

"Hard," Dan said. "He was so shaken, in fact, that he agreed to our suggestions as meekly as you like, his only proviso being that no hint of any plot against him should be noised abroad." He glanced at the half-dozen men around him, the gravity of his features at odds with the gleam of excitement in his eyes. "That's why it is up to us to bring the thing off between us."

"Yes, but bring off what?" someone asked. "Come on Dan, stop being so deuced mysterious!"

Dan's gravity deserted him for an instant. "We are going to set a trap, my friends—and with any luck we shall spring it without anyone getting hurt!"

They were at present in the grounds of the Duc de Raincy's chateau, he told them. It was here that the *chasse* and fireworks display were to have been held later that day in the presence of the king and the Duke of Wellington. And it was here, he was convinced, that Captain Dubois and his cronies would conceal themselves in their bid to assassinate both men.

"The duc is an ardent supporter of the king, and so we have his fullest support. He has let it be known that the fireworks are canceled, which means they must strike this morning. Everything else is going ahead as planned. The king, with his retinue, left Paris late yesterday afternoon, but his journey only took him as far as Bondy, where a house has been put at his disposal."

"But wouldn't this Dubois fellow tumble that something was amiss when the coach didn't turn up here?" drawled a young man who looked incongruously out of place in a stylish caped greatcoat ornamented with huge buttons.

Dan's hooded eyes glinted with anticipation. "Oh, but it did arrive, George—exactly as expected, and carrying a gentleman who bore a striking resemblance to his majesty!"

"Oh-ho! And what of the Duke of Wellington?"

"It would take a better man than me to suggest that *he* might permit someone to impersonate him," Dan said dryly. "The duke arrived as arranged, so we had better make sure that nothing goes wrong."

Charis had begun to warm up a little, but the impossibility of what Dan was suggesting struck a fresh chill into her.

"But there must be miles and miles of grounds! We can't hope to find four men, surely?"

"Not in the ordinary way. But Dubois will have been watching the place, and must by now be so confident of knowing which direction the *chasse* is to take that he will position his men accordingly. Which is why I wanted you here so early. Between us, we should be able to cover all the most likely areas so that when Dubois and his men come—"

"If they aren't here already," someone said, *sotto voce*.

"It's possible," Dan said. "But I don't think so. Dubois is more likely to wait until nearer the time. His cronies aren't exactly bright, and he won't want to keep them waiting about too long, getting careless. The duc's keepers have been instructed to keep out of the way, and I have borrowed some of their smocks. If you put them on you can move about without calling attention to yourselves."

It was almost full daylight now, and a weak shaft of sunlight was filtering through the bare frost-rimed branches of the trees to highlight Dan's tall, lean frame. There was an air of dominance about him as he assigned each to his appointed post. It filled Charis with pride to see how easily he wore his authority, so that no one could possibly feel that he was being given orders.

Only as her own turn came did she grow apprehensive. *If he expects me to mount that wretched horse again, I* shall cry craven and confess all, she vowed in desperation. But he didn't. Instead he turned to her with a half-smile.

"I think I'd better keep you within hailing distance, my boy. Charis will never forgive me if I put you at risk."

She bent down, ostensibly to secure the fastening of her boot. "Oh sisters!" she said carelessly. "They don't understand about adventure!"

"Nevertheless, I have no wish to incur her wrath, so you will oblige me, if you please." His tone was brisk. "I need someone about a hundred yards or so back . . . approximately where you and Parker left the road on your way here. You may ride or walk as you choose, so long as you are quick about it. Keep well into the trees, and if you do see or hear any movement, give your signal and then stay absolutely still, out of sight. Right?"

"Right," Charis said gruffly and, sinking her head into her collar, turned to go.

"Tris?"

She paused, half-looked back. There was a furrow between his eyes, and a kind of rough affection in his voice.

"Be careful! And for pity's sake, don't nod off, and don't use that pistol Parker gave you unless you have. to."

There was a slight constriction in her throat as she nodded and lifted a hand in salute.

ཀ 13 ཉ

Charis crouched halfway up a bank, with a gorse hedge to one side of her and a clear view of the road below. She seemed to have been there for hours, but with the folds of Tris's coat wrapped around her, she was warmer than she could have hoped for.

The effect of the brandy had long since worn off and she had had ample time to reflect upon the irresponsibility of her behavior. As a child—well into her teens, in fact—she had competed fiercely with Tris in everything, and had wished many times that she had been born a boy. But at two and twenty? It was sheer idiocy!

She moved her position slightly to avoid getting a cramp, and the solid weight of the pistol brushed against her leg, an ominous reminder of how much might yet depend upon her. A small frisson that was part fear and part excitement ran along her nerves. She was here now, and must do the best she could not to disgrace Dan.

The weak sun had persisted, and from its position Charis judged that it must be past eight. Her stomach rumbled at the thought of breakfast. Perhaps, after all, Dan had been mistaken, and nothing was going to happen.

Then, in the silence, she heard the sound of a lone curlew. It came from some distance away, and when, after a pause, it was repeated, she knew that the rather effete young man she knew only as George, must have sighted someone. Her heart gave a sudden lurch and then, quite distinctly on the crisp, still air—and not all that far away from her—a twig snapped.

* * *

"Well, major, you was right," said Parker with quiet satisfaction. "That's three of 'em now as we've got in our sights, as you might say. Only Mr. Winslade we haven't heard from."

"H'm. I hope he's all right." Dan shook off the sudden spasm of unease. "We're assuming, of course, that Dubois hasn't recruited more men."

"He won't," said Parker scornfully. "Beggin' your pardon, sir, but we've met his sort before . . . too full of themselves by half! Besides, there's the money . . . he'll not be wanting to split that more ways than 'e has to."

"I expect you're right." Dan grinned briefly, and then frowned. "I could wish they were less spread out, however. I always feel a deal easier if I can actually see my quarry." He stopped suddenly. "What was that?"

The sound came again—a kind of faint, high mewing sound.

"That's young Mr. Winslade now, sir," said Parker. "So what do we do next?"

"We wait until this one shows himself. He has to come this way. Then we quietly pick them off, one at a time."

From their place among the trees they watched and listened. Presently the faint crunch of footsteps became audible and somewhere to their right there was a rustling and a snapping of twigs.

"Any minute now," murmured Dan.

Almost before he had finished speaking a shot rang out, followed by shouts and the sound of running feet.

"God Almighty!" breathed Parker. "Now what?"

The bushes some way ahead of them erupted suddenly and a figure took off at a run, bent low.

"We get after him, for a start!"

Dan was already on his way, thrashing his way through the undergrowth with no thought in his head now but to stop the man from getting away, and with Parker panting at his heels.

* * *

Charis, too, had heard the shot. Her immediate fear was for Dan, and without stopping to think she also began to run, losing her hat on the way, back to where she had last seen him, her hand digging impatiently into the big, clumsy pocket in search of the pistol, and dragging it out. So preoccupied was she that she was almost upon the man before she knew he was there, and he was so intent upon what he was doing that he didn't hear her coming. He was using the trunk of a tree as a shield, and waiting, his own pistol raised.

As she stopped, transfixed, she saw Dan burst into the small clearing, running across her line of vision, his back half-turned to the man, the man aiming his gun . . . Without conscious volition her own arm lifted. . . .

After that, everything seemed to happen at once. She screamed "Dan, look out!", fired at the man, and in the same moment, there was a great explosion of pain in her head and everything went black.

She awoke to a fiendish throbbing in her head that immediately made her wish for oblivion once more. A groan must have escaped her lips, for at once Dan's voice said, not quite steadily, "Thank God!"

Her eyes flickered open, uncomprehending as they encountered a blurred ring of faces gazing down at her, and beyond them the swirling tracery of bare branches, and beyond them yet again, the sky.

But she couldn't see Dan, and though she couldn't think why, it seemed terribly important that she should. She tried to move her head and a thousand stabbing knives sent searing pain in all directions, making her gasp.

"Don't try to move, sweetheart." His face swam into her line of vision—very dear, full of anguished concern.

"What . . . happened?"

"You've taken a nasty crack on the head. Just lie still and you'll feel better presently." His voice was calm now, matter of fact. "Parker has gone to arrange for a litter to carry you up to the chateau."

She tried to remember . . . what chateau? Where was she? But it was too much trouble. Her eyelids grew heavy . . . they began to droop, and as they did so, the outline of a tree . . . a figure beside it . . .

"There was a man," she said distinctly, grappling with fleeting memory. "He had a gun . . ."

"He's gone now," Dan said, soothing her as he would a child.

There came a further moment of excrutiating pain as she was moved, and then Charis remembered nothing more until she awoke to the blissful luxury of a feather mattress, silk sheets to cover her; opened her eyes to a soft opaque light filtering through muslin-curtained windows. For a few moments she lay quite still with a blank, incurious mind, lacking the impetus to proceed further.

It was a small creaking sound somewhere close by that finally aroused her curiosity. She moved her head on the pillow and recollection began its somewhat painful return.

Dan was sprawled in a chair near the bed, legs stretched out, his chin, unshaven, sunk into his chest, his whole aspect one of dejection. The moment she spoke his name, however, he sprang back to life, coming to his feet with an exclamation of mingled elation and relief. He came to sit on the bed beside her, seizing the hand she feebly extended to him.

"Sweetheart! How do you feel? Does your poor head still ache? Oh, you can have no idea how good it is to have you back again!"

Charis smiled sleepily at the extravagance of this speech. "Stilly! I haven't been anywhere . . . only sleeping." She yawned. "Was I asleep *so* long?"

"Almost twenty-four hours," he said with a touch of grimness.

"Heavens!" She stared at his blue-stubbled chin. "And have you been here all that time?"

"Almost all."

"You must be exhausted." Her brow puckered. "I don't really remember . . . I'm not at home, I know." She yawned again. "It's very odd if I've really slept so long, because I still feel quite extraordinarily . . . tired . . ."

She was only vaguely aware of his kiss on her forehead, and of his voice telling her to go back to sleep.

The next time she woke the room was in shadow, lit only by a pair of branched candlesticks. Her head felt much clearer, and instinctively she turned toward the chair, feeling absurdly disappointed to see not Dan, but an elderly woman dressed all in black except for a white lappet cap. She was sewing, but looked up the instant Charis stirred, her lined face creasing into a smile.

"*Eh bien, ma petite!*" she exclaimed. And then, in execrable English, "You feel yourself more better? *Hein?*" She saw Charis's eyes wandering about the room, and chuckled. "*Ah! Votre amoureaux!* I will fetch!"

She whisked away with a swiftness that belied her years, and in a moment returned with Dan on her heels. They did not notice when she left.

"Oh, yes," Dan said. "You look much more the thing, now."

He was very close, his hands encompassing hers as though he would never let them go.

"I do feel much better," she said, feeling unaccountably shy. "Can we talk? There is so much I want to know . . . to explain." She frowned suddenly. "Oh, Dan, what about Tris? He will be so worried . . . and Sir Thomas. What must he think?"

"Stop worrying, my love. It has all been attended to."

She sighed. "I think I must have given you a great deal of trouble."

Dan's fingers painfully tightened on hers; he stared down at them as he lived again those nightmare moments in the forest . . . Charis screaming his name and firing at Dubois a split second before Dubois could fire the pistol already trained on him. Seeing her there, recognizing her voice . . . Dan would never know whether the shock of it had made him that split second slow in shooting the second man approaching her from behind, so that by the time his bullet sank home, the man had already loosed the stone that was aimed at Charis's head.

Charis quite mistook the grimness in his face. She said quickly, "I am *truly* sorry! I never meant to deceive you, but Tris was away and I thought only to help . . . to be near you . . . Instead," she concluded miserably, "I seem to have let you down quite wretchedly!"

Dan looked up at her then. His mouth was awry, and there was an expression in his eyes that she could not fathom as he said huskily, "My dearest girl, you are talking the worst utter nonsense! Don't you know that you saved my life?"

"I did?" She frowned. "Oh, the man by the tree . . ."

"Dubois."

"Was that who he was?" Charis was aware of a slight sinking feeling. "Did I . . . ?"

"Kill him?" Dan read her thoughts with surprising accuracy. "No, you only winged him, but it was enough. The bullet meant for me discharged harmlessly into the air." He gave her a very brief account of what had happened. "So you see, my lovely Charis, the rest of my life is yours to command!"

He had meant only to be tenderly teasing, but for once he failed, and his voice grew suddenly ragged with emotion. She tugged a hand free and raised it to stop his mouth, but he caught it and kissed each finger, until turning the hand palm uppermost, he buried his face in it, his last words muffled—*"If you had died!"*

She lay there with the weight of him across her, feeling curiously helpless in the face of his distress, her free hand stroking his hair, a painful constriction in her throat as she hushed him and begged him not to be foolish when she had never the least intention of dying.

He sat up at last, outwardly composed, only a slightly haunted look at the back of his eyes betraying him. He grinned, half-shamefaced. "A fine tonic I am for the patient! I shall have to answer to Madame Angelique if you take a turn for the worse!"

"Is she the old lady who was sitting here when I woke up?"

Dan nodded. "Madame is the Duc de Raincy's old gouvernante and can be very fierce. She has gone to make you a posset and I shall be banished the moment she returns." He kissed her and stood up. "You are the heroine of the hour, my dearest, and will have to endure much adulation when you are well enough to receive visitors! The king is now here and impatient to make you his thanks. Were he not so anxious to hush this whole affair up, you would no doubt be hailed publicly as a second Joan of Arc!"

Charis smiled sleepily. "Oh, now you *are* being nonsensical!" There was much more that she wanted to ask, but in truth she was growing too tired to concentrate, and the return of Madame Angelique with the posset put an end to all further talk.

But Charis was young and strong and recovered remarkably quickly. Within a day or two she was up and about and the doctor declared that he saw no reason why she should not return to Paris. She was not sorry, for although everyone had been most kind, she found the hospitality rather more tiring than she could have wished.

The king had already departed, having personally expressed his appreciation, and with him went the Duc and Duchesse of Angouleme, and the remainder of his retinue. The atmosphere did become a little less formal with his going, though Charis had been pleasantly surprised in him, finding a great kindness within that poor gross exterior. The Duke of Wellington had been much more bracing in his comments; she suspected that he did not wholly approve of women meddling in such work, but he commended her resourcefulness, nonetheless, in a jolly, teasing way.

Tris was waiting for her on her return to Paris, demanding to know all, and not a little envious at having missed all the sport. Sir Thomas had apparently experienced the greatest difficulty in preventing him from descending upon Raincy, and was only restrained by the need for discretion and the assurance that she was recovering so rapidly that he was likely to pass her on the road.

"And you say this Dubois character got away after all?" he asked eagerly. "Won't he have another go?"

"I doubt it," Dan said. "From the trail of blood he left behind him, I doubt he'll be doing anything much for some considerable time, and with the other three dead, it's my bet he'll take the money and lie low for a while, awaiting events."

"And St. Cloud?" asked Sir Thomas quietly.

Dan lifted a quizzical eyebrow. "I rather think that the King will deal with the marquis in his own way."

So that was that, Charis thought, anxious now to put the whole affair behind her. In fact, were it not for the thought of leaving Dan, she would have been quite happy to return to Brussels there and then. She had received a letter that morning from Lady Rowby and found herself longing suddenly for her comfortable, affectionate presence; she missed, too, Emily's more bracing, chivying ways.

But there was only a week of their stay remaining and it passed surprisingly quickly. All too soon they were attending their last ball before leaving, a fairly grand affair given by a friend of Sir Thomas's, which Charis was pronounced fit to attend; and now, perversely, she wanted time to stand still.

"Surely his grace will give you leave before too much longer to rejoin the Prince of Orange's staff . . . now that Dubois is no longer a threat to him?"

They were waltzing, and Dan's arm was possessively close about her as he whirled her around the room. Her hair, which had been close cropped at the back to facilitate the dressing of her bump, had by now grown over the scar, but remained much shorter than usual, emphasizing more than ever her air of boyish elegance that drove so many of the younger women around her wild with envy.

"I sincerely hope so, sweetheart, though I fear the duke's life will continue to be at risk so long as he remains in Paris . . . and he won't move from here until some alternative is offered to him which can in no way be interpreted as *running away*."

"Sir Thomas says that Lord Liverpool is even more frantic to get him away from here, after what happened! There has been some talk of his assuming command in North America."

"He won't go," Dan said. "Not unless they give him leave to negotiate a peace. That's one war he don't approve of!" He drew her close. "And now, if you please, may we leave Wellington to his fate and consider our own future instead . . . a much more agreeable subject, wouldn't you say?"

She dimpled, her eyes very bright, very green. "It is precisely what I was trying to do, for how can anything be arranged until I know when you are to be released from your obligations?"

"Easy!" He bent, laying his mouth close against her ear. "Marry me tomorrow, and I'll tell his grace to go to the devil!"

An infectious giggle escaped her, and a couple close by them looked askance. "Hush!" she implored him. "We shall make a scandal!"

"No matter. People make scandals in Paris all the time!"

The music ended and they walked off the floor, still laughing.

There was a great stir over near the door; a buzz of conversation, exclamations, and above it all, a tinkling laugh and a tirade of Spanish. "The Marquesa of

Vasconosa," someone said. It had the most extraordinary effect upon Daniel; he froze, so that Charis, with her hand upon his arm, almost stumbled. "Good God, it can't be!" she heard him mutter beneath his breath, and then the crowds parted to reveal a tiny, opulent figure—a pocket Venus with night-black hair luxuriantly dressed and caught at the back into a high Spanish comb over which was draped a mantilla; her gown of black gauze over glittering gold satin was as dramatic as it was revealing, being caught beneath full breasts by a huge emerald clasp, and clinging thereafter in a way that revealed considerably more than it concealed, trailing away finally into a long train. Her eyes, hugely black and slumbrous, surveyed the room until they came to rest at last on Dan. Then her whole face came alive and she flung out to him arms encrusted with gold bracelets.

"*Mi esposo!*" she cried in passionate tones that rang around the room. "*Queridisimo* . . . at last I have found you!" And, as Charis watched in a kind of horrified fascination, the marquesa cast herself upon Dan's breast with the air of a woman plucked from drowning in the nick of time.

~⊸(14)⊷~

Dan had been vouchsafed those few vital seconds of warning, and so was the first to recover. He dared not look at Charis, though he felt the ripple of shock that ran through her, and for a moment he found himself blinded by a red mist of anger. What a cruel jest of fate! Why at this of all times must this specter from his disreputable past come back to plague him?

And then he was pulling himself together, resisting the overwhelming urge to wrap his fingers around the marquesa's lovely Spanish throat, and instead put her from him with all the matter-of-fact cordiality he could muster. "My dear Dominica," he drawled. "What a delightful surprise! But must you always be so melodramatic?"

She pouted, but her eyes were liquid bright upon him. "I have search for you—oh, so long! Why did you not come back to me?"

Charis made a strangled sound, and at once the marquesa turned an imperious look upon her, and demanded to be introduced. It afforded Charis no comfort at all to hear Dan say firmly, "Miss Winslade is my fiancée," nor apparently did it please the marquesa, who broke excitably into a torrent of Spanish.

It was not to be borne; with an indistinguishable apology, Charis excused herself and all but ran from the room, heedless that many eyes were upon her. It seemed that Tris was nowhere to be found, but she ran him to earth at last in one of the rooms set aside for gambling. He greeted her casually at first, then a close look at her

171

face brought him quickly to his feet. He excused himself and came to her side.

"Take me home, Tris," she begged him.

"Not feeling quite the thing, love? Well, I've no wish to say 'I told you so, but you have been overdoing it a bit! Told Dan so." He frowned. "Come to that, where is Dan?"

"I don't want Dan, I want you!" she said on a strangled sob. "Oh, please Tris . . . no questions, I beg of you! Just take me home. You may come back at once, if you've a mind. . . ."

Her pallor alarmed Tristram, but he refrained from quizzing her further; in a moment her cloak had been brought, the coach summoned. It was not a long journey, but she had begun to shake long before they arrived.

In Sir Thomas's salon, Tristram pushed her unceremoniously into a chair and proceeded to pour her a generous measure of brandy. Her teeth chattered against the glass, but by degrees, some measure of composure returned.

Tris perched on the arm of a chair nearby, watching her closely.

"Well now," he said at last. "What's it all about? Have you and Dan quarreled?"

Charis shook her head.

"You had much better tell me, you know. We don't have secrets, you and I . . . not when it's really important! And this *is*, I can tell." He bent low, trying to make her lift her head. "Besides, you know what Emily always says—*'A trouble shared is a trouble halved!'*"

She choked on a sound that was halfway between a laugh and a sob. But before she could steel herself to speak of what had happened, they both heard the sounds of someone being admitted. Tris had not quite shut the salon door and from below came the major domo's sonorous tones and another voice—all too familiar.

"It's Dan!" Charis felt panic rising. "Tris, I can't see him! Not now! Please don't let him come up!"

But the conversation below had ended abruptly, and already Dan's feet could be heard, taking the stairs at the double. Tris frowned and walked quickly out onto the upper landing, closing the door behind him.

The two men faced one another—Tristram slightly wary, not quite sure what was going on; Dan, clearly laboring under intense emotion, and in no mood to brook interference.

"Look," Tristram began, "I don't know what all this is about, but . . ."

"Later, Tris," Dan said crisply, and jerked his head toward the door. "Charis in there, is she?"

His dismissive tone irked Tristram. "Yes—but she don't want to see you," he said truculently.

Dan's smile was bleak. "I don't suppose she does, dear boy, but she *will* see me, nonetheless."

He moved forward purposefully, and the younger man began to feel a little like David facing an implacable Goliath without benefit of a sling. But concern for his sister rose above all other consideration.

"Now look here . . . ." he said again, and then hesitated, wondering what he could say that would make the least impression.

As if Dan could read his mind, he shook his head. "You're a good fellow, Tris. I beg you don't oblige me to send you to grass."

A moment more they faced one another, and then Tristram shrugged and stood aside. "Very well, but if you cause Charis further distress, you'll answer to me!"

"Good God! Do you think *that* is my aim?"

Dan strode to the door and went inside, closing it quietly behind him. He stood with his back to it, one hand still on the knob. Charis had been nervously pacing the floor, but she stopped as he entered and swung around to face him. Her face had always been the mirror of her innermost feelings and now it was all there for him to see—the misery and the anguish, and, now that she had recovered herself a little, there was anger, too. But not surprise.

"I suppose I should feel flattered to observe how quickly you've come after me!" she said, her voice brittle. "But surely it is not kind in you to abandon your beautiful marquesa so soon?" Her mouth went awry. "And after she has taken so much trouble to find you, too!"

"My dear, you are talking nonsense, and you must know it," he said, the harshness of his voice totally at odds with the gentle compassion in his eyes. But she was determined not to be so easily swayed.

"Am I?" she challenged him, head up and turned a little away from him so that he should not see how her mouth trembled. "If only you had told me!"

"Told you what? My past is littered with indiscretions! I've never made any secret of them."

"Perhaps not," she cried. "But this is different!"

"Why? Because of Dominica's affecting little display of histrionics? That is all it was, I promise you. Pure play-acting!"

How lightly he took it! Would it always be so? *This is what I have always dreaded*, she wanted to add, but could not.

But he knew exactly how her mind was working; knew, too, that the way he handled the situation now would make or break their hope of happiness. He moved around the sofa toward her, and she backed away; not far, however, for a handsome Louis Quinze commode lay directly in her path—and, brought up against it with no means of escape, she stood as if trapped, acutely aware of his nearness.

But he made no attempt to coerce her, being content merely to possess himself of her hands, feeling them tremble as they lay imprisoned in his.

"Look at me, Charis."

He spoke with such quiet authority that after a moment she did so, and found that his eyes were steadily searching her face.

"I don't question your right to be angry, and upset—in your place I should probably feel quite murderous—but do you have the least shadow of a doubt about the totality of my love for you?"

For a moment their eyes clung; and in that moment she remembered so many instances, going right back to their first meeting, but most of all she remembered his distress when he thought she might have died. . . .

"No!" she whispered on a sob, and as she swayed toward him and he gathered her close, he seemed to sigh.

"Then what the devil is all this about?" he said, and kissed her with lingering thoroughness.

Later, as they sat together on the sofa, he told her about the Marquesa de Vasconosa.

"At the time I was making fairly regular sorties into French-occupied Spain at Wellington's behest to glean what information I could about enemy movements. During one of these missions I was given shelter by Dominica's husband, a cold, proud aristocrat, much older than her—oppressed by ill-health and a universal dislike of the human race."

Dan smiled and shrugged. "I sometimes think that it was only his overriding passion to rid his country of the French that persuaded him to tolerate me! How Dominica managed to retain her sanity, much less emerge with her spirit uncrushed, I shall never know. It was small wonder, I suppose, that she saw me as something between a shining hero and a savior of her sanity." He said it self-deprecatingly, but Charis could see exactly how it must have been.

"You became lovers," she said unequivocally. It was an observation rather than a question—and when he raised a rueful eyebrow, she added hastily, "Oh, I don't mind so much now."

"You don't?" The eyebrow rose even higher.

"Yes, I do," she admitted. "I mind quite dreadfully,

but I can see that I must learn to accustom myself to an occasional encounter with one of the light o' loves from your disreputable past."

Dan laughed aloud.

"But I am still a little worried about your marquesa."

"Not mine," he said firmly.

"No, of course not, but she does seem to feel that she has some special claim to your affections. Are you quite certain that you didn't make her any promises?" Charis tried not to sound anxious.

"Quite certain. *Mi esposo*, indeed! Such exaggeration is beyond belief! We enjoyed a brief interlude, but that is all it was—and we parted by mutual agreement. In fact, I should be astonished if Dominica has given me more than a passing thought during the past year. Too busy playing the merry widow!"

"Still, I think perhaps you ought to go back to the ball. She is bound to wonder where you have gone, and it isn't very kind to leave her alone in a strange place."

Dan turned to look at her, his sleepy eyes regarding her in wonder. "Have I ever told you what a remarkable girl you are?" She blushed and nodded, smiling. He stood up, pulling her to her feet also. "Come back with me, sweetheart?"

"Oh, I don't think so. . . ."

The door opened cautiously, and Tristram put his head around. "I heard laughter." He glanced from one to the other, looking sheepish. "Not come to blows, after all? Splendid. I didn't relish having to plant Dan a facer!"

There was more laughter and they explained briefly what had happened. Tristram chuckled and vowed that they made him feel positively staid.

"I was trying to persuade Charis to return to the ball with me," Dan said. "But I think I'm in need of reinforcements."

"Of course she'll go! We'll go together." Tristram saw that Charis still looked doubtful. "Best way, love. You

know how the French delight to seize on the least hint
of scandal."

"Yes, of course. How silly of me not to think of that."
She offered an arm to each of them, her good humor
fully restored. "Now—they may say what they will!"

Within a week the Winslades were back in Brussels.

It was as though they had never been away. Emily was
still doing battle with Madame Latour's chef, and despite her grumbles, was enjoying every minute of it.
She subjected Charis to a searching scrutiny.

"Much good Paris has done you, by the look of it!"
she said with one of her sniffs. "Pesky—that's what you
are, my girl!"

"Nonsense, Em," Charis said, trying to ignore the
throbbing at the base of her skull which still plagued
her occasionally. "The journey has left me with a slight
headache, that's all. I shall be fine after a good night's
sleep."

"Headache, is it?" Mrs. MacGrath's tone was frankly
disbelieving.

"Don't bully her, Em," said Tristram, coming swiftly
to the rescue. "You'd have the headache, too, I shouldn't
wonder, if you'd spent hours on end shut up in a stuffy
coach with the rain hammering down on the roof." He
gave her one of his most beguiling smiles. "Now, if you
were to make Charis one of your special tisanes. . . ."

"Oh, you and your smooth tongue!" But she bustled
off at once, calling for Meg to set a kettle on to boil.

Charis let out a sigh. "Thanks, Tris."

"Think nothing of it. Orders from Dan." He gave her
a quick hug. "You *are* all right, love?"

"Yes, of course. The doctor did warn me that I might
experience discomfort for some time." She returned his
hug and then pushed him away. "Go along. I know you
must be longing to see your little Celestine. Give her
my love and tell her I'll see her tomorrow."

Tristram was in fact feeling unexpectedly nervous.

He had written to Celestine during his absence, and had received one letter in return—a shyly formal little missive which conveyed between the neatly penned lines the merest hint of her youthful ardor.

But he need not have worried. She had heard the carriage arrive and was standing half-diffidently in the back vestibule gathering sufficient courage to mount the stair in hopes of seeing him. Tristram's first instinct was to sweep her up into his arms, but feared that such impetuosity might alarm her, so instead he took her hands and bent to kiss them gently.

This proved too much for Celestine. She had waited for what seemed like a lifetime for him to return, and at the sight of him something in her snapped. She moved restively, and murmured a soft, "Oh, please!" and the urgency in her communicated itself to Tristram, so that, with a smothered exclamation, his chaste salute became something quite different.

"This house is no place for that poor child!" declared Emily on the following morning when she brought Charis's breakfast to her bed despite protests.

"Don't fret yourself that I'll be making a habit of this," she said, plumping down the tray on Charis's knee. "Though I'm not sorry to have you back, and that's the truth of it!" She returned to her theme. "Mrs. Grant does her best, but that child's mother is not as she should be, and that's putting it kindly."

"Oh dear, is she no better, then?"

"Better?" Emily flung back the curtains and arranged their folds with assiduous care. "Didn't I find her up here in the sitting room only a few days since, hovering in that way she has, and looking all worried. Hoped we weren't finding the children a nuisance, she said!"

Charis made a small sound of distress. "What did you do?"

"What could I do? I told her they were as good as gold, and persuaded the poor body to return to her own rooms! But that's not the point." Emily's hands were folded primly in front of her, a sure sign that she was displeased. "In my opinion, it's her husband that someone should be sending for!"

"Yes, well we shall have to see," Charis said evasively. "I'm not sure whether it is our place to interfere."

Lady Rowby, when appealed to, said that she would mention the matter to her husband, who might well have some suggestion to proffer.

Her ladyship was delighted to have Charis back. Like Emily, she had been a little concerned to find her looking so pale, but her improvement with each day that passed proved sufficient to reassure her that the trifling accident to which Charis had alluded must have been the cause and not, as she had at first feared, a quarrel between herself and Daniel.

"There is no sign of Dan's coming back to Brussels, I suppose?"

"Perhaps, before too much longer," Charis said, her expressive young face providing further proof, if proof were needed, that all was well in that quarter. "I daresay you know already that the Duke of Wellington is almost certain to leave Paris in the very near future?"

Lady Rowby nodded. "Rowby talks of Lord Castlereagh's being needed back in London, and feels that the duke may well become his replacement at the Congress in Vienna."

Charis said that Sir Thomas was of the same mind. "And if it proves to be true, then Dan's work in Paris will be at an end."

"Which will please you, no doubt." Her ladyship beamed at Charis. "The Prince of Orange won't be sorry, either. He was complaining to Rowby only the other day, in a jovial sort of way, about the continuing absence of his newly appointed aide. Not," she added dryly, "that military duties weigh very heavily with his royal highness. It is simply that he had been finding Town dull of late with some of his English friends away on visits—although we grew no less festive."

"I wonder how the prince will feel when that same aide requests leave to marry within a short time of his return?" mused Charis.

Lady Rowby's eyes lit up. "Have you then settled upon a date?"

"Not exactly." An involuntary picture of the marquesa, who was still in Paris, popped into Charis's mind. Not that she entertained the smallest qualm about Dan, she told herself, as she added firmly, "But I think we shall not delay too long."

"That is excellent news, my dear."

But Christmas came and went, and it was almost the end of January before the Duke of Wellington finally quit Paris for Vienna, leaving Dan free to return to Brussels. Even then, all was not certain for Wellington was debating the possibility of taking Dan with him.

"Fitzroy and his wife are to remain here in Paris with Kitty for the present—to deputize for me, as it were," the duke mused. "I shall have young Lennox, and Freemantle, of course, but I'll miss Fitzroy damnably. . . ."

He was quick to note the carefully veiled expression in the major's eyes. He said shrewdly, "But perhaps Miss Winslade would not be best pleased if I kept you from her yet again? Eh?"

Dan's manner was sanguine as he assured his grace that Charis was fully conscious of his duties and obligations, and could be counted upon to understand. "But I am less sure of how his royal highness would take the news."

"Ah, yes—the Prince of Orange. You do well to remind me," said the duke regretfully. "I was, after all, responsible for your appointment in the first place— and from what I hear, there are times when Young Frog may well benefit from a steadying hand. A pity, but I fear I must adhere to my original principle."

And so Dan returned to Brussels, to a joyful reunion. Charis had resolved not to mention the marquesa, but

Tristram was less nice in his notions, and quizzed him facetiously about the gorgeous widow.

Dan's sleepy eyes rested upon Charis for a moment, and although she met them with every appearance of equanimity, he thought he detected just a hint of apprehension clouding the clearness of her gaze.

"Oh, Dominica very soon lost all interest in me," he said, affecting a deep sigh. "I found I couldn't withstand the opposition."

"Oh-ho!" Tristram chortled. "That's coming it a bit strong! A bouncer, if I ever heard one."

Charis agreed, playing along with the game and laughing in spite of an irrational need to be reassured.

"I don't see anyone cutting you out unless you wanted them to," Tristram persisted.

"True, but then I *did* want someone to—and when that someone is no less a personage than His Majesty's Ambassador to the Court of France, who is known to have an eye for a beautiful woman—"

"The marquesa has transferred her affections to *Wellington*?" Tristram began to laugh.

"She left for Vienna on the very same day," Dan said blandly. "Of course, it's not for me to say whether or not that was pure coincidence, but she has been seen on his arm rather frequently of late."

"Oh, you are incorrigible!" Charis exclaimed, almost angry with him for teasing her so.

Dan kissed the tip of her nose. "And you, my dear doubter, made the temptation irresistible!"

"I wasn't doubting you! Truly, I wasn't!" she protested, blushing, and Tristram, looking from one to the other, deemed that it was time to leave.

Major Hammond was not the only person to return to Brussels at that time. Early in February the Comte de Mallon surprised everyone by turning up at the Latour residence. He arrived as Charis was paying her daily visit to Madame Latour—a habit she had adopted as much for Celestine's benefit as any other, for the increasing strain of her mother's condition was taking its toll of the young girl's stamina both physically and mentally.

"If her father doesn't come home soon, I'm going to the Hague to seek him out!" Tristram had said recently in a sudden burst of frustration.

Charis could not but sympathize, though she hoped he would not act precipitately. She therefore greeted the count with rather more warmth than she would otherwise have accorded him, seeing him as someone who might at least attempt to use his authority. His reaction to her greeting was such that she hoped she had not given him a false impression, and she rushed at once into begging him to give them an account of his visit to Vienna.

He shrugged. "It was all very gay, very frivolous—like one great, unending waltz! One hopes that your Duke of Wellington will take the Congress firmly in hand, but I did not wait to find out. In time, unremitting gaiety begins to fill one with ennui. Did you not find something of the kind in Paris, Miss Winslade?" His knowing eyes smiled into hers. "Or did the presence of Major Hammond alleviate any such tendencies?"

It was the perfect opportunity to impress upon him that Dan's presence in Paris had made all the difference, and that they hoped to be married very soon now. He received the news with a faint ironic lift of the eyebrows, and transferred his attention to Madame Latour, who, after greeting her cousin with a faint spark of enthusiasm, had fallen once more into reverie. The count frowned.

"Poor Marie! She is no better, I think?"

"No. If anything, I would say that she is worse. Lord Rowby has written most urgently to Monsieur Latour, but as yet there has been no reply."

"Well, you know my opinion of that man!" His worldly-wise eyes glinted inquiringly. "And the young ones? Does their little affair progress?"

Charis sighed. "Their feelings are unchanged, but as matters stand, Tris finds himself in something of a quandary. It is a situation requiring much patience—a quality for which he is not in general renowned!"

"To the devil with patience. I saw the child for only a moment when I arrived, but it was enough to show me that she begins to wear a haunted look."

"I know, but what can Tris do? Celestine *is* little more than a child, and Madame is in no condition to make decisions, nor in this case would it be proper for her to do so."

The count was at his most ironic. "Then let him run away with the wench! It will be a five days' wonder, and as soon forgotten!"

Charis feared it might yet come to that, but only as a last resort. She hoped the count would not put the idea into Tristram's head . . . if indeed it were not already there! But she could not answer for his actions should the problem drag on indefinitely.

But Fate was about to intervene. At the beginning of March, word reached Brussels that Napoleon had successfully effected an escape from Elba, intent upon fulfilling his prophecy that he would return to Paris with the first violets of spring.

❧❦ 15 ❧❦

Bonaparte had done it again. He had set Europe by the ears. In Vienna the Congress stopped waltzing and the powers hastily set about piecing together some kind of joint agreement. They waited—and waited in vain—to hear that his landing in France had been resisted. Instead, news eventually reached them that one by one the French generals were rallying to their erstwhile emperor without a shot being fired in anger.

Toward the end of March, Sir Thomas arrived in Brussels, and found himself very much in demand, having actually witnessed Napoleon's arrival in Paris.

"Utter chaos, my dears!" he told a select dinner party at Lady Rowby's that first evening, his manner as gently laconic as though he were discussing some trivial domestic mishap. "But no more than one could expect. The king and the royal family scurrying out under cover of darkness, bound for Ghent . . . couriers dashing everywhere . . . great carts of baggage and furniture! Highly diverting!"

"How did the people take it?" Charis wanted to know, remembering her own experiences of their sanguine attitude to events.

"Much as you might imagine. Everything closed down, except for the cafés, of course . . . and they were crammed to the doors and spilling over onto the pavements! Shouts everywhere of 'Vive l'Empereur!' There must have been thousands cheering him as he arrived!"

"I wish I had been there!" exclaimed Tristram, leaning across the table in his excitement. "Did you actually see him, sir? How did he seem?"

"Very fat," said Sir Thomas in his drollest way. "Tired and rather bored. But that didn't prevent the audience at the opera from giving him a twenty-minute ovation when he appeared in his box at a gala performance!"

"What dreadful turncoats they are!" said Charis in disgust.

"No, my dear. Simply realists." He smiled gently at her. "The French royal family have shown little evidence of caring one jot what happens to the ordinary people in the short time that poor Louis Gros has been back on the throne—one cannot blame them if they now see Bonaparte as a glamorous figure who will give them back their pride!"

Dan had not been at his aunt's dinner. He had his hands more than full dealing with the prince, who had been thrown into a huff by the news that Wellington was expected to supercede him as Commander-in-Chief of the British-Netherlands forces, appointed by the Allied European Powers.

"I'm having the devil's own job with him!" Dan told Charis on one of his brief visits to her. "Slender Billy in a huff is no joke, I can tell you! And his father is little better. Wellington is desperate to get all the fortresses properly garrisoned, and King William does nothing but make objections."

"Anyone would think that the king wanted the French back in Belgium," Charis said. "I suppose there is little doubt that Napoleon will try to take it?"

"None at all, I should say." Dan sounded far from displeased. "At least the prince has now written to Wellington, expressing his willingness to surrender his command, and the duke has written back, plying him with all kinds of good advice. Also, Lieutenant-General Lord Hill is coming out to keep an eye on slender Bill—a good choice, for he quite likes Daddy Hill! But I'll be a lot happier when Wellington actually gets here.

If he's too long about it, his impetuous young subordinate will be straining at the leash, eager to start the war without him! In his wilder moments he has even talked of invading France to rompé Bonaparte before he ever sets foot in Belgium."

It was fast becoming clear to Charis that Dan's enthusiasm for the forthcoming confrontation had superceded all thoughts of marriage for the present, and so, without making a fuss, she quietly packed her trousseau away into boxes and resigned herself to a period of waiting.

But although the news about Napoleon had a momentary sobering effect upon the English visitors still merry-making in Brussels, very few showed the least disposition to pack their bags and leave. After all, troops were pouring in almost daily now, and with them came a great many more sightseers and pleasure seekers eager to join in the fun. As though stimulated by all this additional attention, Brussels blossomed in the spring sunshine; an ever-increasing number of colorful uniforms proliferated among the silks and muslins in the park, and amid the underlying excitement which increasingly pervaded the atmosphere, Charis found her talent as an artist much in demand once more.

She was driving home one afternoon, well pleased with the outcome of her latest commission, when a familiar skirl of excited greeting made her rein in and look about her. On the far side of the street a flurry of palest blue muslin was hastily disentangling itself from a scarlet coat sleeve.

"Heavens! Lavinia!"

Her cousin emerged, laughed up at her escort, and ran toward Charis, clutching at her elegant chip-straw villager hat which was threatening to blow away on the breeze.

"Charis! I don't believe it!" she gasped. "I was this minute on my way to see you!"

"But . . . how is this? Oh, why didn't you let me

know you were coming? Is Aunt Lizzie here, too?" The questions tumbled out.

"We are all here . . . thanks to Ceddie, who is now become an ensign in the Guards. Only fancy! He pestered Papa until he gave in . . . Mama almost had a fit! She has always doted on him, as you know, and was immediately convinced that if she wasn't here to watch over him, something awful would happen. It was only this conviction that induced her to brave the sea crossing!"

Lavinia's escort was once more at her shoulder—tall, broad-shouldered—a vision in scarlet and gold lace, with curling black hair and a handsome set of whiskers. She rested a proprietorial hand on his arm.

"I daresay you won't know Captain Garrard? He commands Ceddie's company—or whatever it is that captains do!" She wrinkled her nose at him. "James, this is my cousin Charis."

The captain bowed, smiled, and said everything that was proper, but Lavinia hardly let him finish. She had been regarding Charis with some envy, and broke in: "Lud—how dashing you are . . . driving yourself about the town! What Mama will say, I can't think! I could scarce believe my eyes when I first saw you!"

Charis chuckled. "I wouldn't call my poor little gig dashing, exactly, but it serves me well enough. I would that I could take you both up, but as you can see. . . ." She waved an expressive hand.

"Oh, that's all right," Lavinia said airily. "You may take *me*. James won't mind not coming, will you, James?"

The young man looked a little put out at being so summarily dismissed, but he took the hand so imperiously held out to him and dutifully helped Lavinia up into the gig, accepting as his reward a brilliant smile and a promise that she would save him a waltz at Lady Charlotte Greville's ball on the following evening.

"You haven't changed, I see," Charis said dryly as

she took up the ribbons and set the gig in motion. "Still ordering young men around!"

Lavinia giggled. "Of course. It's very good for them. Makes them all the more eager to please!"

Charis laughed and the remainder of the short journey was taken up almost entirely by her cousin's chatter about the family doings, which included the surprising news that Nugent was engaged—"to as Friday-faced a creature as you ever saw! Exactly right for Nugent!"

Charis felt obliged to remonstrate, though she felt that her argument lacked conviction. "Are they also in Brussels?"

"Oh yes! You wouldn't catch Nugent missing an opportunity to pontificate on such a momentous event!"

Emily was out when they arrived home, so Charis took her cousin into the salon, where they made themselves comfortable while continuing their cozy gossip, Lavinia with her feet tucked up in one corner of the sofa, all pretensions to sophistication abandoned.

"I had half-expected to find you married by now," she confessed archly. "Such a sly puss, stealing the delectable Major Hammond from under all our noses! I declare, I was more than a little miffed when I first heard . . . but now I don't mind a bit! I am having the most tremendous fun!"

"Well, I'm very glad," Charis said, "because I didn't set out to steal Dan. It just . . . happened! Oh, wouldn't it be splendid if we could be married while you are all here? We had hoped . . ." Her eyes clouded. "But all now depends on Boney. Dan is kept so busy that nothing can be arranged at present."

Emily came in at this point, exclaimed at seeing Lavinia, and when all had been explained to her, said grudgingly that she supposed they would be wanting to take tea.

A few moments later the door opened again.

"That was quick, Em," Charis said without raising

her head. When there was no immediate answer she looked up. Tris was standing in the doorway. He was wearing the blue uniform of the 16th Light Dragoons.

"I simply had to volunteer," he said, looking exceedingly sheepish. "Lord Rowby agreed that I might do so."

Charis couldn't speak; her throat was choked with conflicting emotions—pride, anguish, even anger that he hadn't consulted her, and most of all, fear. Not you, Tris! she longed to cry out. Oh, please! Not you, too!

But Lavinia, who eschewed any but the most trivial of emotions, and who saw war as the most splendid adventure, carried the moment through by flinging herself upon her cousin and declaring that it was the most romantic of things ever . . . only imagine both he and Ceddie having the same rush of patriotic fervor! This involved a lot of complicated explanation, which gave Charis time to pull herself together.

Finally he was walking across the room with one arm still casually draped across Lavinia's shoulder, still listening to her chatter. But his eyes were on Charis, pleading for understanding.

"Say you don't mind, love," he said quietly.

"Mind? Why ever should she mind?" Lavinia looked from one to the other. "Charis, you *don't* mind, do you?"

"I think he's quite mad," she said in a tight little voice, her teeth set on edge by Lavinia's mindless chatter, but immediately she regretted her words, for in spite of his efforts to conceal it, there were little eddies of excitement behind Tris's pleading expression that reminded her irresistibly of a much younger Tris trying to talk his way out of one of his scrapes.

"Well, I think it's splendid!" Lavinia's voice ran on. "Quite apart from any other consideration, there is nothing like a uniform for giving a man an air of consequence! Oh, come on, Charis," she coaxed. "You must agree that Tris cuts as fine a figure as one might see anywhere?"

Charis, seeing him through misty eyes, resigned herself to the inevitable and forced a smile to stiff lips. "The very pink of perfection, in fact," she agreed, pleased to find that her voice was quite steady. Her eyes still held his, and as the mist cleared she was rewarded by the warmth of his smile. "Does Emily know?"

The sheepish look returned. "Not yet. I crept past her door."

"Well, I advise you not to let her see you while she has the tea tray in her hands," she said jokily, "or she's likely to drop the lot!"

But it was Meg who brought in the tray, staggering under its weight, with Emily at her heels admonishing and issuing instructions at the same time. "Carefully now . . . no, no, not like that! Don't be rushin' it, for pity's sake, or you'll have the whole lot sliding off! That's the way of it. . . ." They were well into the room now. "Just lay it down, nice and gently does it— *Mercy me!*" She had seen Tristram at last.

Charis leaped forward as Meg squeaked with fright, and as her hand steadied it, the tray landed on the table with a jangle of crockery.

". . . giving a body frights like that! At my time of life, anything could happen!"

It was some time later. Emily had been pushed into a chair, soothed with tea that had a drop of something in it guaranteed to steady the nerves, and she issued her parting thrust as she bustled out at last, shoulders hunched, with an air of injured pride that disguised her distress.

Lavinia couldn't see what all the fuss was about. She sipped her tea and listened to Tristram.

"Lord Rowby has been jolly decent about it. Said he admired my sentiments and that if he were my age, he'd want to help account for Boney too . . . made it all easy for me."

"But won't he be awfully short-handed?" Charis wanted to know. "If you go, there will only be Mr. Neill and Ned."

"He says not. He heard today that Sir Charles Stuart is moving from the Hague to Brussels, so there should be plenty of Embassy people to share the burden of work."

With Brussels fast becoming the hub of everything, his Britannic Majesty's Ambassador was not alone in seeing the advantages of removing his business thither. And among those who did so was Monsieur Latour.

He chose an unfortunate moment for his return. Celestine, distracted by the thought of Tristram's going into danger, had been so unwise as to blurt the whole of her anguish out to her mother, who in consequence became more confused and bewildered than ever—a condition that the arrival of her husband did little to alleviate.

Charis was witness to the scene that ensued, having been summoned by Mrs. Grant to try to pacify Celestine while she did her best to handle the mother.

Charis was in the act of leading Celestine from the room when Monsieur Latour arrived, and her first impression was of an austere man, trimly bearded, who carried his slight frame with arrogance. As she hastily introduced herself, he signified curtly that he wished to be alone with his family, who seemed sadly in need of a steadying influence. Mrs. Grant gave a little nod of resignation and unhappily Charis withdrew. What exactly happened thereafter was never fully clear, though Mrs. Grant was able to throw a certain amount of light on events. Monsieur had, it seemed, arraigned all three women before him in the salon, and demanded explanations, in the course of which poor Madame had inadvertently mentioned the Comte de Mallon's name . . . and in the ensuing angry scene, Celestine's love for

Tristram had also come to light. Monsieur, burning with a self-righteous warth, forbade any further contact between the two young lovers, announced his intention of turning the Winslades out of his house at the earliest opportunity, and blamed Mallon for everything.

Then he had locked his sobbing daughter in her room before retiring to his own chamber to brood upon the cruel fate that had saddled him with a half-crazed wife and an undutiful, hysterical daughter just when his business affairs had begun to show signs of recovery.

There was to be a fete in honor of the King and Queen of the Netherlands that evening at the Hotel de Ville, and as the Prince of Orange was called upon to attend his parents, Dan had been given leave to ride in early from Braine le Comte so that he could escort Charis personally to the fete.

He was in excellent spirits, due in no small measure to the news that the Duke of Wellington was in Brussels at last.

"Now we shall see an end to all the shilly-shallying. Old Hookey'll have everyone jumping in no time, just you wait and see!"

He was so like a small boy with a treat in prospect that Charis smiled in spite of her worries. She told him about Tris and found that he wasn't in the least surprised by her brother's spirited response.

"He should have come to me. I'd have got him in to my old company. Mind you, with so many raw troops, the duke is like to have a hard time of it; I daresay Our Division will get split up. Still, Tris rides well and is full of go, and with Vandeleur as his Brigade Commander, he won't go far wrong!"

"That is supposed to make me feel better, I daresay," she said with an exasperated sigh.

"Well, it should." He grinned. "Especially as I've heard that Lord Uxbridge is to command the cavalry and they couldn't ask for better, even if his appointment does raise a few eyebrows! He's got plenty of dash, and that's what we'll need!"

But Charis had reached the limit of her patience. "No more, I beg of you!"

Dan looked at her in some surprise as she snapped the words out, her voice tight—a little shrill.

She shrugged helplessly. "It may come as a sad disappointment to you, but I have had more than enough of military matters to last me for the present!"

A rueful smile came into his eyes. "Boring on, am I?"

"No . . . Oh, no! I didn't mean that, precisely. . . ."

"But you would much rather that I admired that exceedingly becoming gown," he said softly, "which I know I haven't seen before, and which compliments your eyes so perfectly!"

He attempted to draw her close, but she resisted, suddenly angry.

"*No!*" she cried again. "Oh, how could you think me so light-minded as to care a jot for anything so trivial!"

"Well then?" He still held her, but loosely, and his narrowed eyes, looking down at her, were uncompromisingly keen.

She felt trapped, and not a little silly under that unwavering scrutiny, but nor could she look away.

"It's just . . . I feel so shut out." The words sounded feeble, said aloud. Impulsively she added: "Oh please . . . *if you would only say you love me occasionally!*"

Dan cursed himself for a fool. His hands slid up her arms to cup her face. "Sweetheart . . . I'm sorry! How can you possibly love such a blockhead!" The words were punctuated with kisses, and by the time she had protested that it was she who was wicked and foolish when she had meant to be so sensible, and he had reassured her, it was some little while before they grew sensible again.

Charis had meant to tell Dan about the happenings earlier in the day, but it seemed a pity to spoil the mood, and as there was nothing he could do about it, she decided that the matter would keep until tomorrow when she could maybe tell Lady Rowby, and ask her advice.

Meanwhile the evening, both personally and in every other respect, seemed destined to be a huge success—with a great many people already at the Hotel de Ville when they arrived.

In one of the anterooms she encountered Aunt Lizzie with almost her whole family in train.

"My dear child, is it always like this . . . the rooms so hot and crowded? And almost everyone a foreigner!"

Charis suppressed a chuckle at the plaintive tones. "Did you expect otherwise, Aunt Lizzie? This is Belgium, after all . . . not London!"

"Well, of course, I know *that*! But I know too that a great many of our friends were to be here, only I can't seem to find any of them!"

Charis stifled a sigh. She could just see the top of Dan's head across the room. He seemed to be engaged in animated conversation.

"Perhaps they are all in the ballroom," she said. "Come along and I'll take you there. It will be much less crowded, apart from anything else."

"You seem remarkably at home, cousin," Nugent observed, as he ushered his fiancée through the crush with a solicitude that amused Charis all the more as the young lady in question—a Miss Camberely—was exactly as Lavinia had described her, built to withstand a cavalry charge. She met Lavinia's eyes and looked away quickly.

"I suppose I am," she said.

When, later in the evening, the Duke of Wellington arrived with his suite, an almost palpable sensation of relief spread throughout the room. He was in excellent form, his distinctive laugh being frequently raised above the hubbub. He greeted Charis with the greatest amiability, and commended Tristram for his enterprise. "Rowby misses him, I know, but we shall need plenty like your brother if we're to do the job, Miss Winslade!"

Ned was missing Tristram, too.

"I d-do my best," he said with a rueful shrug. "But I can't t-talk to people like Tris does. Besides, he made such light work of everything, always funning! I don't mind t-telling you, it's a bit grim with only Neill for company most of the time."

"Oh, poor Ned!" Charis commiserated. "You really must come around to us whenever you feel like it, even though Tris isn't there." She grinned. "Emily does miss having him to fuss over, and you know you have always been one of her favorites!"

"May I?" His face, so prone to blush, grew pink with pleasure. "Thanks awfully."

It was some time after supper, when Charis had been temporarily separated from Dan, that she saw the Comte de Mallon approaching with an air of purpose. She had already favored him with a quadrille, and handsome though he might be in his colonel's uniform, she had no wish to encourage him further. If he was going to be tiresome. . . .

But something in the gravity of his expression as he drew close, drove all such thoughts from her mind. And his clipped tones did little to alleviate the sudden unease that filled her.

"Miss Winslade! Thank God I have found you so quickly. I must ask . . . nay, beg you to come with me at once! An urgent message has come from my cousin's home." He made an indecisive gesture. "The servant was incoherent, but it seems he asked that you or I, preferably both, should go there with all speed. Your brother is not here tonight, I think?"

Charis remembered the trouble earlier and a small frisson of fear ran along her nerves. "Something has happened? Celestine?"

"She is safe, I think, but it is not good." His handsome features were set in lines of grim intolerance. "Come—are you with me? If we might just slip away quietly. . . ."

At any other time Charis would have demurred, but the urgency in his manner communicated itself to her. She looked desperately about her, but Dan was not to be seen. And then she caught sight of her cousin.

"Oh, Nugent! Please, would you be so good as to find Major Hammond, and tell him that I have been summoned home most urgently! The Comte de Mallon is to accompany me, but if he can possibly get away, I may have need of Dan's support!"

Nugent looked at the flamboyant figure at her side with some disapproval. "Really cousin, I don't think—"

"I'm sorry. I don't have time to listen to your thoughts!" she said. "Just find Dan, if you will, and give him my message!"

In the darkness of the carriage, with only the creaking of the springs to disturb the silence, Charis waited for the count to tell her more. When he failed to do so, she found her imagination painting pictures that were insupportable, until she could bear it no longer.

"Monsieur—if you know something further, enlighten me, I beg of you! I have the feeling that you *do* know more than you have said."

She heard him draw in his breath in the darkness. Then his voice came, heavy with an awful irony. "There was some trouble earlier today, I believe? Following upon the return of Monsieur Latour?"

"Yes."

"The messenger brought a note from Mrs. Grant. It would appear that, as a result of what happened then, my cousin this evening visited the kitchens where she procured a knife—with which she has stabbed her husband!"

∾◖ 16 ◗∾

"But, my dear child," exclaimed Lady Rowby. "How dreadful for you!"

"It wasn't pleasant," Charis admitted.

In fact, sitting now in her ladyship's salon amid blessed normality, she could almost persuade herself that it had been no more than a particularly bad nightmare. Except that just thinking about it brought back the awful reality.

"It was much worse for Mrs. Grant, of course, for it was she who first heard the servant's screams and rushed to discover the cause, and so was witness to the whole terrible scene. And for the servants themselves, of course."

Lady Rowby cast a compassionate glance at her young friend's pale face. "If you would rather not speak of it?"

Charis forced a wan smile. "I think, in a funny sort of way, that it's a relief to talk."

"Dan has told us some of it, of course. He said that there could be no doubt of it's being Madame's hand that performed the dread deed."

"None at all. Her fingers were locked around the knife handle when Mrs. Grant found her, the blade still plunged in his neck, and she was muttering incoherently that her daughter's life should not be ruined as hers had been by his intolerance and injustice."

Her ladyship drew in a sharp breath.

"I keep telling myself that if only I had done more—sooner . . ." Charis said shakily.

"You mustn't blame yourself, my dear," Lady Rowby was quick to reassure her. "I don't think anyone fully appreciated the extent to which her mind had deteriorated."

"No," said Charis. "Or that she was so addicted to laudanum, which undoubtedly accounted for her fits of vagueness, and may even, according to the doctor, have contributed to her growing mental instability."

"Well, at least she is now at peace." Lady Rowby sighed. Charis shut her eyes and swallowed hard, trying to dispel the sick horror that came over her once more as the memory of those last hours returned—her arrival at the house with the count to find all the lights blazing, the doctor already there, that one brief unnerving glimpse into Monsieur's room before the door closed upon the count and the doctor, leaving them to pursue their grim deliberations.

Charis had kept herself occupied meantime by comforting the distraught old major-domo, while chivying the remaining servants into going about their business or withdrawing to their own quarters. She had persuaded Mrs. Grant that there was little more she could do, having seen Madame, as passive now as a child, safe to her room where her aged, tiring woman had taken her in hand. She had even coaxed the volatile chef into agreeing to make hot restorative drinks and bring them to the salon. Mercifully, Celestine had slept through the whole thing and there seemed little to be gained by rousing her before it became necessary.

Dan was a long time arriving—Nugent had been slow to deliver her message—and when he did come, he was angry, more angry than she had ever seen him as she poured out the gist of what had happened.

"Mallon had no business to involve you!" he said. "The Latours are not your concern."

Charis, her nerves already stretched, was incensed by his attitude. She had looked for loving sympathy, support—and instead he shouted at her. With only the salon door between them and Mrs. Grant, who had fallen into an uneasy doze, she besought him to keep his voice down, and drew him into the doorway of a small anteroom.

"The count did not involve me. It was Mrs. Grant who asked me to come, and I should have been ashamed to refuse!"

She was not to know that it was the sight of her white face, and haunted eyes, and her beautiful gown, now crumpled, that had been responsible for his outburst—that and the fact that it was Mallon who had been at her side instead of himself when she needed help. Jealousy was an emotion comparatively new to Dan, and he did not immediately recognize it for what it was.

"Well, if you have now done all you can, there is surely no need to remain any longer," he said stiffly.

"Oh, but I can't leave now! Mrs. Grant will need me more than ever once the initial shock has worn off. She has been through the most terrible experience . . . and Celestine will have to be told . . . and there is Madame to be dealt with. . . ."

"Oh, good God!" he exclaimed softly. "Surely there must be someone else?" He wanted to take her in his arms, to carry her away from all the distastefulness and the scandal that would follow, but her shoulders were very straight and her mouth wore a stubborn look that he had seen before—and he knew that he wouldn't really have her any other way.

But before he could tell her so, there were footsteps on the stairs and Mallon and another man who must be the doctor came into view. The latter nodded curtly, said that he would return first thing in the morning, and left.

"Well, Major Hammond." The count's voice was more clipped than usual. "This is a bad business."

"So it would seem," Dan said politely. "You have my commiserations." And after a slight pause, "What will you do?"

The count shrugged. "For the moment, I shall remove the ladies from here first thing in the morning.

My own house on the outskirts of town will serve for the present—there is more room than enough to accommodate them—and poor Marie will be well cared for. I, myself, am very seldom there just now, but there are any number of servants with little or nothing to occupy them."

But when morning came, there was no Madame to be cared for. One dose of laudanum too many had relieved her of the unbearable burden of life.

The scandal was on everyone's lips for a few days, but with so many other things happening it was soon relegated to the back parlors of the more prim matrons.

The Latours, husband and wife, were laid to rest without ceremony, attended by only a handful of people.

Celestine, stunned by the suddenness of it all, was not present, having already been removed to the Comte de Mallon's mansion, which lay between Brussels and Hal in peaceful countryside. It was here that Tristram came the moment he received word, and found her looking alarmingly frail in her blacks. The worst of the tragedy had been kept from her, but enough of its import got through to haunt her imagination with conjecture. Yet her composure, said Mrs. Grant, had not once, to her knowledge, faltered, which did not seem natural in a young girl.

But Celestine's calm did not survive Tristram's arrival by more than a minute. The mere sight of him, so handsome in his regimentals, his arms held out to her—and she flew to him and was held close, the brittle shell of her control splintering into fragments. As the sobs racked her body, he vowed in a shaky voice that the moment he was free of his present obligations, they would be married, and she would never have cause to be unhappy again.

She stared up at him with tear-drenched eyes. "But you will be in such danger, *mon amour*! And 'ow am I to bear it if you are killed?"

It was a new experience for Tristram to have someone so totally dependent on him; quite different from his relationship with Charis, for close though that was, and always would be, it was based on a kind of equality—a sharing of mind and spirit. But Celestine looked to him for her whole existence, and he found it an awesome responsibility. But she must not know it.

"Devil a bit!" he chided with determined cheerfulness. "I've been in and out of scrapes all my life, and no harm done! You ask Charis. And as for Em—why, she's rung enough peals over me to fill a cathedral—and swears that I bear a charmed life!"

After much more in this vein, he left her in a more hopeful frame of mind, but "I don't care to think of her out there with only Mrs. Grant for company," he told Charis with a protective gravity that she found surprisingly touching. "Not that Mrs. Grant isn't a jolly sensible sort, but she don't exactly exude a sense of fun!"

Charis doubted if fun was much in Celestine's mind at the present, but she knew what he meant, for the tragedy had taken its toll of Mrs. Grant also. "Still, I don't see what may be done about it for the present. It wouldn't do for Celestine to come back here. . . ."

"I should say not!" Tristram interjected.

"But I will go to see her as often as I can, and try to take her mind off her troubles."

"I know I can count on you, love. Of course, it was jolly good of Mallon to take her in, as it were, only he ain't there most of the time, and though he's written to her sisters, heaven alone knows how long it'll be before we hear anything. One of them lives in America, I believe."

He saw Charis was looking at him with a curious expression and he grinned as he took up his dashing bell-topped shako with its red and white plume and draped cording, and set it jauntily on his head.

"I know! The thought of me as a man with responsibilities *does* take a bit of swallowing! Scares the hell out of me when I think about it, I can tell you!"

She sighed and wondered where Dan was at that moment. With a slight constriction in her throat, she realized that they hadn't really been alone together since that awful night. He seemed to be away a good deal—and when he was around, there was often a small crease between his eyes which vanished on the instant whenever he found himself to be under observation.

She knew that he hadn't wanted her to stay on in their part of the house once the rest was virtually shut up, but as she had tried to explain, no objections had been raised as to their remaining until such time as the other children were traced.

"It's ridiculous! I shouldn't have thought that you'd *want* to stay. It can't be very pleasant for any of you."

"Oh Dan!" She didn't want to quarrel with him. "We don't really have much choice. I doubt there's a room to be had in all of Brussels, let alone an apartment! And we *are* quite separate from the rest of the house."

"You could go to Aunt Sybil's," he said, coaxing her with some of his old persuasiveness. "I might even get to see more of you there!"

It was tempting—very tempting. And when he smiled at her in that lazy way that set his long, sensitive face alight, she almost agreed there and then. But what would Emily say to such an idea?

"Let me think about it," she pleaded, and saw a little of the light die out of his eyes.

Emily was forthright as ever.

"Well, of course, it's for you to decide," she said with a sniff. "Though I can't see why you should want to go uprooting us all when there's no need! And what I'd do with meself in a strange household I don't know, I'm sure."

"I thought you got on very well with Lady Rowby's Mrs. Dalgleish."

"Getting on is one thing," said the old lady cryptically, "and sharing a kitchen is quite another!"

And that, Charis decided with reluctance, was that.

As May wore on and the weather grew warmer, Brussels seemed to grow ever more festive—picnics were added to all the other entertainments that abounded, and assignations made in the romantic atmosphere of ballroom or theater were brought to a happy conclusion in the shady forest of Soigies or on some secluded riverbank. Flirtation was the order of the day, and seldom was a floating muslin gown to be seen without an accompanying scarlet uniform; heads close together beneath frivolous parasols; roman sandals twinkling under hems edged with rows of frills.

There was a giddiness in the air that was infectious. And Lavinia was in the thick of it, loving every moment. Every day it seemed that more troops arrived, but she refused to believe that anything would come of it.

"Mama says that the duke wouldn't be giving half so many balls if he really expected Boney to march on Belgium," she told Charis blithely as they set out in an open carriage for the point-to-point races at Enghien with several young guardsmen in attendance and her Captain Garrard very prominent among them. "But I shan't repine if he never comes."

But he will come, thought Charis. There were all kinds of conflicting rumors about where Napoleon was— about what the duke expected to happen, or not to happen. An occasional adverse rumor would send the nervous scurrying to pack, but for the most part the pretty young ladies, like Lavinia, were determined to fill each sun-drenched day with gaiety.

But there was an air of unreality about it all and Charis knew that Wellington wouldn't be assembling such a comprehensive force without good cause. Nor would Dan be disappearing for days on end.

Enghien was particularly gay that day—red coats everywhere one looked. Charis, as usual, had taken her sketch book and was soon to be found sitting with her back against a tree trunk, busily capturing the lively scene. She had come in for much teasing in the beginning, but it soon became accepted that Miss Winslade was intent upon recording each event for posterity. This was not, in fact, far short of the truth, for she had already assembled a fairly comprehensive collection of sketches covering all the relevant aspects of life in Brussels at that time.

As always, she had a small group of interested lookers-on—admirers, Lavinia called them—and she was laughing at a remark made by one of them when the book was forcibly removed from behind her by a hand she knew at once.

"Oh, I say . . ."

The chorus of protest was totally ignored, as she turned to look up into Dan's eyes. They were half-closed, at their most inscrutable, as he put a hand firmly, insistently, beneath her elbow to urge her to her feet.

She scrambled up with something less than grace and flung a breathless, laughing apology over her shoulder in the general direction of the startled guardsmen, as she allowed herself to be propelled willy-nilly out of their reach.

"Oh, this is monstrous!" she cried in mock horror as he urged her onward, half-running to match his long stride, until they were out of sight of the last amused onlookers. "Release me this instant or I shall scream for help!"

"Will you, now?" he murmured, turning her in his arms and claiming her mouth with a completeness that robbed her of all her remaining breath. "You were saying?" he queried much later, softly against her ear. "About screaming?"

A gurgle of laughter escaped her. "I'm thinking about it!" And then, "Oh, my dear disreputable love, I had begun to think you no longer cared!" She lifted her eyes to his. "Or that you were somehow disappointed in me?"

Dan's arms tightened around her in a most satisfying way. "No," he said. "Just damnably jealous."

"Jealous? Oh, how absurd!" She strained back against his arms. "Of whom, pray?"

"Of anyone who looks at you as those young gallants were doing just now," he said after a slight pause, and she was almost sure that he was being evasive. "Absurd, as you so rightly say. It is an emotion that I have known little of until lately."

"Oh, then you will know exactly how I felt about your marquesa?" she said triumphantly as they turned to wander along beneath the trees. "Where is she now, I wonder? Not with the duke still, that's for sure!" Her eyes twinkled wickedly. "His interests now lie in quite a different direction!"

"Tattle monger!" he taunted her. "I can remember a time when you'd never have noticed such a thing."

She laughed. "Well, to be honest, I wouldn't have done so now, had Aunt Lizzie not drawn my attention to his marked partiality for Lady Frances Webster."

"Trust Lady Weston to notice!"

They had come some way and were now well out of earshot of everyone else. He stopped and turned her to face him, his expression suddenly grave.

"Sweetheart, I want you to promise me that if the worst happens—if things look like they're going badly—then you will take Emily and Meg and get out of Brussels as fast as you can."

Her eyes widened a little. "You know something?"

"Only what one might expect—that the French troops are massing along the frontier. But—" the harrassed little lines were back between his eyes and she put up a finger to smooth them away—"and this is not for public knowledge . . ." She nodded. "There's a very heavy mass of cavalry forming—more, I think, than his lordship was expecting—and Murat is reported to be on his way from Italy to command it. Also, Soult has accepted the office of Major General under the Emperor. That should take care of the waverers!"

There was a sick feeling inside her. "Then there will be a battle?"

"Oh yes." Dan ruffled her hair absently. "Pray God we are ready for it."

"When?"

He shrugged. "That, my dearest love, is one of the great imponderable questions."

But back in Brussels, Dan was his old urbane self, dancing the night away with Charis at yet another of his lordship's balls as though he had nothing at all on his mind.

At the end of May the duke was due to review his cavalry at the site of a great natural amphitheater near Grammont. All the fashionables were making plans to drive out to view the spectacle—and it occurred to Charis that, since Tristram would be on parade, Celestine might care to go and watch also. It would do her good to get out.

The day was very warm as her little gig took the road to Hal, turning off the road at last to traverse the avenue of trees leading to the count's mansion.

As had become her habit, she drove around the side of the building so as to approach the house through a small conservatory.

It was only as she was about to step into the salon beyond, that she heard voices—the count's and another, raised in anger. Mallon must have ridden over from Mivelle. Just for a moment she hesitated, not wishing to intrude, and in that moment the count's voice came very clearly: "You must be mad, coming here! I want no part of your crazy scheme!"

"But you would not deny, *mon colonel*, that without their commander, the Allied armies would fall apart like a pack of cards," came the harsh reply.

"Sapristi! But such an act is without honor—and as such ranks little short of murder."

Charis was frozen where she stood, trying not to believe the meaning of what she was hearing.

She turned to creep away and in so doing, caught her sleeve on a potted fern so that it rocked on its stand.

The conversation stopped abruptly. Charis, incapable of movement, waited with a sense of fatalism as the footsteps came closer—and the door was flung open.

"Who is there?"

The Comte de Mallon was framed in the opening, his flashily handsome face taut—looking doubly imposing in the Belgian light blue and red of a Colonel of Hussars.

"Miss Winslade!" His voice was, like his face, taut, with none of its accustomed charm. "Do you make a habit of entering my house at will?"

The accusation was so unexpected that she did not at first reply. She was on the point of turning to leave after stiffly begging his pardon, when her glance was trapped by a pier glass set in one of the salon's alcoves; it showed her a reflection that made her blood run cold, the reflection of another uniformed figure in darker blue, though she scarcely noticed what he wore—it was the face that took her attention.

He was the Frenchman, Dubois.

She must have made some sound, for the count was suddenly looking at her more closely, was following the direction of her glance.

"Eh bien," he said, with a little shrug of inevitability. "I think perhaps you had better come inside, my dear Miss Winslade."

✠ 17 ✠

Dan rode into Brussels, bone-weary, after yet another foray across the border. It had not been an official intelligence mission, those could be safely left to Colonel Colquhoun Grant, his intelligence chief, in whose precise judgment Wellington could always place his trust.

But it was as a result of something Grant had reported that Dan had been alerted to a possible renewed attempt by Dubois to assassinate the duke. It hardly seemed likely on the face of it that anyone, even Dubois, would attempt anything so crazy, but the man described by one of Colonel Grant's contacts had sounded remarkably like the Frenchman—and he was certainly fanatical enough to have a shot at it.

Tris had to call Dan's name twice before he looked up.

"Hullo. I didn't expect to see you here." Dan roused himself to be agreeable. "Thought Uxbridge would have you all performing complicated maneuvers, ready for the Grand Inspection tomorrow!"

Tris grinned wryly. "Don't speak of it! I'm only here briefly with a message from his lordship. What with the heat and the dust and the horses, not to mention these damned tight collars, it's all we can do to stagger to our beds at night, I can tell you! You know, I never realized how much polishing and downright sweated labor went into turning a troop out in prime style!"

Dan laughed at the feeling in Tris's words. "That'll teach you to go for a soldier, my boy!"

"Oh, I wouldn't have missed it for worlds!"

"Well, far be it from me to keep you from your duty, lad." Dan sketched a lazy salute, but as he prepared to ride on, Tris hesitated. "I say, Dan, it's none of my business to know how close the Frogs actually are—and I ain't fishing . . ." He grinned. "But I surprised one disappearing into the hedgerow on my way here. If I hadn't been carrying urgent papers I'd have gone after him, I can tell you!"

"Where was this?" Dan's voice was deliberately casual.

"Oh lor! About five miles this side of Schendelbeke, I suppose. Does it matter?"

"I shouldn't think so. Probably an advance scout sent to spy out our strength. Did you happen to get a good look at him?"

"Only his back, I'm afraid. Thick-set, an officer, I think."

"Going which way?"

Tristram thought toward Hal, and on this they parted, and Dan, nudging his mount into a gentle trot, grew thoughtful. He wasn't a great believer in coincidence. A French army scout on a routine mission or Dubois on more sinister business?

In the Rue Royale, his deliberations were received with keen interest.

"You think the man was Dubois?" The duke asked when he had finished.

"He might just be fanatical enough to try. He was, after all, remarkably close to Schendelbeke," Dan mused, "and it's hardly a secret that the building of the bridge over the river at the point is connected with your review tomorrow."

"Well, we shall just have to see he don't get away with anything, shan't we?" said the duke.

We meaning me, I suppose, Dan thought as he took his leave. It occurred to him that Charis should be warned not to leave the confines of Brussels for the present.

But he was too late.

"Miss Charis drove out to see that poor wee girl from upstairs more than an hour since," Emily told him in the slightly disapproving manner she always adopted when describing those more independent traits in her charge's character. "What with her goings-on, and Master Tristram taking leave of his senses, I've little enough to occupy meself these days."

Dan listened with every appearance of patience, but could not wait to be away.

He rode as fast as his already tired mount would allow out along the Hal road, his eyes and senses constantly on the alert. But he turned at last down the avenue leading to the Comte de Mallon's mansion without having encountered anyone or anything unusual.

It was only as he mounted the steps to the front door that he heard the shot—it came from the rear of the house, and without waiting to lift the knocker he turned and ran, leaping over flowerbeds and brushing aside shrubbery. There was a conservatory door—open.

All his years of experience now preached caution. He stepped in and across to the door leading into the house. There was silence, and then a faint murmur of voices. Slowly, he turned the handle.

Charis stared down at the motionless figure at her feet—and, incongruously, her mind was obsessed by the stain even now spreading outward and soaking into the soft blue-patterned carpet. Someone would have to clean it up before it dried—such a pity to ruin what was clearly an expensive, tasteful addition to a room filled with evidence of good taste.

The door from the hall opened a fraction and a startled servant appeared. "Get out!" snapped the count with ill-concealed rage, and then, hardly less tersely as the door closed again, "Sit down, Miss Winslade. You look damnably pale."

I expect I do, she thought, feeling her way in a kind of daze to the nearest chair, and forcing herself to breathe deeply and evenly several times in order to quell the sudden nausea that threatened. After all, not a few moments since, she had expected to be the one stretched out on the carpet.

Dubois had not recognized her at once. When he did, there had been more in his eyes than mere anger at being discovered by her in a highly compromising situation, or even the uncertainty of knowing how much she had overheard of his plans—what she already knew was enough to damn him.

As he told the count in a hard, expressionless voice that she must die, his fingers had moved instinctively to massage the place near his shoulder where her bullet had festered for three whole days before he could find a surgeon to remove it, and the fever that had followed, and the hole that even now refused to heal properly and felt at times as though a knife was being gouged into him—all this he laid at her door.

"I think this obsession of yours with killing has addled your wits, captain," the count had said coldly. "Give it up, for God's sake, and I will engage to restrain Miss Winslade until you are clear over the frontier."

"It's not *my* wits that are addled, *mon colonel*—nor am I so fickle as to be driven from my duty by the lure of flimsy petticoats and a pretty face. She knows too much about me. The last time we met she was in a man's rig and had a gun in her hand!"

"This I do not believe!" There was a calculating gleam in the look that Mallon turned on her. "Or, yes, perhaps I do." He laughed unexpectedly. "You are full of surprises, Miss Winslade, are you not?"

"*Merde!*" exclaimed the furious captain. "This is no time for pleasantries! The opportunity to kill Wellington has presented itself and I do not mean to be thwarted a second time by this—" He called Charis an exceedingly foul name, which she did not understand—though the reference was clear.

The count's mouth thinned. "You are a crude man, captain. However, that is your problem. Mine is somewhat more complex. Does this assassination have official blessing?"

"No, but I shall be thanked soon enough when it is seen how everything will be altered."

"You think so?" mused the count. "You know, I am not so sure."

Dubois sneered and his voice grew menacing. "Well, we shall just have to wait and see. Meantime, I suggest that you make up your mind which side you are on—because I don't aim to leave anyone here to tell tales, and you're a fool if you do."

Charis had looked the count full in the eyes then, shock momentarily robbing her of fear. "You are going over to Napoleon?"

One eyebrow quirked ironically. "My dear mademoiselle, I have always been Napoleon's man. In my humble opinion, his breadth of vision is quite unparalleled in living memory!"

"Then all this time you have been living a lie?"

He smiled faintly at this. "I have been living as I must, dear lady. After all, while Napoleon was on Elba, there seemed little point in courting unpopularity. One must perforce bend a little with the wind."

Such an amoral attitude dismayed Charis profoundly, but she was given no opportunity to remonstrate. Dubois was growing impatient. Time was pressing and he could see no reason for further delay.

"Look, colonel, if you are too squeamish to carry the thing through yourself, just hold her for me—that's all I ask. It needs but a small tap on the jaw, and I will finish her off peaceful-like in the conservatory."

"Perhaps that would be best. If she were a stranger, it would not matter, but . . ."

Charis couldn't believe she was hearing the words. But as he strolled forward to stand behind her, his face was wiped clean of expression. His hands on her arms were almost caressing as they slid down to encompass her wrists. Every instinct urged struggle, but she would not give them that satisfaction. The fingers of one hand wrapped her wrists around like a steel band—his breath was warm against her ear. "Do you have any last prayers, Miss Winslade?"

Almost in that same moment, the shot rang out . . .

Dan opened the door without a sound. A sofa lying across his path blocked his view slightly, but not sufficiently to prevent his seeing Charis slumped head down in a chair with Mallon standing at a nearby table, engaged in laying down a pistol. The air reeked of spent powder. Dan leaped forward with a howl of almost animal rage intent upon hurling himself at the count for the sole purpose of choking the life out of him.

It was Charis's voice that stopped him—faint, but perfectly clear. The next moment, like a whirlwind, she was in his arms, sobbing his name over and over again, incoherent in her relief.

"Very affecting," drawled the count from behind them. "But if you could restrain your very natural relief for the moment, I feel that we should repair to an adjoining salon so that my servants can clear up the mess in here."

Only then did Dan turn and see the body of Dubois sprawled on the floor. The questions sprang to his lips and were forestalled.

"Later, my friend," said the count.

And later it was, when all the explanations had been gone into, that Dan said tersely, "The fact remains, monsieur, that you have been intriguing against the Allied cause all along, whether with Dubois or others. You realize that it is my duty now to ask that you surrender yourself into my hands and come back with me to Brussels."

The count inclined his head with deep irony. "You may ask, certainly."

"Dan, you can't!" cried Charis, looking from one to the other. "He saved my life!"

She shuddered, remembering again that moment when she had waited for certain death, her hands pinioned by one of the count's—her body pulled back against his, and Dubois walking toward her, a look close to pleasure on his face—remembered the look of almost ludicrous dismay that replaced it as the count's pistol appeared in his free hand. . . .

"You can't have him arrested!" she cried again.

Dan turned to look at her, his eyes narrowed to a fierce intensity. Then, without a word, he turned back to Mallon. "Very well, you may go. It can make little difference now, and we are not at war quite yet."

"But soon, eh?" The count bowed again. "My thanks, major—and to you, *chère mademoiselle*." His gaze rested0 on Charis rather longer than was necessary, and then he became brisk suddenly. "If you would perform one small favor for me?"

Charis saw that there were tired creases around Dan's eyes and that he was frowning. She said quickly, "What is it that you wish, monsieur?"

"My young relation, Celestine, and the good Mrs. Grant—they should not remain here any longer, I think. Do you suppose you could find someone in Brussels to take them in?"

"My aunt will house them," said Dan. "If they can be ready quickly, they can come with us now."

After that, things moved very quickly. Celestine and Mrs. Grant and their baggage had been piled into the count's town coach and they were instructed to keep it for their use.

"But what of you, cousin?" Celestine asked shyly, for she was still a little in awe of him.

The count glanced at the others, and said dryly, "Oh, I shall be much occupied with military matters from now on, my child. If I am spared, you may be sure that you will see me again. If not, then I have made provision for you."

Charis moved across to her own gig, which was waiting with a groom in charge. As Dan went to retrieve his horse, the count followed her, his hand extended to assist her to climb up. But he held on to her hand for a moment.

"I would like to think that you forgive me, mademoiselle."

She hesitated, coloring a little. "I am not sure that I can," she said gravely. "Nor can I approve what you do, monsieur. But I do not wish you any ill."

"*Eh bien!* Then I must be content." His bold eyes held hers, smiling faintly. He saw, across her shoulder, the major riding toward them purposefully. "Your fiancé does not love me, I think." The bold eyes glinted. "We will give him cause for his jealousy, yes?"

Before Charis could protest, he had lifted her hand to his lips in a lingering caress. Then he laughed and helped her gallantly up into her gig. "It will do him no harm, *chère mademoiselle*. I would that I might stand in his shoes!"

He stood back and saluted. "*A bientôt.*"

❦ 18 ❧

The moment had come, as they had all known it must. The lights were still streaming out from the windows of the Duke of Richmond's house in the Rue Blanchisserie where one of the most brilliant balls in a season unparalleled as to the number and quality of its balls, was slowly drawing to a close, though a few determined couples still circled the ballroom floor.

Hours earlier, that same room had been crowded; had echoed to the skirl of the pipes as the tartan-clad Royal Highlanders had danced strathspeys and sword-dances—and everyone cheered.

Uniforms abounded—scarlet and blue, rifle green, and magnificently braided Hussars, and the ladies, not to be outdone, were equally fine. But there was a strained gaiety about it all. When the Duke of Wellington arrived at about midnight, the rumors of the day seemed to be confirmed, for every now and then one of the officers would slip away, leaving his partner with blank unseeing eyes that were curiously at odds with the music and the frenetic chatter around about.

Small silences became interspersed with wild bursts of laughter.

Charis felt that she could not bear it. Aunt Lizzie was in floods of tears, having just seen her precious Ceddie dash off in high good humor, promising to "give Boney a hiding, Mama!" And even Lavinia, who had until now seen it all as a grand adventure, had grown uncommonly quiet as her handsome bewhiskered captain followed Ceddie from the room.

Dan had appeared only briefly at the ball; as aide to

the Prince of Orange, he was kept busy carrying dispatches back and forth.

But he had remained at the ball long enough to claim one brief, pulsating waltz. He had been in a strange mood ever since that awful day more than two weeks ago, by turn offhand and fiercely possessive—and always busy, so that she had no time to reassure him. Only once had she tried to explain the count's behavior—his eyes had glinted beneath those lazy lids, as he said that she need have no fear—he understood perfectly.

Even Lady Rowby had become a little concerned; with Celestine now under her roof, she saw rather more of Charis than before—and of Dan on his brief visits home.

"Everything is all right, my dear?" she had hazarded with some diffidence. "Oh, I know that we are all on edge—I couldn't tell you how many times the Courcys packed and unpacked their bags before they finally left for Ostend and the packet home; and I fear many others will follow before long. But Dan doesn't seem in the least like his old carefree self."

And he wasn't—Charis was forced to admit it—and to admit if only to herself that somehow she was responsible. I will make it up to him, she vowed silently. If I could only have a few minutes alone with him as we did at Enghien. . . .

To keep herself busy meantime, she used the skill God had given her. As the troops continued to pour into Brussels, she soon became a familiar sight among them. It had happened almost by accident—one of the old-timers had called out to her on one of her early morning drives. "Beg pardon, miss, but ain't you the young lady as draws people's likenesses?"

She had smiled and said that she was, and before she knew it, she was besieged by requests for "a picture for me mum, miss" or "just a small likeness to send to the missus—in case Froggy gets me!"

It became a labor of love and brought her many new

friends. The drawings had to be small enough to go into their packs—and though she steadfastly refused payment, saying that it was her own contribution to the proceedings, she did become the recipient of many small tokens of their gratitude.

"Can you never do anything by halves?" Emily grumbled. "Just look at yourself—all eyes! What the major will say when he sees you, I don't know—or Master Tristram, for that matter—except that his head is full of cavalry charges and the like!"

"I'm all right, Em," Charis said with a tired smile. "It won't be for long—and those gallant boys—some of them are so pitifully young!"

Now those boys were already forming up in the Place Royale as she danced her waltz with Dan. He held her much closer than decorum would normally allow, but on this night decorum had gone by the board. The young people had thrown open the windows to the night air, which was so hot and still that hardly a curtain stirred.

"Don't speak!" he murmured against her ear. "Just let me hold you."

She closed her eyes against the prick of tears and all too soon heard him groan, "Oh God! Slender Billy is beckoning! I must go, sweetheart!"

"Yes, of course," she said, smiling steadily. "I mustn't keep you from your duty! Only—you will be careful, won't you?"

When he had gone, she sought out Lady Rowby and said that she rather thought she would go home. "Aunt Lizzie is going now—so I can go with her."

When she got home, Tristram was there. He had been to visit Celestine and was visibly shaken.

"Do look after her, love," he said. "She's had so many blows in a short time, and I do worry about her."

Emily bustled in with one of her special fruit cakes carefully wrapped in a cloth. "And there's half a chicken—your sister's been visiting those peasant folk again!"

"Thanks, Em." He lifted her up in a bear hug until she protested, but her voice was gruff.

Brother and sister walked to the door, hands joined, and only released them with reluctance. "I shall pray for you," Charis said in a tight voice. "And don't you dare get into any trouble!"

He ruffled her hair, kissed her, and went running down the stairs.

There was no hope of sleep—with the windows wide open, the noise from the Place Royale seemed to grow in momentum as she sat listening. She had persuaded Em to go to her bed some time ago, and soon found the solitude unbearable. The drums beating to war echoed in her head and finally she went out to see for herself as the sky was paling into dawn.

The Place was a confused ghostly gray mass of men, horses, wagons, trumpet blasts and drums, and the sound of running feet as men came tumbling out of their billets at the last possible moment.

So this was how it really was, she thought—this was how an army prepared to go to war. In spite of her fear, a strange excitement gripped her. Men recognized her, shouted cheery farewells as she picked her way through all the tangle of equipment being assembled by the commissariat trains.

As the sun came up she was still there watching the regiments move out with a steady tramp of boots, including Dan's old regiment, "The bloody, fighting Ninety-fifth," the shout rang out, "The first in the field and the last out of it!" Would he miss being with them? From the park came the strain of the pipes—coming nearer, the feet a rhythmic thunder, the kilts swinging. Probably some of them were the men who had danced at the ball earlier.

Charis waited stolidly until the last regiment had vanished. Then she went home.

Later that day she went to visit Aunt Lizzie, who was all but prostrate but refused to leave while Ceddie was "out there," perhaps getting himself killed! Nugent had less compunction—he must and would, he said, take Miss Camberely home.

"Go then," said Lavinia tartly. "We shall manage on very much better without you!"

"Are you sure you wouldn't rather go home?" Charis asked her.

"Would you?" Lavinia shot back at her.

Charis smiled wryly. "No. I have too many ties to hold me here."

"Well, so have I. A poor thing it would be an' I deserted Ceddie or . . . or James—" she looked defiant—"or even Tris, come to that!"

"Yes, of course." Charis was brisk. "Well, if you wish to make yourself useful, Lady Rowby is to open her house to provide for the wounded as several other ladies are doing. There will be lots to do."

"The very thing! Only wait while I fetch my bonnet. Mama is sleeping soundly. I made her take a little laudanum."

They met hardly anyone on the way to Lady Rowby's. The streets, so full the night before, were now ominously silent—with wagons and tiltcarts lined up for the transportation of the wounded.

Lavinia was soon set to scraping lint while Charis volunteered to collect as many blankets as she could procure. Tents were to be erected at the Namur and Louvain gates to accommodate the wounded—and here, too, equipment was needed.

From then on it was a matter of waiting—from the distances came the sound of cannonading and people ran from their houses to listen. But very little happened in the next two days, but for a few alarms and excursions— the Duke of Brunswick was brought in by his heartbroken Brunswickers—and once, a troop of Belgian cavalry galloped through the town in disorder shouting that all was lost. But after the inevitable panic, with many people hurrying to leave town, life settled back once more.

But then came the wagonloads of wounded and with them, those who could walk or stagger from the battlefield.

From this moment on, the girls worked with hardly a moment's respite. Charis was amazed to see Lavinia, who had never soiled her hands with the least chore, on her knees in the dust of the road binding up ugly, congealing wounds with strips of lint, of petticoats ruthlessly torn into shreds.

Emily and Meg had forsaken their household duties and like Charis they now spent most of their hours in staunching wounds and helping the walking wounded to shelter.

The Belgian doctors were working magnificently in their shirt-sleeves. Sisters of Mercy moved quietly from one soldier to another, murmuring words of comfort as they worked.

Rumors abounded—the Allies were retreating, the French were closing in on Brussels, they had been repulsed—but it all passed Charis by, her brain, her senses had grown numb from the sight of so much suffering.

And then came the thunder and the lightning and the rain—such rain. It drenched everyone in seconds, and the dust turned to mud in the streets.

"Go home, Miss Winslade," called one of the doctors as he trudged wearily from one house to the next. "You have done more than enough for one night."

Obeying him by rote, she stumbled toward the Rue Ducale. A figure lay, half-propped up against some railings. He was young—a Highlander no older than Ceddie—and a glance was enough to show her that he was close to death. She bent to speak to him, and his eyes focused on her with a gleam of recognition.

"The . . . artist lassie!" he gasped. "Will you . . . do me a portrait . . . for my mother . . ."

Charis felt the tears choking her throat. "I have no paper."

"In—my sporren . . ."

She stumbled blindly and drew out a small writing case. She worked swiftly, with shaking hand, shielding the paper as best she could from the rain. As she held it up to him, his eyes were beginning to glaze, but he smiled with the sweetness of a child—nodded, and died. Feverishly she slid the drawing back into the case and returned it to the pack, swallowing the nausea that rose in her, suppressing the thought that perhaps somewhere Tris or Dan might be dying just like this.

Then she stumbled on, half-running, until she was turning the corner into the Rue Ducale—and ran head-on into a broad unyielding masculine chest.

"Oh damn!" she gasped.

There was an infinitesimal pause and then a voice deep with emotion murmured, "Unlady like—but pardonable in the circumstances!" and strong hands were steadying her, warm through the thin soaking muslin of her dress.

She looked up into loving eyes that devoured her from under lazy lids.

"Oh Dan!"

"The very same. Strange how life has a way of repeating itself!" He peered closer. "Tears, sweetheart?"

"The rain," she lied valiantly, and slid into unconsciousness.

She came to at Lady Rowby's, on a bed in one of the few rooms not given over to the wounded. And Dan was beside her, the lines in his face etched with dirt—but he had never looked more handsome.

"Did I faint?"

"You did, young lady." He sounded severe. "Aunt Sybil tells me you've been doing far too much!"

She made a dismissive gesture. "No more than anyone else. Dan, how does it go? The battle, I mean."

He grimaced. "Not well. But Wellington has now

fallen back on Waterloo, where he always meant the decisive battle to be, I think. We have lost a lot of good men, but we *shall* do the thing, never fear!"

Charis hardly knew how to ask. "Tris? Have you . . . is he . . . ?"

Dan grinned. "The last I saw of him, he was plastered in mud but still very much in one piece. Like me, I suspect he bears a charmed life!"

"Anyone else we know? Ceddie?"

She knew from his face that it wasn't good. "He's alive, but the poor brave lad has lost a leg."

"Oh no! He's hardly more than a child!"

Dan paused. "And Captain Garrard's dead—in the same action."

"Oh no! Poor Lavinia—and Aunt Lizzie! I must go to them!"

"Not now. Later, when you have rested." Dan was firm as his hands cupped her face. "Nothing must happen to you." And then: "Sweetheart, I can't stay. I only came in with a message from Slender Billy. But it will all be over soon now, and we shall be married at once—no more delays—no fuss—just married! Is that understood?"

"Yes, Major Hammond," she said meekly. They were both covered in mud, but it didn't seem in the least incongruous.

"Good." He bent his head and kissed her in that long lingering way that melted her heart. "Now I car go and get this war finished."

The room was very quiet after he had gone. Charis knew that she too ought to get up and go home. Instead, she lay thinking about Dan riding back into the thick of the battle. And suddenly, unexpectedly, the thought held no terrors for her. Impossible to explain it rationally, this feeling she had—that, no matter what, Dan would come back to her. But the feeling was there, warm and comforting.

She turned on her side and curled up with the confidence of a child. And in a moment she was asleep.

JOIN THE REGENCY READERS' PANEL

Help us bring you more of the books you like by filling out this survey and mailing it in today.

1. Book title:_____

Book #:_____

2. Using the scale below how would you rate this book on the following features.

Poor		Not so Good			O.K.			Good		Excellent
0	1	2	3	4	5	6	7	8	9	10

Rating

Overall opinion of book . . . . _____
Plot/Story . . . . _____
Setting/Location . . . . _____
Writing Style . . . . _____
Character Development . . . . _____
Conclusion/Ending . . . . _____
Scene on Front Cover . . . . _____

3. On average about how many romance books do you buy for

yourself each month?_____

4. How would you classify yourself as a reader of Regency romances?
I am a (   ) light   (   ) medium   (   ) heavy reader.

5. What is your education?
(   ) High School (or less)   (   ) 4 yrs. college
(   ) 2 yrs. college   (   ) Post Graduate

6. Age_____   **7.** Sex: (   ) Male   (   ) Female

Please Print Name_____

Address_____

City_____State_____Zip_____

Phone # (   )_____

Thank you. Please send to New American Library, Research Dept, 1633 Broadway, New York, NY 10019.